A Lucy Stone Mystery

BACK TO SCHOOL
MURDER

Leslie Meier

KENSINGTON BOOKS
http://www.kensingtonbooks.com

KENSINGTON BOOKS are published by

Kensington Publishing Corp.
850 Third Avenue
New York, NY 10022

Library of Congress Card Catalog Number: 96-80345
ISBN 1-57566-216-7

First Kensington Hardcover Printing: October, 1997
10 9 8 7 6 5 4 3 2 1

Printed in the United States of America

CHAPTER ONE

"Unexpectedly, at home," typed Lucy Stone. "Chester Neal, aged 85 years." She paused and brushed away an annoying strand of hair. It was stifling in the newspaper office and it wasn't even nine o'clock.

"Ted? I'm not sure about this wording. Shouldn't we put 'suddenly' instead of 'unexpectedly'? How can death be unexpected when you're eighty-five?"

"I'd say it was pretty unexpected for Chet," replied Ted Stillings, the fortyish publisher, editor, and chief reporter for *The Pennysaver*.

"Really? How did he die?" asked Lucy, leaning back and fanning herself with the press release from McCoul's Funeral Home.

"Fell off a ladder."

"A ladder? What was he doing on a ladder at his age?"

"Picking apples, of course."

"Oh."

"And from what I hear, the family's pretty upset. Especially his father."

"His father!" exclaimed Lucy.

"Just kidding," said Ted, patting his pockets. "Camera bag, beeper, pens, notebook ... I think I've got everything. I'll be over at district court, covering the arraignments. The morning after Labor Day is always pretty busy. If something comes up, call my beeper number, okay?"

"Okay," said Lucy, turning back to the obituaries. Poor Chet would be missed by a lot of people in the little seaside village of Tinker's Cove, Maine. He belonged to the Masons, the Chamber of Commerce, the Men's Forum, and the Village Improvement Society. He was also a deacon at the Community Church and a trustee of the Broadbrooks Free Library.

"Hi, Lucy! Isn't this weather awful?"

Lucy looked up from the computer and welcomed Karen Baker with a broad smile. Karen's face was pink with the heat, and her blond pageboy hung limply.

"Hi, Karen. Never fails. As soon as summer is officially over and the kids go back to school, we get a heat wave."

"You know, I think you're right. What are you doing here? I didn't know you were working at the paper."

"It's just for a few days. Ted asked me to fill in for Phyllis. Her mother's sick. What can I do for you?"

"I've got an announcement for the PTA Bake Sale this weekend. Am I too late for this week's paper?"

"Not a bit," said Lucy, quickly checking the scribbled announcement for date, time, and place.

"What have you done with little Miss Zoë?" asked Karen. Her daughter, Jennifer, and Lucy's next-to-youngest daughter,

Sara, were best friends. Zoë, Lucy's two-year-old, was a favorite with both Jenn and her mother.

"She's at the new day-care center, over at the Rec Building. It's pretty nice."

"That's what I hear," said Karen.

"Actually, I'm wracked with guilt," said Lucy, casually propping her chin on her hand.

"They'll take good care of her. Sue Finch is in charge, isn't she?"

"It's not that. I'm suffering guilt pangs because I don't mind leaving my baby. Not one bit. I love it here. Isn't it great? I feel as if I ought to be wearing a little hat like Rosalind Russell in *His Girl Friday.*"

"I never noticed it before, but you're right. This place sure has plenty of atmosphere," said Karen.

Lucy followed her gaze as she took in the dusty venetian blinds that hung from the plate glass window, and the framed front pages commemorating VICTORY IN EUROPE, JAPAN SURRENDERS, and the famous Niskayuna Mills fire that hung on the walls. The space behind the counter was divided into two areas: Ted's with its ancient oak roll-top desk and swivel chair, and Phyllis's, temporarily Lucy's, with an ugly battleship gray steel desk topped with a computer. A police scanner sat on the counter, occasionally emitting hisses and cackles.

"Notice that smell?" asked Lucy. "That's hot lead. From the old linotype machine. Ted says you only smell it in hot weather. But the best part is the bathroom. I get it all to myself—nobody follows me in." At two, Zoë liked to follow her mother everywhere.

Karen chuckled sympathetically. "I know what you mean. It's been a long summer, hasn't it? Seemed like the kids would never go back to school. I had to restrain myself when that beautiful big yellow bus pulled up this morning . . . I was tempted to kiss Moe!"

Lucy grimaced. Moe was a very ugly, very fat school bus driver. "So, how are you going to fill your idle hours, now that the kids are back in school?"

"Well, this morning I took a long shower, and then I had a second cup of coffee and read the newspaper. But I can't really afford to continue this fabulously luxurious lifestyle. I've got to give Country Cousins a call." Like a lot of women in Tinker's Cove, Karen worked part-time for the giant catalog retailer, Country Cousins. "What about you? Are you coming back this year?"

"Probably." Lucy sighed. "'Thank you for calling Country Cousins. My name is Lucy. How may I help you today?'" she recited. "You know what I'd really like? A job that's not just a job. Something interesting and challenging, you know?"

"Sure. Why do you think I've stuck with the PTA all these years? There, I'm somebody. I'm Madam President. Not just 'Karen-what-would-you-like-from-our-catalog.'" She shrugged and tucked a strand of damp hair behind her ear. "Good jobs are hard to find around here."

"I know," agreed Lucy, pausing a moment to listen to the scanner. Just a routine traffic stop. "If I went back to school, I could teach English. I only need a few credits, you know."

"That's a good idea, Lucy. Quite a few of the old fossils at the high school are coming up for retirement."

"Really?"

"Yeah. And you could substitute in the meantime. It's decent pay, and no commitment. If the kids are sick or something, you don't have to go in . School schedule, too. You only work when the kids are in school."

"Maybe I will sign up for that course."

"Which one?"

"Over at Winchester. Tuesday and Thursday nights. 'Victorian Writers (1837–1901), with a special focus on Elizabeth Barrett Browning and Robert Browning.' I saw it when I typeset the ad. I was so tempted—I majored in English lit, you know. But it seemed awfully expensive."

"Education is a good investment," said Karen. "Especially if you could eventually teach. They start at over twenty thousand, plus benefits and summers off. Why, that new assistant principal at the elementary school—Carol Crane—I bet she's barely thirty and she's making forty-two thousand."

"You're kidding." Lucy turned to listen to the scanner. Her attention had been caught by a change in the dispatcher's tone. Usually flat, reciting routine phrases and codes, it had suddenly become imperative.

"Seventeen and Nineteen, report to One-One immediately. Do you copy?"

"What's One-One?" asked Karen.

"Let me see," said Lucy, reaching for a laminated sheet tacked above her desk. She scanned the list and raised an eyebrow. "The elementary school."

"All available units, report to One-One stat, do you copy?"

The two women's eyes locked as they listened to a chorus of voices responding with the single word, "Copy."

"Uh, base, this is Seventeen."

"Seventeen's the chief," explained Lucy.

"Copy, Seventeen. Go ahead."

"Uh, we need fire and rescue over here."

The two women simultaneously took a quick breath.

"Copy. Will relay that message."

"Uh, base?"

"Copy, Seventeen."

"Call the state police for assistance—uh—just get the bomb squad out here real fast! Copy?"

"A bomb at the elementary school?" Karen was incredulous.

"That's what it sounded like," said Lucy, a catch in her throat.

"Jenn's there. And Sara. I'm going over there," announced Karen, hurrying out the door.

"Damn. I'll be along in a minute. I have to call Ted."

Lucy scrabbled frantically among the mess of papers on her desk for the Post-it with Ted's beeper number. She finally found it and punched in the digits. Then she waited, hand on the receiver, for Ted to call back. Her fingers tapped nervously as the minutes ticked by. Sirens filled the air and emergency vehicles screamed down Main Street, blurs of red and yellow as they raced past the office. It was all she could do to wait. She wanted to get to the school, to make sure Sara was all right. Finally, after what seemed like an eternity but was only two minutes, the phone rang.

"Ted! It's about time you called—there's a bomb at the elementary school!"

CHAPTER TWO

"What did you say?" Ted asked.

"A bomb!" Lucy yelled into the phone. "At the elementary school!"

"Calm down, Lucy," Ted instructed patiently. "Take a deep breath. Now, tell me where you got a crazy idea like that."

"I heard it on the scanner. The Chief called the bomb squad."

"It's probably a hoax," said Ted. He had been covering the news in Tinker's Cove, what little there was, for nearly twenty years. He'd reported on plenty of fires and auto accidents and the occasional domestic abuse incident, but he'd never yet covered a bombing.

"Ted, I'm not going to sit here and argue with you. Maybe there isn't a bomb, maybe it is a hoax, but Sara's in that building and I'm going over there!"

From the way his ears were ringing, Ted was pretty sure Lucy had slammed the phone down. He was standing in the courthouse lobby, leaning against the wall next to the pay phone, still holding the receiver in his hand. As he replaced it, he heard the distant wail of a siren. Even if it was a hoax, he decided, it was still a story. In fact, it was a definite first for Tinker's Cove.

Shouldering his camera bag, he hurried outside and quickly crossed the parking lot to his ancient VW beetle. In seconds, he was on his way to the school.

At the door, Lucy hesitated. She didn't have a key, so she would have to leave the office unlocked. Then again, crime wasn't exactly a big issue in Tinker's Cove, where people routinely left their doors unlocked. Hoping for the best, she turned the dangling OPEN sign to CLOSED and pulled the door shut behind her. Then she ran across the sidewalk to her Subaru wagon and jumped in. Looking over her shoulder, she made a big U-turn across Main Street and pressed the gas pedal to the floor. She didn't care if she got a ticket but she didn't think it was likely—all the cops were at the school.

As she raced down the quiet streets, images she had seen on the TV news crowded her mind and she tried to push them away. The Oklahoma City bombing; the fireman cradling a limp baby in his arms. The bloodied children who minutes before had been safe in the day-care center. The World Trade Center, where workers staggered down endless flights of smoke-filled stairs, emerging with soot-blackened faces. The twisted steel wreckage of a Jerusalem bus, and a city street turned into a morgue. "No," she whispered to herself. "Not here. Not my baby."

Turning onto Oak Street, she was almost surprised to see the tall, red brick school building standing exactly as it had for fifty or more years. Today, it shimmered in the heat, and rays of sunlight bounced off the glass windows. To Lucy, it seemed fragile, like a mirage that could shatter and disappear at any moment.

Lucy blinked and reassured herself that everything was all right, for now. Every rescue worker in the county seemed to have answered the call; the driveway and parking lot were filled with fire engines and other emergency vehicles. Hoses had been laid, several ambulances stood by with their lights blinking. There was no place to park so she pulled the Subaru onto the lawn and braked.

A shrill alarm bell sounded as she climbed out of the car and her heart skipped a beat. Seconds later the students began exiting the building in neat lines, led by their teachers. Years of fire drill training had paid off. She scanned the children's faces, searching for Sara and soon spotted her small, chubby figure. She was holding hands with Jenn, and following her teacher, Miss Kinnear. Lucy gave her a little wave.

The children were soon arrayed in orderly rows on the lawn, where they stood waiting for the usual signal to return to their classrooms. The signal didn't come. Instead, the principal, Mrs. Applebaum, made her way heavily across the driveway. She stood facing them on sturdy stockinged legs, her feet stuffed into sensible shoes. She smoothed the white collar that trimmed her size 20 washable polyester-cotton dress and raised a bullhorn to her plain, pleasant face. The sun bounced off her glasses.

"I am very proud of you today," she began. "You have all behaved very well, and the school was evacuated in record time. The fire chief tells me it is not safe to go back into the building just yet. I am going to ask you all to step back. Teachers, when I give the signal, will you please have your classes move across the lawn to the baseball field—as far back as you can go." She paused, making sure everyone was paying attention, raised her arm, and said, "Now."

The group receded across the lawn to the outfield and reformed once more.

"Very good," said Mrs. Applebaum. "Now, I'm going to ask you all to sit down. We are going to sit and wait until it is safe to return to our classes. Teachers, since this is the first day of school, I want you to check and make sure all your students are accounted for."

Spotting Karen among a handful of anxious mothers clustered together on the lawn, Lucy approached them. "What's going on?" she asked.

"They haven't said, but it must be serious for them to evacuate the building," offered Anne Wilson.

"There doesn't seem to be a fire," said Vicki Hughes. "What could it be?"

Lucy's and Karen's eyes met.

"Maybe it's a water leak or something," said Anne.

Lucy nodded. She wanted to believe it was something as harmless as a water leak. "The kids are behaving awfully well."

"They sure are," said Karen, pulling her oversized T-shirt from her sticky body and flapping the loose fabric. "It's sweltering out here."

"I'm glad I sent my boys off in shorts this morning," offered Vicki. "Some of those kids are wearing long-sleeved shirts and corduroy pants."

"Their back-to-school clothes," said Lucy. "I guess they can't wait to wear their new things, even if it's ninety-five in the shade."

"Ladies, I'm going to ask you to move back, if you don't

mind," said Officer Barney Culpepper, crossing the grass toward them.

Barney had been Lucy's friend ever since they'd worked together on the Cub Scout committee. Over the years Barney had added some weight, and nowadays a sizable belly hung over his heavy police belt. His hair was still thick, but the buzz cut he favored was turning decidedly gray. He planted his feet firmly and hitched up his pants.

"Hi, Barney. What's up?" asked Lucy.

"Well, you didn't hear this from me," said Barney, leaning forward conspiratorially, "but they've found a device attached to the school clock."

"A device?" asked Anne, stepping closer.

"Like a bomb?" whispered Vicki.

"That's what they think," said Barney, nodding. "They think it's set to go off when the lunch bell rings. At eleven-thirty."

Lucy looked at her watch. "That's in ten minutes!"

"Right. That's why I want you to move back."

"No problem." The women scurried across the green grass and joined the children on the baseball field.

"There's Ted," said Karen, pointing to the driveway where a battered yellow VW was pulling up.

"It's about time," said Lucy. "He almost missed the biggest story in Tinker's Cove since . . . I don't know when."

The women watched as Ted made his way over hoses and around squad cars and approached the men in charge: Fire Chief Stan Pulaski and Police Chief Oswald Crowley. Their heads bobbed and hands waved as they conversed, and Lucy wished she could hear what they were saying.

A sudden commotion among the children drew the women's

attention; kindergarten teacher Lydia Volpe was running through the seated students, her hand at her mouth.

"Uh-oh," said Karen.

The women watched the awkward pantomime as Lydia pointed to the building and then tried to run in, but was restrained by two firefighters.

"What's that all about?" asked Vicki.

"Somebody's still in there," said Lucy, who never hesitated to jump to a conclusion.

"Oh my God," breathed Anne.

"Who could it be?" asked Vicki.

"You know, I didn't see Tom Spitzer with the rest of the kindergarten kids," said Anne, whose daughter was in Lydia's class.

"You're right," said Vicki, scanning the group of kids. "He's not there." All the mothers knew Tommy; he had been born with cerebral palsy and was a familiar figure at school gatherings with his aluminum crutches and his brave little grin.

"Maybe he's home with a cold or something," said Karen.

"I hope so," said Lucy, glancing at her watch. It read eleven twenty-six. Four minutes.

"I don't think he's home," said Anne, indicating the front of the school, where two members of the bomb squad were hurriedly pulling on padded suits and helmets. They were just entering the building when they were almost knocked off their feet by a small blond woman in a pink suit. She dashed past them and disappeared into the evacuated building.

"Who was that?" asked Lucy. "That wasn't Tommy's mother."

"That was Carol Crane, the new assistant principal," said Karen. "What time is it?"

"She's got three minutes, if my watch is right," said Lucy.

"I can't stand it," moaned Anne. "What if she doesn't make it?"

"How's she going to find him?" asked Vicki, wringing her hands. "He could be anywhere."

Lucy looked down at her watch, holding her breath as the sweep hand lurched from numeral to numeral. The children were unnaturally silent, sitting with their classmates on the lawn. The teachers gathered together in little groups. The rescue workers stood by, manning their stations. Ted fingered his camera. All eyes were fixed on the green double doors of the school.

The big hand of her watch fell on the six, and Lucy reached out and gripped Karen's arm. Karen covered Lucy's hand with her own.

The doors swung open, and Carol Crane staggered out, followed by the two bomb squad members. She was clutching little Tommy tightly to her chest.

The students began cheering as Carol ran down the steps, supported by the two helmeted men. A sudden, thunderous boom silenced them, and everyone watched as the first-floor windows ballooned out and shattered. Clouds of thick, dusty smoke billowed out of the empty window frames. Carol was thrown to the ground by the force of the explosion, and she fell on top of Tommy, protectively covering his body with her own. The two bomb squad members were also thrown forward onto their knees, but quickly scrambled to their feet. Carol, with Tommy's small body folded beneath her, lay quite motionless.

CHAPTER THREE

The seconds following the explosion were absolutely quiet. No one coughed or moved, not even a bird sang. The children sat in stunned silence on the grass with the sun beating down on them. Everyone stared at the blasted building, waiting for the inevitable collapse. But time ticked on and the school remained standing, a scarred backdrop for the drama unfolding in front of it.

The paramedics had rushed to aid Carol and Tommy. They carefully rolled Carol onto her back and began to examine her. She appeared to suddenly regain consciousness; her hand flew to her head and in the silence everyone heard her first words.

"Is Tommy okay?" she asked.

They were already transferring the little boy to a stretcher, but before they could fasten the straps, he popped up into a sitting position.

"I was locked in! I couldn't get out!" he exclaimed, shaking with outrage. Then he burst into tears. A female paramedic hurried to him, patting him on the shoulder and wiping his tears.

Then, all eyes were drawn to Carol Crane as she awkwardly and painfully got to her feet, assisted by one of the helmeted rescue workers. She staggered a bit, then turned slowly and faced the crowd of students and teachers, who began cheering and applauding.

Carol stood there for a moment, a tiny fragile figure in pink surrounded by the uniformed paramedics. She gave a little wave and turned to bend solicitously over little Tommy's stretcher.

As she watched the drama unfold, Lucy felt tears pricking her eyes and blinked them away.

"That is one brave lady," said Karen, fumbling for a tissue and blowing her nose.

"The whole building could have come down on top of her," said Anne.

"She risked her life to save Tommy," added Vicki.

As they watched, Tommy was carried to a waiting ambulance and placed inside. Carol climbed in after him, assisted by the paramedics, and the doors closed. Then the ambulance proceeded slowly down the drive.

"No lights or sirens," said Karen. "They're probably just taking them to the Cottage Hospital to make sure they're okay." The women nodded, knowing that if they had been seriously injured they would have been rushed to the trauma center in Portland.

"What a relief," said Vicki, blowing her bangs out of her eyes and fanning herself with a paperback novel she had been clutching for dear life.

"What book is that?" asked Lucy.

"I don't know," admitted Vicki. "I was just holding it. I

think I wrecked it." She looked down ruefully at the crumpled romance, whose cover still pictured the busty heroine swooming in her muscle-bound lover's arms, and giggled.

The tension that had gripped everyone was suddenly gone. The children were growing restless on the lawn. Some of the younger boys began wrestling, and a few very bold boys began chasing each other. The teachers ignored them, laughing and talking with each other while the rescue workers were congratulating their fellows, shaking hands and slapping each other on the back. Only one person didn't seem to be sharing in the general mood of celebration.

Sophie Applebaum, the principal, stood watching as the ambulance came to the end of the driveway and turned onto Oak Street. When she turned to consult with Chief Pulaski, Lucy caught a glimpse of her expression. She didn't appear relieved, or grateful; she looked thoroughly disgusted. Then, giving her head an abrupt little shake that made her tightly permed gray curls bounce, she once again raised the megaphone.

"Attention, students. Attention."

She waited and the students gradually fell silent.

"Today has been a very unusual day and I want to thank you all for your cooperation. I'm going to ask you to be patient just a little bit longer. Chief Pulaski tells me the building may not be safe, so we cannot go back inside. The buses will arrive in a few minutes to take you all home."

A few of the older children began cheering, but were quickly silenced with a stern look from Mrs. Applebaum.

"You will remain with your teachers until school is dismissed. If there is no adult at home, please tell your teacher and we will make special arrangements."

She lowered the megaphone with a trembling hand, and

Lucy saw the toll the morning's events had taken on her. Her usually rosy cheeks were pale, and her face seemed flaccid and droopy. The school nurse also noticed the principal's distress and hurried to her side.

"There's no sense making the kids wait for the bus," said Karen. "Why don't I take the girls to my house? Are you going back to work?"

"I guess I should," said Lucy. "I forgot all about it."

"No wonder. We had quite a bit of excitement, didn't we?"

"Too much if you ask me. I'll get Sara and meet you at your car."

Lucy hurried across the coarse grass to Sara's class and got Ms. Kinnear's permission to take her daughter home.

"This has been quite a shock for the children," said the young teacher, nodding wisely. "I'm sure we'll have counseling available for the students who have trouble dealing with their emotions. If Sara seems upset, or afraid to go to school, I hope you'll take advantage of it."

"I will, thank you," said Lucy, taking Sara's hand. She gave it a little squeeze, and impulsively bent down to kiss Sara on the head.

"Mom, not in front of everybody," Sara complained.

"Sorry," apologized Lucy. "Mrs. Baker has invited you to spend the afternoon with Jenn—how does that sound?"

"Okay," answered Sara.

She seemed less enthusiastic than usual, and Lucy wondered if she had been frightened.

"What did you think of all this?" asked Lucy. "Were you scared?"

"I wasn't scared. It was a rip-off!" announced Sara with a scowl.

"What do you mean?"

"I thought the whole school was going to blow up and then we wouldn't have to go back for a long time. But look—it's still right there." Sara pointed indignantly, one hand cocked on her hip.

Lucy followed her finger. The school did seem to have survived the explosion with only minor damage. The office windows were blown to bits, but the sturdy brick building appeared otherwise intact. Nevertheless, Tommy had had a close escape. There was no telling what might have happened if Ms. Crane hadn't saved him.

"Shame on you!" scolded Lucy, grabbing her by the hand and hurrying her along. "Think of poor Tommy! We're all very lucky it wasn't worse."

Sara straggled along beside her mother, a stubborn pout on her little round face. Lucy looked down at her precious and adorable little girl and smiled. In her heart, she couldn't blame her. What normal child wouldn't miss the freedom of summer vacation, and wish for a reprieve?

CHAPTER FOUR

Bill Stone pulled his pickup truck alongside the mailbox that stood at the end of the driveway and pulled out the day's assortment of catalogs and bills. Setting it beside him on the seat, he turned smoothly into the driveway and parked in his usual spot by the back porch.

The house seemed oddly quiet with the kids in school. Through the summer he'd gotten in the habit of coming home for lunch and then taking the kids for a swim at nearby Blueberry Pond. Taking a break in the middle of the day made sense—he found he accomplished more by working in the cool of the evening rather than the heat of the afternoon. It was one of the compensations of the lifestyle he and Lucy had chosen. He knew he could make more money if he worked for a big corporation the way his father did, instead of struggling along on his own as a restoration carpenter and contractor, but then he wouldn't be able to spend much time with his family.

He hardly ever saw his father when he was growing up; Dad often worked late and was frequently away on business trips. Bill remembered his father's look of surprise when he asked him for driving lessons.

"You're too young to drive," his father had said.

"But Dad, I'm sixteen," Bill had replied.

"That's impossible," declared his father.

It wasn't until he'd checked with Bill's mother that the senior Mr. Stone accepted the fact that his son was really sixteen. Somehow Bill had grown up without his father even noticing.

Bill was determined that wouldn't happen to him. Even so, despite his best efforts, it seemed that the kids were maturing awfully fast. Toby was starting his freshman year in high school, and Elizabeth, now twelve, was already developing ominous curves and bulges. Where had the time gone? Sara was eight, and even little Zoë wasn't a baby anymore. If he asked her how old she was, she delighted in holding up two chubby fingers.

Climbing out of the truck and mounting the porch steps, he mopped his brow with a crumpled red bandanna. It was sweltering. He considered going for a quick dip, but abandoned the idea. It wouldn't be much fun by himself. Instead, he went into the kitchen, sat down at the round oak kitchen table, and leafed through the mail, putting the bills aside for Lucy. A heavy vellum envelope bearing the engraved name of NICHOLS, NICHOLS AND BROWN caught his eye. It was obviously from a law firm, and as a small businessman he knew such letters rarely brought good news.

Grunting, he slid his callused thumb under the flap and withdrew a word-processed letter. Randy N. Wiggins, whose round signature made Bill suspect he was a rather junior member of the firm, regretted to inform him that his client, Nelson Widemeyer, was filing for protection from his creditors under the provisions of the bankruptcy act. Needless to say, both Mr. Wiggins and Mr. Widemeyer regretted the necessity of this action.

Bill sighed and tossed the letter aside. He regretted it, too, especially since Ned Widemeyer owed him a final payment of $15,000 for converting an old one-room schoolhouse into a summer home. This wasn't going to do Bill's credit any good—he himself owed a good portion of that money to the local lumberyard and hardware store.

Placing his hands on the table, Bill pushed himself to his feet and opened the refrigerator door. A tall, green bottle of beer caught his eye. What the hell. He knew he shouldn't drink so early in the day, but who could blame him? He twisted the cap off, chugged most of the contents, and yanked open the meat drawer.

He must have pulled harder than he'd intended, because the drawer flew out of its shelf and fell, spilling slices of plastic-wrapped cheese all over the floor.

"Shit," he said, stooping to pick up the mess. After he was finished, he made himself a ham and cheese sandwich, topped it with a handful of chips, and grabbed another beer. Then he went out to the porch and sat down on the creaky old glider. That's where Lucy and Zoë found him, snoring loudly, when they arrived home a few hours later.

"Daddy!" exclaimed Zoë, as Lucy boosted her up the porch steps.

"*Shhh*, you'll wake him up," cautioned Lucy, but not meaning it. She wanted him to wake up. She was furious that he was sleeping, obviously ignorant of the explosion.

"*Unh*," mumbled Bill, then he lurched upright.

"Don't mind us," said Lucy, with an edge to her voice. "We didn't mean to disturb you."

"It's the heat," said Bill. "I must have dropped off."

"I guess you didn't hear the news," said Lucy, glancing pointedly at the beer bottle on the floor. The gesture was lost on Bill.

"What news?" he asked, still groggy as he got to his feet.

"Somebody blew up the elementary school." Lucy tossed off the sentence, pulling open the screen door and disappearing inside.

"You're kidding, right?" asked Bill, following her.

"No, it's true," said Lucy, opening the refrigerator and pouring a glass of juice for Zoë. She set it on the table and lifted Zoë into the high chair. "I was there when it went off. Thank God it didn't do much damage."

Bill scratched his chin. He was having trouble absorbing this. "Was anybody hurt?" he finally asked.

"No. They evacuated the building. Tommy Spitzer, you know him, the little boy with crutches, got trapped inside somehow. Carol Crane, the new assistant principal, rescued him just in time." Lucy began to sniffle, and reached for a tissue. "I was so afraid. What if . . . ?" She left the sentence unsaid, unwilling to voice her worst fears, and dissolved into tears.

Bill wrapped his arms around her. "This is incredible."

"It was horrible," Lucy cried. "I couldn't believe it was happening, but it did."

Bill pulled away. "A bomb! Here in Tinker's Cove!" he exploded, pounding a fist on the kitchen counter and staring out the window over the sink. "I'd like to get my hands on the maniac who did this . . ."

In imitation, Zoë pounded her fist, making the juice glass jump.

"What good would that do?" asked Lucy, picking her up and sitting down at the kitchen table, setting the baby on her lap. "Don't you think there's been enough violence already?"

"Who's in charge over there, anyway? How could they let something like this happen?"

"You make it sound like it's the school's fault there was a bomb."

Zoë was tired. She gave a big sigh and relaxed against her mother. Lucy wiped her juicy mouth with a napkin.

"Well, maybe it is. They sure managed to get somebody pretty mad. Mad enough to blow the place up." Bill sat down heavily at the table and flapped the envelope. "You know what this is? Widemeyer declared bankruptcy."

"How bad is it? Are we in trouble?"

"We'll manage." Bill snorted. "It's kind of funny. I thought that was just about the worst thing that could happen and then you told me about the bomb. It sure puts things in perspective."

"It sure does." Lucy's expression was sober. A little line formed between her eyebrows. "What kind of maniac would want to hurt innocent children?" she demanded, stroking Zoë's downy head.

"Listen, Lucy. I'm sure the police will catch whoever did this," said Bill, sounding a note of caution. He knew Lucy tended to get involved in local crimes, such as the wave of arson that had swept through the town a couple of years ago.* "There's no need for you to try and solve this yourself."

"Maybe you're right," said Lucy, surprising him with her agreement. Then she continued, in a thoughtful tone. "Maybe it was someone angry at the school. Somebody who didn't get a

*Tippy-Toe Murder

job, or got fired or something like that." Realizing Zoë was asleep, she carried her upstairs and put her in her crib.

When she returned to the kitchen, Bill tried to pick up the argument, but was cut off by the grinding gears of the late-afternoon activity bus as it made the climb up Red Top Hill. Since Toby was on the soccer team and Elizabeth was playing field hockey, they usually took the late bus home. Bill and Lucy heard the brakes squeal as the bus stopped at the end of the driveway. Seconds later, Elizabeth and Toby burst into the kitchen, laden with backpacks and sport bags which they dropped at their feet.

"There was a bomb at the elementary school!" exclaimed Toby.

"It blew up!" added Elizabeth.

"I know. I was there," said Lucy. "How did you hear about it?"

"Everybody was talking about it. Is it true Miss Crane was a hero for saving Tommy Spitzer?" asked Toby.

"It's true."

"Sara has all the luck—she won't have to go to school," complained Elizabeth, throwing herself into a pressed oak chair. She sprawled across the table, leaning on her elbow. At twelve she was skinny and lanky, with knobby knees and short, dark hair. Lucy allowed her to shave her legs, but she drew the line at plucking her eyebrows, much to Elizabeth's disgust.

"There wasn't much damage to the building," said Lucy. "I don't think she'll miss more than a few days at most. So, how's eighth grade?"

"Boring," said Elizabeth, blowing her bangs out of her eyes. "I wish I was in high school, like Toby."

"High school is better," said Toby, opening the refrigerator door and waiting hopefully for a delicious snack to jump out and surprise him.

"Close the door, you're wasting electricity," said Bill.

"Mom, how come there's never anything good to eat?"

"Probably because you ate it all. Have a bowl of cereal."

"Yuck," said Toby, opening a cupboard and moving boxes around. He finally chose one and poured himself an enormous bowl full, adding at least a pint of milk.

"Why is high school better?" asked Lucy.

"You get to change classes—no matter how boring a teacher is, you only have to stand it for forty-five minutes. And they're not all boring. Mr. Cunningham is really pretty interesting. He told us we're going to do all kinds of neat stuff, like make hydrogen sulfide. It smells like rotten eggs." Toby paused, and began shoveling cereal into his mouth.

He was sandy haired, and almost as tall as his father. Always hungry, he ate a prodigious amount of food. His room was usually littered with empty glasses and plates, testament to his frequent snacks.

"You're disgusting," observed Elizabeth, watching him eat. She was chewing on a stubby black-lacquered fingernail.

"Don't insult your brother," admonished Lucy. "He's growing, and so are you. Don't you want something to eat?"

"No, I'm too fat." Elizabeth tentatively touched her chin, checking for pimples.

"You are not," insisted Lucy. "You need to eat good foods to stay healthy. How about an apple? Or some yogurt?"

"I'm not hungry. Is Mr. Cunningham the same Mr. Cunningham who coaches field hockey?"

"I guess."

"Well, if he is, he's a pretty neat guy—for somebody who's really old."

"He must be all of thirty," said Lucy, catching Bill's eye.

"There's a new kid," offered Elizabeth.

"Really?" Lucy was interested. Newcomers were rare in the little town.

"His name is Lance. He comes from California."

"Sounds like trouble," said Lucy, exercising her New England reserve. "What does he look like?"

"He's got a great tan—and a nose stud."

"What color is his hair?" Lucy was suspicious.

"It's not purple or anything," said Elizabeth.

"That's nice."

"It's kind of orange."

"Oh," said Lucy, shaking her head. She looked up as the door flew open and Sara marched in, stamping her feet.

"What are you so mad about?" asked Lucy, sticking her head out the door and waving to Karen, who beeped the horn before continuing down the driveway.

"We've got school tomorrow," said Sara, pouting.

"Are you sure?"

"It was on the car radio."

"It's for the best," said Lucy in a soothing tone. "If they had to close the school, you'd have to make up the time—on Saturdays or something."

"It stinks!" said Elizabeth emphatically.

"At least you got out of school today," said Toby philosophically, setting the empty bowl in the sink.

"We had to sit in the hot sun and roast."

"What about Ms. Crane? She was a hero, braver than any of

the firemen," said Elizabeth, who occasionally exhibited feminist tendencies.

"She's mean. I saw her yelling at Mr. Mopps."

Lucy raised an eyebrow. All the kids loved the school custodian, whose real name was Mr. Demopoulos. Since he was usually seen pushing a mop, and the kids had trouble pronouncing his real name, they settled on calling him Mr. Mopps. He didn't seem to mind.

"Well, she's his boss and Mr. Mopps has to do his job. I've got to get supper started, but you've all got time for a swim."

"Good idea," said Bill. "The truck leaves for Blueberry Pond in five minutes."

"Wait for me!" shrieked Sara as they all clattered off to change into swimsuits.

"Take your bags—don't leave them here in the kitchen," yelled Lucy, but the kids were already gone. She shrugged and turned to Bill. "Thank goodness the bomber didn't seem to know what he was doing."

"You said it." Bill's agreement was heartfelt.

"I love the kids—you know I do." Lucy sighed and bent to pick up the backpacks. "But summer vacation was plenty long enough."

CHAPTER FIVE

When Lucy arrived at *The Pennysaver* office at nine the next morning, three phones were ringing, Ted was yelling into a fourth while scribbling furiously, and a man she had never seen before was bent over an oversized computer screen in the back corner.

"It's about time you got here!" hissed Ted, covering the mouthpiece with his hand. "The device itself was amateurish, you say? *Unh-hunh*. What about domestic terrorists? The Maine Militia? Not their style, you say? Okay. Well, thank you for your time." He hung up the phone and tilted his head toward the man in the back. "Lucy, this is George. He's our paginator," he said as he punched numbers into the phone.

Lucy gave George a little wave, and sat down at her desk. "Am I late? I thought I was supposed to come in at nine."

"Damn!" exploded Ted, slamming down the receiver and making her jump. "They lost my film. Can you believe it? Lucy—

go right over to Capra's Photo and make them find my film, okay?"

"Right now?"

"Lucy, I'm not sure you understand the newspaper business. It's not a guideline, it's a deadline! Get going."

"Okay," said Lucy, diving for the door.

When she returned, proudly holding up a red and yellow envelope, Ted snatched it from her and spread the photos out on the counter. Lucy stared at them; the camera had captured in stark black and white the tension preceding the explosion and its aftermath. There were the chiefs, Pulaski in a white cap and Crowley in a dark one, conferring anxiously. A controlled Mrs. Applebaum speaking through the megaphone. A frightened little girl holding tightly to her teacher's hand. There was a sequence of pictures illustrating Carol Crane's exit from the school with Tommy in her arms, and then being helped to her feet by rescuers, little Tommy lying at her feet.

"This is it!" exclaimed Ted, tapping a photo. "Page One."

"That's weird," said Lucy.

"What? What's weird?"

"Don't you see it?"

"See what?"

"She looks just like Jackie Kennedy after JFK was shot. See the smudges on her skirt. The way her hair falls?"

"You're right," said Ted.

"She was even wearing a pink suit—but these pictures are black and white so you can't tell."

"Well, it was a good photo then and it's a good photo now. George, make sure this goes above the fold, okay? We ought to sell a lot off the stands with a catchy photo like this. Headline! We've got to have something snappy."

"BOMB THREATENS SCHOOL," suggested Lucy.

"Nah. Everybody already knows that. We need an angle."

"TEACHER SAVES KID? TEACHER SAVES CRIPPLED KID?"

"Crippled?" Ted rolled his eyes. "You do have a lot to learn. Crippled is a definite no-no."

"Oh," said Lucy, chastened.

"Try this, George. I want a twenty-four-point teaser. MINUTES BEFORE EXPLOSION . . . Then, DARING RESCUE SAVES STUDENT. What's the biggest we've got? Sixty point? Will it fit?"

"Looks good," said George, studying the screen.

"Then go right to my lead. Make that bigger than usual. Eighteen point or something, and transition down, okay?"

"Got it."

"Save some space for the story about the investigation. I'll write that now. Lucy, I need you to typeset some last-minute legals that came in yesterday. I think I put them on your desk."

"Okay," said Lucy, switching on the computer.

"And by the way," Ted added. "Phyllis called. Her mother will need her for longer than she thought. She's got breast cancer."

"How awful."

"Yeah. Phyllis sounded pretty upset. So, is that okay with you? Nine bucks an hour. Wish I could go higher, but I can't."

"That's fine," said Lucy, doing a quick calculation. Even accounting for day care and taxes, she'd be clearing more than $200 a week. She smiled to herself as she found the legals and started typing them into a computer file.

She was so absorbed in her work, she didn't look up even once until Ted asked if she would like some coffee.

"I'm going over to Jake's. Can I get you something?"

"You're done already?" Lucy was amazed. She hadn't finished typing out a few brief legal notices and Ted had written an entire news story.

"Unfortunately, there wasn't much to tell," he explained. "They don't seem to have much to go on."

"I thought they could get a lot of information from the bomb itself."

"Well, since it blew up, there isn't much evidence left. And let's face it. It isn't as if we've got the Israelis working on this. Bombs are few and far between in Maine."

"Can't they send it to the FBI or something?"

"They are—but like I said—it's not like there are known terrorist groups they can link the bomb to."

"What about the Maine Militia? They were involved in that standoff with the Penobscot Indians, weren't they?"

"Yeah, but if you remember, they weren't exactly shy about claiming credit for their activities. In fact, they're always looking for publicity. If they did this, you can be sure they would have sent out press releases claiming responsibility. It's probably the work of some lonely nutcase who got his instructions off the Internet. Amateur hour. It's too bad. We're going to be feeling aftershocks for a very long time."

"What do you mean?"

"It's just that the schools have enough problems. Money's tight, special-needs costs are going up, parents want to know why Johnny can't have calculus and computers and football, too. The conservatives complain that the schools are undermining morals by teaching sex education. And the liberals don't want the kids reading *Huckleberry Finn* because they believe it's racist. No matter what they do, somebody's mad at them, and now this happens."

"That's like Bill. He was blaming the school for the bombing."

"A lot of people feel that way, believe me. The administration shouldn't have let it happen. How did the bomber get access to the clock? And how come Tommy was unaccounted for? People are going to be asking a lot of questions. So, how do you take your coffee? Cream and sugar?"

"Black," said Lucy. "Thanks."

As Ted was leaving, he held the door for Karen. She bustled in, obviously in a hurry. There were dark circles under her eyes.

"I'm late," she announced. "Can you do me a big favor? I need to know when the school committee is holding their next meeting."

"Sure," said Lucy. "I typed it yesterday." She tapped away on the keyboard, closing one file and opening another. "Here it is. Monday, the eleventh."

"That's what I thought. Thanks." She turned and started to leave.

"Wait a sec," Lucy called. "Why did you want to know? Are you all right? You look terrible."

"Couldn't sleep a wink. Every time I started to drift off, I'd dream about the bomb and wake up. I kept dreaming the same thing—how I was walking past piles and piles of rubble and there were children's voices calling for help. I heard them crying but I just kept walking. It was horrible."

"It was only a dream. Everybody's fine. Tommy's home, resting, and Ms. Crane is back on the job."

"This time. But what if it happens again? That's why I'm going to the school committee meeting. As PTA president, I've had a lot of calls from parents. They want to make sure this doesn't get brushed under the rug and forgotten. They want answers, and so do I."

"The police are investigating. Ted said even the FBI is involved."

"That's all very well and good but this never should have happened in the first place. A lot of people think Mrs. Applebaum isn't running a very tight ship."

"Really? I like Sophie," said Lucy.

"Well, you've known her for a long time. Some of the younger mothers think she's getting too old. They think someone like Carol Crane ought to be in charge. Listen, I've got to go," she said, glancing at her watch. "See you at the meeting!"

Lucy went back to the legals, typing in an announcement for a Zoning Board of Appeals hearing. As her fingers flew over the keys, automatically copying the details of the request for a variance, she recalled her first encounter with Mrs. Applebaum. She had gotten Toby's first progress report from kindergarten teacher Lydia Volpe and had been disturbed to see that his fine motor skills needed improvement. She made an appointment with Lydia and, perched on a tiny chair, went over the results of Toby's "readiness inventory." There seemed no doubt about it. Toby was definitely not as bright as she and Bill had thought; he was going to have a difficult time in school.

Leaving, she walked slowly down the hall, wondering what the future held for her darling little boy. She and Bill had such high hopes for him, and now it seemed he would probably have to repeat kindergarten.

"Is something the matter?" asked a pleasant voice.

Looking up from the linoleum-tiled floor, Lucy saw Mrs. Applebaum studying her with an expression of concern. Before she knew what had happened, she was pouring out her problem.

"My little boy—he's in kindergarten. His fine motor skills need improvement!" Lucy blurted it out, blinking back tears.

"Come into my office," said Mrs. Applebaum.

Sitting Lucy down in a chair, she handed her a box of tissues and a glass of water.

"You met with Mrs. Volpe? And she showed you all sorts of charts and tests?"

Lucy nodded.

"Did you ask her for a comparison to other boys the same age as your son?"

Lucy shook her head.

Mrs. Applebaum smiled. "Well, if you had, she would have shown you another chart. And you would have discovered that ninety percent of all four-and five-year-old boys have poor fine motor skills. It's just the way they are. Your son is probably very normal."

"Really?"

"I'd bet the school budget on it. What's your son's name?"

"Toby Stone."

"I know Toby. He's a firecracker. I wouldn't worry about him." She patted Lucy on the shoulder and helped her to her feet. "Don't worry. Toby's doing just fine. He's smart and healthy and has lots of energy—he's running and jumping. The fine motor skills will come in a year or two."

When Lucy left Mrs. Applebaum's office, she felt as if a huge weight had been lifted from her shoulders. Toby was normal after all. Everything was going to be all right. And it had been. By the time he was in third grade, Toby was at the head of his class. In eighth grade he had gotten all A's, except in sewing, which was compulsory for both boys and girls.

He apparently never did develop those fine motor skills.

Lucy smiled to herself and closed out the legal file, shipping it to the paginator with a few key strokes.

She was stretching her arms when Ted came in, carrying a paper tray of coffees. He was sitting down, his feet propped on his desk, prying the tight plastic lid off the paper cup when the phone rang. Lucy took the call.

"It's the printery," she told him. "They're going to shut down early today so they can install some new software. Can you ship the paper now?"

"Are we done, George?"

"All done, boss. I'll take the disk right over." He popped a disk out of the computer and tucked it in his pocket. "See you next week."

"Well, that was lucky," said Ted, sipping the hot liquid. "Some days it's three or four in the afternoon before we're ready to go to press. With luck, we'll be on the stands this afternoon."

Lucy sipped her coffee and glanced around the cluttered office. She liked it here, she decided. It was exciting, and fun. She had a lot to learn, of course, but she was a quick learner. Already, she felt at home.

"Hi, Barney!" She smiled as Officer Culpepper closed the door behind him and approached the counter.

"I've got an announcement here, about Cub Scouts," he began.

"Sorry," she said. "The paper just went to press. It will have to go in next week's issue."

"That's okay," said Barney, lifting off his police cap and running his thick fingers through his bristly hair. "There's no hurry."

"Anything new in the investigation?" asked Ted, casually sipping his coffee.

"Not really," said Barney. "State police are handling the investigation, of course. They don't tell us much. Mostly, we're just supposed to keep the parking places in front of the station clear for them. You know how it is." He sighed.

Ted nodded. He understood the resentment the local cops felt for the state police. They got stuck cleaning up the messes and doing the legwork, and the state cops got all the credit.

"I did notice something interesting," said Barney. " 'Course, if they ever found out I told you, I'd be in big trouble."

"They won't find out from me," said Ted, putting down his coffee and leaning forward in his chair.

"Well," said Barney. "We've got this new 9–1–1 system."

"I know. I wrote a big story about it," said Ted.

"Right. One of the features of this system is that whenever we get a call, the computer tells us the location of the caller. That's so if somebody passes out or something, we can still help them."

"Yeah," said Ted.

"I happened to look at the log for yesterday. And you know what I found out?" Barney paused to adjust his belt, which was sagging under the weight of his gun and radio. "The call reporting the bomb came from the school."

"What!" Ted sat up suddenly, spilling coffee on his khaki pants. "From inside the school? You're sure?"

Barney nodded.

"Dammit! Why couldn't you have told me sooner? That's big news—that's a breakthrough in the investigation!" He hit his forehead. "I can't believe it. The one time I get breaking news, it's too late. The paper's already gone."

"Can't you get them to hold it? Stop the presses, or something," asked Lucy.

Ted gave her a withering glance. "What do you think this is—a movie or something? We don't have our own press. I can't stop anything. Frankly, I'm lucky the Portland paper puts up with me—my press run is so small." He patted at his pants with a napkin. "I think I'll go change my clothes."

As Lucy and Barney watched, he trudged across the office and out the door.

"Gosh," said Barney. "I didn't mean to upset him."

"Don't worry. You can't take Ted too seriously. If I got upset every time he yelled at me, well, I'd be upset an awful lot. It's just the way he is. One minute he's a screaming maniac and the next he's forgotten all about it. Really."

"If you say so," said Barney.

"You're sure about this? That the call came from the school?"

"Oh, yeah." Barney nodded.

"But who could have done it? Not one of the teachers?"

"Not likely. Chief seems to think it was a kid."

"A kid?" Lucy was incredulous.

"Kids have changed." Barney nodded sadly. "Over at Gilead they charged a fourteen-year-old with rape."

"I just don't believe a child could have done it, and especially not one from Tinker's Cove. If they're real daredevils, they ride their bicycles against traffic for thrills."

"I know what you mean," said Barney, who was a frequent visitor to the school and knew most of the kids by name. He gave a Halloween safety presentation every October, he taught the kindergarten students to call for help by dialing 9–1–1, and he set up a bicycle safety workshop complete with a working traffic light in the gym every spring.

"Still," he added, "times are changing and kids aren't what

they used to be. These are strange days." He set his cap on his head and opened the door. "Take care, Lucy."

Left by herself in the quiet office, Lucy tried to sort out her emotions. She was shocked to learn that the call had come from inside the school—she had assumed the bomb was set by some weirdo with a grudge. Someone who hadn't been hired for a job, or maybe someone who had to repeat second grade and blamed all subsequent failures in life on that first disappointment.

If the call had come from inside, the bomber had to be either a student or an employee. No one else had access to the phones. Lucy didn't think a student could have done it. For one thing, the school only taught grades kindergarten to four. Even the oldest students were only nine or ten years old, a trifle young to be handling explosives.

There didn't seem to be any likely suspects among the staff either. Most had been at the school for years; only Ms. Crane was new, having been hired the previous spring when the former assistant principal won the jackpot in the state lottery and quit suddenly. Rumor had it she was enjoying her new life in Bali very much.

Come to think of it, thought Lucy, something was different at the school. It was no longer quite the happy, relaxed place it had been when Toby started kindergarten there. She remembered the look of disgust on Mrs. Applebaum's face after the explosion. Did the principal have her own suspicions? And what about Mr. Mopps? Sara had heard Ms. Crane scolding him. Could he have set the bomb?

Lucy sighed and began tidying up her desk, sifting through the pile of papers and throwing out the old news releases. Coming across the night school announcement from Winchester College, she reread the description of the Victorian literature course. "A close examination of the work of the major figures in English literature of the Victorian period (1837–1901), with special emphasis on the poetry of Robert and Elizabeth Barrett Browning."

She adored the Brownings, and had read everything she could find about them, delighting in every detail of their famous courtship and elopement. It would be wonderful to learn more about the Brownings and their contemporaries, she thought, and to do it in the company of kindred souls. Fellow students who shared her enthusiasm for the Victorians.

Well, why not, she asked herself. Now that she was earning some money, there was no reason she couldn't sign up for the class. The college was even offering a reduced rate to Tinker's Cove residents.

Then again, Bill had gotten that letter from Widemeyer's lawyer, announcing his bankruptcy. Maybe this wasn't a good time to spend money unnecessarily. Bill had been worried, all right, but he'd said they would manage. The money she was earning was a windfall; it wasn't really part of the family budget. They hadn't expected it, they wouldn't miss it, she rationalized.

Besides, when was the last time she had done something for herself? She couldn't remember, if she didn't count the chocolate bars hidden in the freezer. Furthermore, the course wasn't just for her pleasure and amusement. It would give her some of the credits she needed, and in a year or two, she could become a certified teacher. She picked up the phone and made the call.

CHAPTER SIX

It was nearly four when George returned, thumping down several bundles of folded papers. With a practiced flick of his thumb he snapped the plastic strips that held one bundle together and handed a copy to Lucy.

"Here it is—hot off the press," he said, grinning at her.

"Wow," said Lucy. She unfolded the tabloid and spread it flat on her desk.

"Looks good, doesn't it?"

"It sure does," said Lucy, looking at the familiar *Pennysaver* with new eyes. "It really does. It looks great."

"I thought you'd like to see what you've been working on."

"Thanks," said Lucy.

"See you next week," said George, giving her a little nod.

Left alone, Lucy studied the paper, slowly turning the pages. She was excited to see how it had all come together. The dramatic photo of Carol Crane on page one was a definite interest grabber.

Turning the page, she smiled to see the meeting announcements she had typeset, right on page two. And a few pages later, the obituaries. There was even a photo of Chester Neal; his hair was parted low over one ear and combed up over his bald patch. The legals were tucked in just before the classified ads. And the ads— she had taken some of them over the phone. She looked for Franny Small's refrigerator, "Sears Kenmore in Mint Condition," and Harold Higham's puppies, "Shepherd Mix—Good Tempera- ment." When she found them, she was oddly pleased.

What must it be like for Ted, she wondered. Every week he saw his own thoughts and words transformed into print and read by hundreds, maybe even thousands, of people. If she was this excited to see her want ads, what would it be like to write a story, a real news story?

She refolded the paper and straightened it, giving it a little pat. Then she tucked a couple of extra copies in her bag, locked up the office, and went to pick up Zoë at the day-care center.

Driving along with the toddler babbling happily beside her, Lucy tried to think of something quick and easy for dinner. She was used to having all day to prepare supper—with plenty of time to roast a chicken or mix up a casserole. Now, it was already a quarter past five, and the family usually ate at six. She didn't have time for potatoes, and even macaroni took nearly half an hour—fifteen minutes for the kettle of water to boil and then ten or twelve minutes for the noodles to cook.

Couscous was quick and she had quite a lot of it thanks to a buy-one-get-one-free special. Couscous and salad and what? Lucy tried to remember what was in the freezer.

The freezer! She hadn't defrosted anything. Braking, she made a quick U-turn and headed back to the supermarket. She would have to pick something up.

Pulling into the IGA parking lot, Lucy hoisted Zoë onto her hip and hurried inside. Cruising the meat case, she grabbed a package of ready-to-cook chicken strips then dashed over to the freezer section, where she found bags of Oriental vegetable mix. She joined the other working moms in the express line, and checked out their choices for future reference. Stir-fry was popular, so was rotisserie cooked chicken from the deli, and frozen pizza.

Paying for the groceries took her last few pennies. Lucy hurried back to the car and pulled into the driveway at a quarter to six. Sara was skipping rope in the yard and came over to the car.

"There were dogs at school, Mom," she said, proud to have some news to impart.

"That's nice," said Lucy, bending over the car seat to unbuckle Zoë. "Did you pet them?"

"No." Sara was clearly disappointed. "The policemen wouldn't let us."

"Police dogs? What were they doing?" asked Lucy, balancing Zoë against her chest as she reached for the bag of groceries.

"Smelling."

"Smelling what?"

"Everything." The little girl studied her shoes, then raised her head. "Mom?"

"What, honey?"

"Can we get a dog?" This was a consistent item on Sara's wish list.

"No, sweetheart. Elizabeth is allergic to dogs."

"Elizabeth's in trouble." Sara gave a sly little smile. "Daddy's mad at her." She turned and skipped across the yard, humming a happy little tune.

Lucy shook her head and mounted the porch steps. As soon

as she opened the door, she heard Bill's raised voice. She followed it to the family room and found Bill, crimson-faced, confronting Elizabeth and a leggy teenaged boy sitting side by side on the couch.

"This," said Bill, turning toward her, "is Lance."

"Hi, Lance," said Lucy, giving him a grim little smile.

"Lance has been paying a visit to Elizabeth," said Bill, through clenched teeth. "They came home from school together."

"That was hours ago," said Lucy.

"Exactly," said Bill, turning on his heel and leaving the room. "You're her mother. You've got to do something about this."

Lucy sat down on the hassock, still clutching Zoë and the groceries.

"You must realize why your father is upset," she began, appealing to Elizabeth.

"He doesn't trust me! It's not fair! He didn't even give me a chance to explain."

"It's just not a good idea for you to entertain friends unless a parent is home—we'll have to make a rule that you can't have guests after school unless one of us is home."

"That stinks." Elizabeth crossed her arms across her chest and slouched down on the couch. Beside her, Lance looked distinctly uncomfortable.

"Well, until we can work out something better, that's the rule. I thought you had field hockey practice—what happened?"

"I skipped it."

Lucy raised her eyebrows. "From now on, there's no more skipping practices. Understand? Now, Lance, I'm sure your family must be looking for you."

"Mom, Lance lives on the other side of town. Can you give him a ride home?"

Even Elizabeth knew this was pushing it. Lucy stared at her for a minute.

"I don't think so—I've got to get supper started. Lance, why not give your folks a call, and then you can start walking. And you, miss," she said, handing a rather soggy Zoë over to Elizabeth, "can change Zoë and keep her occupied while I cook."

Lucy escorted Lance to the kitchen. He did have a deep tan, she observed, and the little gold bead in his nose wasn't all that unattractive. Personally, she didn't like orange hair, but she couldn't deny that the boy had a certain cocky charm.

While he phoned, she got a pot of water boiling for the couscous, started browning the chicken in a frying pan, and began assembling the salad.

"I'm sorry, Mrs. Stone," said Lance. "I didn't mean to get Elizabeth in trouble."

"You didn't—she's perfectly capable of getting in trouble all by herself," said Lucy, showing him the door.

"Sara," she called up the stairs as she ripped open the vegetables. "Set the table, okay?"

It was nearly six-thirty when Lucy called the family to the table for dinner.

"About time," said Bill, clearly disgruntled.

"I'm starving," said Toby, helping himself to most of the couscous. "I thought we'd never eat."

"Toby, that's way too much. Put some back so your sisters can eat, too. If you want, have a piece of bread instead."

"I hope this isn't going to happen every night," said Bill. "How much longer are you going to be working on the paper?"

"I'm not sure," admitted Lucy. "Phyllis's mother has cancer. She may need her for quite a while."

"Why don't you tell Ted you'll finish out the week but he'll have to get someone else after that," suggested Bill, passing the salad to Sara.

"I couldn't do that," said Lucy, surprised at how strongly she felt. "Who would he get?"

"I don't know—and I don't care. This isn't working out." Bill's tone was definite. "The kids need you. The house is a mess. Things are out of control."

"Other families manage. I think it's just a matter of adjusting. If everyone pitches in, it will all work out."

"Why should we have to pitch in?" asked Bill, his voice rising. "The house and the family are your responsibility. I don't ask you to hammer shingles for me!"

"That's not exactly true," said Lucy. Her voice was getting louder, too. "I do the books for you and handle the correspondence. I help the kids with homework and a million other things. I don't think it's too much to ask for a little help with the housework and cooking. Especially since I really enjoy working at the paper!"

Bill's jaw tightened. The kids were very quiet, as they always were when their parents quarreled. Lucy suspected it was a survival technique that had been passed down through the chain of evolution. Lion cubs and little hyenas probably kept clear of their snarling parents, too.

"And before you say another word," added Lucy, "you might as well know that I've signed up for a night class at Winchester College. It's something I've wanted to do for a long time."

Bill didn't say anything. Instead, he got to his feet and left the table, leaving most of his meal untouched.

Lucy pushed her plate away and slid her chair back from the table. "I'm not very hungry either," she said, getting to her feet and addressing the children. "Finish your dinner, and then you can wash the dishes."

For once, no one argued.

Having delivered her ultimatum, Lucy went out to the back porch. She stood there, leaning on a post. The temperature had dropped a bit, and a soft breeze was stirring. Between the heat and her job, she realized, she had neglected the garden. Picking up a hoe that stood by the back door, she marched across the yard.

Opening the wire gate and surveying the vegetable plot, she sighed. The tomatoes definitely needed attention—the plants were slipping from their supports, weighted down with ripening fruit. A number of overripe Big Boys had fallen to the ground and split open. What a waste, she thought. She began picking the red, ripe fruits, inhaling the spicy, pungent scent of the foliage. In just a few minutes she filled a plastic beach pail that Zoë had abandoned. What am I going to do with all these, she asked herself, slowly sinking to the ground.

In summers past, she had always made tomato sauce, filling the gleaming quart jars with her own savory, herb-filled recipe. Some years the garden produced barely enough tomatoes to make sauce, and she'd had to buy more at Andy Brown's fruit and vegetable stand. But this year, the garden had been extremely productive. The plants were loaded with ripe fruit, and there were plenty of green tomatoes coming. If she got tired of making sauce, she could switch to green tomato relish and piccalilli.

If she got tired. Who was she kidding? She was exhausted. She didn't have the time, or the energy, to make tomato sauce. In fact, truth be told, she didn't want to make tomato sauce. She didn't want the mess of skinning and seeding them. She didn't want to burn her fingers on the hot jars. And most of all, she didn't want to process the jars in a hot water bath until the kitchen was so full of steam she was afraid the wallpaper would peel off. She was sick of making tomato sauce.

From inside the house, she heard Zoë wail. Time to go back. She slowly stood up and, carrying the bucket in one hand and the hoe in the other, walked across the toy-strewn yard to the porch. Things change. Time doesn't stand still. Life is full of choices, and she was going to make some new ones. This year, she'd bag the tomatoes and let the kids take them into school to give to their teachers. She'd take them to the food bank. She'd put them on a table by the road. She'd even put them on the compost heap. But she'd be damned if she'd make another batch of tomato sauce.

CHAPTER SEVEN

Later that night, a loud clap of thunder woke Lucy and she lay in bed listening as rain pounded down on the roof. Bill was snoring softly beside her. Lucy had always tried to follow her mother's prewedding advice not to go to bed mad, so she had made a point of seeking out Bill before she turned in for the night. She found him in the little attic office where he kept his files and drafting table.

"Gosh, it's hot up here," she said as she ducked to pass through the small doorway.

"I've got the fan going. Once you get used to it, it's not bad," he said, looking up from a lined yellow pad covered with figures.

"Are you upset about Widemeyer? Does he owe you a lot?" Lucy was feeling guilty about spending so much money on the course. If they really needed the money, she could withdraw and pay only a small penalty.

"It'll be okay." Bill put down his pencil. "I just hope it's not the beginning of a trend." Bill had seen New England boom in the eighties only to crash in the nineties, and didn't want to have to repeat the process.

"I know things have been kind of crazy lately," said Lucy.

"Kind of." Bill picked up an antique agate doorknob he used for a paperweight and fiddled with it. "These days I never know what I'll find when I get home from work and I don't like it. This job of yours is not working out."

"Maybe not. But I want to give it a try. Besides, Ted only needs me for a couple of weeks." Lucy hoped it would be longer, but Bill didn't need to know that. She bent down and nuzzled his ear.

He reached his hand around her waist and pulled her down on his lap.

"We haven't done this in a long time," said Lucy, gently pressing her lips against his. "Am I getting too heavy?"

"No," said Bill, pulling her closer for another kiss. "I'd say you're just about right."

The next morning the temperature was cooler and the air was crisp. Fall was definitely in the air, and Lucy was the very model of a modern working mother. She made hot cocoa and oatmeal for the kids' breakfast. She packed lunches for herself, Zoë, and Sara. She put out lunch money for Elizabeth and Toby. She unearthed a lasagna she had frozen months before, when Bill had impulsively decided to take the whole family out for dinner, and set it on the counter to defrost. It was amazing what you could accomplish if you were organized, and got up an hour ahead of the rest of the family, she told herself.

By the time she had arrived at *The Pennysaver*, after dropping off a rather clingy Zoë at the day-care center, she felt as if she had already put in a full day's work. She set a bag of tomatoes on Ted's desk and began sorting the mail.

"Hi, Lucy," said Ted as he entered. "How's it going?"

"So far, so good," said Lucy, fighting the impulse to yawn. "I thought the paper looked great."

"Not bad," said Ted. "If only we had more weeks like this."

"You don't mean that." Lucy was shocked.

"Yes, I . . ." He paused, shamefaced, and shook his head. "No, I don't. Hey," he said, opening the bag of tomatoes, "are these from you?"

"Yeah, the garden's in overdrive." Lucy paused. "You know what Sara told me? They had police dogs over at the elementary school."

"I know. Explosive-sniffing dogs. They checked all the closets and desks."

"Isn't that kind of closing the barn door after the horses have gone?"

Ted shrugged. "They seem pretty convinced that a student set the bomb."

"That's crazy. The oldest kids there are fourth graders. They're practically babies."

"There is a widespread belief that half the kids in America are surfing the Internet looking for instructions on how to build bombs at home. The other half are crashing into adult chat rooms, looking for porn."

"Most kids in Tinker's Cove don't even have computers."

"Maybe, but the fact is that the phone call came from the school."

"What about the staff?" Lucy paused. "What do you know about Mr. Mopps?"

"Not much, except that the kids seem to like him. He's been there for years."

"Isn't Greece a violent sort of country?" asked Lucy.

"I think it's been pretty peaceful lately. Besides, he doesn't come from Greece. I think he grew up in Brooklyn. Why? Do you suspect him?"

"Sara told me that Ms. Crane was chewing him out over something."

"Well, I don't think it was for blowing up the school." Ted put the bag of tomatoes on the top of his desk and sat down, flicking on his computer. "I'd like this story to break, but not just yet. I could use some new developments early next week, so I can get them in next week's paper."

Lucy shook her head in disgust. "Have you no shame? I'd like this thing solved as soon as possible, so I don't have to worry about the kids." She began typing entries into the meeting calendar. After a few minutes she raised her head and asked Ted, "Do you know a kid named Lance? He's new in town. From California."

"I think Adam has mentioned him." Adam was Ted's son; he was the same age as Toby and the two were good friends.

"He was at our house last night. Caused quite a brouhaha."

"I'm surprised. Adam seems to like him."

"It wasn't Lance's fault. Bill's not ready for his little princess to have a boyfriend."

Ted smiled. "No father ever is. I remember Sue's father absolutely glaring at me at our wedding. He's never really accepted me."

"Lance is different from most of the kids around here. He

seems older, more sophisticated. Kind of urban. If it was one of the kids, it might have been him."

"How could he do it? He goes to the high school."

"The elementary school was open all summer while they were doing that asbestos removal project. Anybody, including Lance, could have slipped in and set the bomb. I bet it wouldn't take more than a minute or two."

"What about the phone call?"

Lucy leaned forward and wagged a finger at Ted. "I've been thinking about that. The person who made the call wasn't necessarily the same person who set the bomb. The bomber could have gotten one of the students to make the phone call. All a kid has to do is tell the school secretary he forgot his lunch and she'll let him use the phone."

"You may be on to something, Lucy." Ted picked up the phone. "I think I'll give Crowley a call and pass along your idea, just in case he hasn't thought of it himself." He chuckled. "Especially if he hasn't thought of it himself."

"You shouldn't tease the poor man."

"Aw, Lucy. I've got few enough pleasures as it is. Don't take this away from me." He spoke into the receiver. "Chief Crowley? Ted Stillings. How's the investigation going? Got your bomber yet?"

The phone interview didn't take long; Chief Crowley was not known as a conversationalist.

"Well?" asked Lucy when Ted had hung up.

"He said the dogs didn't turn up anything. He wants to question the third and fourth grade students, but Mrs. Applebaum won't let him. He's going to go over her head to the superintendent, and if need be, he'll petition the school committee on Monday."

"That's going to be some meeting," predicted Lucy.

"You bet," said Ted, starting to peck away at his keyboard.

Lucy busied herself with the obituaries. Next thing she knew, it was time for lunch. The afternoon flew by as she organized the old papers in the morgue, answered the phone, and kept an ear cocked to the police scanner.

Just before leaving work, she called Toby at home and asked him to put the lasagna in the oven. She picked up Zoë at the rec center and proceeded to the middle school, where Elizabeth had field hockey practice.

That morning, no longer trusting Elizabeth not to sneak off with Lance, Lucy had decreed she would pick her up after field hockey practice. She had instructed Elizabeth to wait for her on the school steps, but they were empty when she pulled up. She drove around the school to the parking lot beside the playing fields, but there was no sign of her there either. Lucy did see the coach, Mr. Cunningham, talking with one of the players. She approached them, all the while keeping an eye on Zoë, who was strapped in her car seat.

"Hi!" she began. "I'm Elizabeth Stone's mother. I don't see her anywhere."

"Lizzy's probably in the locker room. Sami, would you go in and tell her that her mom's here?"

"Sure, Mr. C." Sami obediently trotted off, her plaid kilt bouncing and her blond ponytail streaming behind her.

"Lizzy's a promising player," said Mr. Cunningham. He was tall, and stooped a bit to talk to Lucy. She thought he was rather homely, with a beak of a nose and a silly mustache, but she could see why Toby and Elizabeth liked him. He seemed relaxed and friendly. "I think she'll make a real contribution to the team."

"Really?" Lucy raised an eyebrow. "Somehow I don't think of her as a team player."

"Lizzy?" He sounded surprised. "She has a natural flair with the stick," he said, walking along with her to the car. "Did you play?"

"Me? No," said Lucy, with a little laugh. "I'm not much of an athlete."

"Well, field hockey's different. It's a great game and the girls love it. It's a chance for them to let out some of that teen aggression."

"No wonder Elizabeth's good at it," said Lucy, grinning as she hopped back in the car and started the engine.

Pulling around to the front steps once again, she saw Elizabeth waiting for her. Zoë laughed and bounced in her safety seat while Elizabeth loaded her book bag and sports bag and hockey stick into the car.

"How was school?" asked Lucy, wondering if Elizabeth was still mad about the night before.

"Okay," admitted Elizabeth, staring straight ahead.

At least she answered, thought Lucy. Encouraged, she plowed ahead. "Mr. Cunningham seems nice. He said you're a natural at field hockey."

"Yeah, he's great. He makes practices fun, you know?" She smiled, and Lucy's heart lifted. It was like the sun coming from behind the clouds after a long gray spell.

"I was surprised you let him call you Lizzy."

"He said Elizabeth is too long—he can't yell it across the field very well."

"I think it's kind of cute," said Lucy.

Elizabeth groaned. "You won't tell Toby, will you?" she asked anxiously. "I don't mind Mr. C. calling me Lizzy, but he's the only one. I don't want Toby doing it." She turned and stared out the window, chewing on a fingernail.

The clouds were back, thought Lucy, pulling into the IGA parking lot. Leaving the girls in the car, she hurried inside and picked up a loaf of garlic bread, an action-packed video, and a box of microwave popcorn.

When she arrived home, she was greeted by the rich, cheesy aroma of the baking lasagna. She tucked the garlic bread in the oven beside it, quickly assembled a salad, and served dinner promptly at six. At half past six the dishwasher was humming and she was on her way to the seven o'clock class at Winchester College, having left the video and popcorn for Bill and the kids.

CHAPTER EIGHT

Winchester College was a venerable liberal arts college located on the outskirts of Tinker's Cove. With its spacious campus, the college was both part of and apart from the town. Students were often seen on Main Street and frequented the shops and restaurants, where their parents' dollars added to the local economy. Some Tinker's Cove residents found work at the college as secretaries and maintenance workers.

For the most part, however, the college was a community unto itself. The professors tended to live in houses near the campus, and socialized with each other. The college sponsored numerous concerts, lectures, and plays throughout the year, but few Tinker's Cove residents ventured onto campus to attend. They were working people, for the most part, and such high-brow entertainment didn't have much appeal for them. The division between town and gown was very real.

When Lucy parked her car and crossed the quad to Tyndall

Hall, where her class was to meet, she felt as if she was entering exciting new territory. It was still quite light, but there was a sense of peaceful calm on the campus. One or two students bicycled past her on the walk, while a few small groups were scattered about on the grassy quad, sitting and chatting. From the open window of a dorm she heard snatches of a rock song.

Maybe this is what it's like for an American to visit England, she thought. You know the language, you know the customs, but it's not your native country. What did these students think of her as they passed? Did they think of her at all? Did she look ridiculously old?

She was dressed much the same as many of the female students in jeans and sneakers, with a light corduroy jacket against the evening chill. A few of the boys seemed to show a bit of interest when they noticed her, walking a bit taller and looking at her as they approached on the walk. But when she was close enough for their eyes to meet, and for them to see her age, they quickly looked away. So much for the theory that young men find older women attractive, she thought.

When she reached her classroom, however, she felt more at home. The students were a mixed bag—a few undergraduates, a handful of senior citizens, and the rest in their late thirties or early forties. Middle-aged, middle managers, middle class—they had the hopeful look of people who were feeling the squeeze and were determined to do something about it.

Lucy slipped into one of the seats with an oversized arm for note taking, smiled at the familiar-looking woman next to her, and waited for class to begin. She didn't have long to wait. At a few minutes past seven the professor strolled in.

Quentin Rea, as he was listed in the course catalog, was not a tall man. He was slight and wiry. But when he removed his

Harris tweed jacket, Lucy noticed he was nicely muscled across his shoulders and back. She guessed he was a bit younger than herself—there was no trace of gray in his hair, which he wore rather long. It was light brown, streaked with blond, and he had a habit of tossing it back. His face was lean, and like some fair men, his beard was surprising heavy. Lucy was willing to bet there was a luxurious growth of hair on the chest beneath that pale blue Oxford cloth shirt.

Ashamed of herself because she was not in the habit of mentally undressing men, however attractive they might be, she turned her head away and met the eye of the woman next to her.

"Dishy, don't you think?" said the woman.

"I don't think I will have any trouble paying attention," said Lucy, with a wink.

"All right," began Professor Rea, after taking the roll. "Why the Victorians? Everybody used to think they were hopelessly dusty and musty, and all of a sudden they're popular again. Any ideas?"

An older man in the back of the room raised his hand, and the professor nodded at him.

"I read somewhere and it struck me at the time that we have all been influenced by the Victorians. A lot of our ideas and manners, even the way we celebrate Christmas, have been passed down to us from the Victorians. Most of us know people who grew up in that period."

Lucy nodded, thinking of her friend Miss Tilley, the retired librarian of the Broadbrooks Free Library. Only Miss Tilley's very dearest friends dared address her by her first name, Julia. She was certainly the living embodiment of Victorian ideas and notions.

"It was the beginning of the modern age—railroads, electric

light, telegraph—they were all invented then. Industrialization was in full swing," offered another man.

"It was a time when roles were changing," Lucy found herself saying. "Then it was the industrial revolution, today it's the information age. The Victorians had to adjust to a new way of living, just like we do."

The professor nodded in agreement. "All true, all true. But if you ask me, the Victorians are popular because we've figured out that all that propriety and formality was nothing more than a coverup. They were obsessed with sex."

He paused, giving the students an opportunity to chuckle.

"Oh, sure, they concealed the piano legs, but we know from their diaries and collections of dirty postcards that they were really a bunch of filthy, dirty-minded little prigs."

While the professor waited for the giggles to subside, he began distributing copies of a reading list.

"Now, I know the first thing you are going to ask is what happened to the Brownings. Well, they're on page two. Your first assignment is Carlyle's *Sartor Resartus*. Don't panic, you won't have to read the whole thing. And we will get to those wonderful sonnets, I promise. They're for dessert, and as any proper Victorian would tell you, it's meat before sweet. Now, what do you know about Thomas Carlyle?" He scanned the class, looking for a volunteer.

"He was Scottish," offered a pretty young thing in the front row.

"That's true. It's a beginning," he said, with an encouraging smile. "What else do you know about him?"

The student squirmed. "Well, he was known as the 'Sage of Chelsea.'"

"Very good. Anyone else?"

"The Clothes Philosophy," offered the older man in the back of the room. "The idea that old ideas, even religions, should be discarded like old clothes."

Lucy regarded the man with new interest. Already she was enjoying the exchange of ideas with her classmates, and the professor's ready wit.

"Ah, yes," said the professor. "Perhaps D. H. Lawrence, a twentieth-century writer who struggled mightily to free literature from the constraints of the Victorian period, said it best when he wrote, 'Gods die with the men who have conceived them . . . Even gods must be born again.' Thank you, Mr. . . . ." He paused and looked down at his class list. "Mr. Irving. And on that note, I think we will end for tonight. I will see you all again on Tuesday."

Checking her watch, Lucy saw the professor had dismissed the class a little early. With luck she might get to the bookstore before it closed at nine. She was heading for the door, when he stopped her.

"Mrs. Stone, that was a very insightful comment."

"Really?" Lucy felt a bit uncomfortable at being singled out.

"Yes, it was." He gave her a lopsided little smile, and the corners of his eyes crinkled. "I wonder if you would like to continue the discussion with me at the student union. I usually stop there after class for a cappuccino."

"Oh, that would be nice," began Lucy, as an embarrassed blush crept over her face, "but I really want to get to the bookstore before it closes. Thanks anyway."

It was only afterward, as she stood in line with her arms full of books, that she wondered why she had been so unnerved by the professor's invitation. After all, she was reasonably attractive and this wasn't the first time since her marriage that another man had expressed interest in her. The problem was, she realized with a shock, until now she hadn't felt tempted to accept.

Trudging toward the parking lot with her heavy bag of books, Lucy was surprised to see Josh Cunningham.

"What are you doing here?" she asked.

"I was just catching up on my reading," he said, shortening his steps to walk beside her. "I need to keep up with new developments in chemistry and biology, but I can't afford the journals—teacher's salary, you know. So I come here every now and then and use the science library. Can I carry those for you?" he asked politely, indicating the books.

"Oh, I can manage. Thanks, anyway," said Lucy, thinking he was awfully nice. "You have another one of my children, you know."

"Who?"

"Toby. He's in ninth grade."

"Toby is yours, too? He's a nice boy."

"I like to think so, but I'm keeping my fingers crossed, just in case."

"Growing up is tough. Sometimes they make bad choices." Josh shook his head mournfully. "Even kids from good families."

"Is that what you think happened with the bombing? Was it one of the kids?"

"I hope not," he said earnestly. "We're a pretty small school system, almost like a family. I don't think it could have been one of ours, but you never know. Kids can really surprise you."

"That's for sure," said Lucy, stopping at the Subaru. "This is my car."

He took the books while she fumbled for the keys.

"You know, Mrs. Stone . . ."

"Call me Lucy."

"Okay, Lucy. I guess you're taking a class? At night?"

Lucy nodded. "Victorian literature."

"Well, if you're going to be using the parking lot at night, I'd suggest you have your keys ready. That way a mugger wouldn't have time to attack you. And you really ought to park under a light, if you can. And stay away from the bushes."

Lucy looked around the dark, shadowy parking lot that was surrounded with tall trees and leafy shrubs. She rarely worried about her safety in Tinker's Cove, but she realized Josh had a point.

"It was still light when I parked," she said, finally pulling the keys from the bottom of her purse and unlocking the door. "Thanks for the advice."

She took the books and climbed in the car.

"No problem," he said, giving her a little wave as she started the engine. "Get home safely."

CHAPTER NINE

When Lucy and Zoë arrived at the day-care center on Friday morning, Sue Finch was leaning on a counter near the row of cubbies that stood ready for the children's jackets and lunch boxes, reading *The Pennysaver*.

"Good morning," she said, looking at Lucy over her half-glasses. Raising a jet black eyebrow she asked, "So, what's the story that Ted didn't print?"

Lucy grinned. One of the best things about working was seeing Sue every morning. The two were longtime best friends, but nowadays they rarely had time for leisurely chats at the kitchen table over a cup of coffee. Sue, who was a member of the town's recreation commission, was the moving force behind the day-care center in the recreation building basement.

"Moms need affordable, high-quality care," she had told the Board of Selectmen, the Finance Committee, and finally the entire town meeting. Everyone, Sue included, was amazed when the normally tightfisted voters approved the funding and the center opened with Sue as director.

" 'It's all in *The Pennysaver*,' " said Lucy, repeating the paper's familiar slogan. She set Zoë down and unzipped her jacket. Then she pulled a brown paper bag from her tote bag and gave it to Zoë. "Give these to Aunt Sue, okay?"

Zoë toddled toward Sue, holding out the bundle.

"Is that for me?" asked Sue, taking the bag. "Tomatoes! Thank you, Zoë." The little girl beamed with pride, then turned and scooted over to the play kitchen.

"There was one thing that didn't make the paper," said Lucy. "Barney said the call to the police reporting the bomb came from the school."

"Hmmm," said Sue, thoughtfully massaging her chin with a perfectly manicured hand.

Watching her, Lucy decided that if she didn't like Sue so much, she would have to hate her. Here she was messing around with fingerpaint and Play-Doh all day and she looked ready for a day on the town in her black slacks, sleeveless white turtleneck, and black patent leather sandals. A smart black and white plaid jacket completed her outfit.

"That means someone inside the school did it? I can't believe that." Sue shook her head. "What do you think about our Ms. Crane? Pretty gutsy, I'd say."

"You were on the search committee that hired her, weren't you?"

"I was," said Sue proudly. "Did we do good?"

"You did good," said Lucy. She watched as Zoë began putting pots on the play stove. "Don't you want to hear about my class? I think it has possibilities."

"To you, maybe. To me," continued Sue, smoothing her

glossy pageboy hairdo, "Victorian literature is about as appealing as doing my taxes. Cleaning the cat box. Washing windows."

"I get the idea," said Lucy. "Each to her own. But I bet even you would find the professor rather attractive."

"Really?" Sue cocked her head to the side.

" 'Dishy' is the word I heard used."

Sue was focusing on two little boys across the room. "Justin, I really like the way you're sharing that truck with Jason." She turned back to Lucy. "How old?"

"Not too old, not too young." Lucy lingered over the words.

"Lucy!" Sue's eyes grew big and round. "You sound as if you're interested in him. Are you considering signing up for some extracurricular activities?"

"Absolutely not!" Lucy exclaimed. "I would never, ever do such a thing."

"Methinks the lady doth protest a bit too much," said Sue, hurrying over to the dress-up area. "Jill, you can wear the bride's veil now, but in a few minutes it will be Tiffany's turn, okay? Tiffany, why not try the policeman's hat for a few minutes, until Jill is ready to give you the veil." She turned back to Lucy, a skeptical expression on her face.

"Believe me, it never even occurred to me. In fact, he asked me out for coffee and I turned him down." Lucy nodded virtuously.

"If I were you, I'd keep turning him down."

"He'll never ask again."

"Don't bet on it. When I was in college, there were professors who were absolutely relentless. They had to get their hands on as many of the girls as possible—I think it was a contest or something. It was rumored they had a scoreboard in the faculty club."

"I remember a few professors like that, too. But I think things have changed. They call it sexual harassment and you can file a complaint."

"Maybe." Sue didn't seem convinced. "Is everything okay with you and Bill?"

"Sure." Lucy's tone was a bit defensive. "It's just one of those rough times that all couples go through. He's having a hard time adjusting now that the kids are growing up. He wants everything to stay the same. He doesn't like me working."

"You know, I see that a lot." Sue grabbed a paper towel and mopped up the snack table, where the little bride had just spilled a cup of grape juice. "When the moms first bring their kids here, they're happy and excited. But pretty soon they start getting a worried look and the next thing you know we're getting a letter from the lawyer advising us that divorce proceedings are in progress and not to release the child to anyone but the mother."

"I don't think it will come to that," said Lucy, looking absolutely stricken. "At least, I hope not. I was really joking about the professor."

"I'm exaggerating," said Sue, patting her arm. "It's only happened once, maybe twice."

"You had me worried," said Lucy, laughing with relief. "The way I see it, we're going to need two incomes. College isn't that far away for Toby and Elizabeth, you know."

"Don't I ever." Sue's daughter Sidra had graduated from Bowdoin in June. "We'll be paying off those loans until it's time for us to retire." Hearing a wail from across the room, she looked up. "Justin, you don't really want to hit Eloise with that truck. You want to share the truck with Eloise. See? Eloise is going to load the truck with blocks, and you can dump them out."

Glancing at her watch, Lucy saw she was already a few minutes late. Giving Sue a wave, and Zoë a peck on the cheek, she hurried out. Mounting the steps to the sidewalk, she noticed a vending machine filled with issues of *The Pennysaver*. It was old news today, but the page one photo of Carol Crane was still compelling.

Caught by the camera, she was a picture of courage under stress. Slightly disheveled, her stocking torn, a streak of dirt across her skirt, she seemed a very fragile heroine. Bending over little Tommy Spitzer, her body conveyed a message of care and concern. But the expression on her face, raised to the camera and the crowd beyond, was exalted. She might have been Saint Joan, defying the flames.

Lucy shook her head and hurried down the street to the newspaper office. As she marched along, she thought of the Clothes Theory that Mr. Irving had mentioned in class the night before. It seemed an odd name for a philosophical theory about religion. An odd idea, really. People changing religion to suit their needs, just like they changed their clothes. A Christian Conservative would wear a suit and tie. A liberal Unitarian would wear blue jeans. Atheists were doomed to wear sweat suits. Lucy smiled at her cleverness as she pulled open the door and confronted Ted.

"I know I'm late," she began.

"No problem," said Ted with a casual wave of his hand. "I was just on my way to the post office. I'll be right back. We've got a bulk mailing to get out."

When he returned, he was carrying several plastic trays for the mailing, plus a big bundle of letters held together with a thick rubber band.

"This is odd," he said, setting the trays on the counter. "We don't usually get this much mail." He went over to his desk and reached for the letter opener.

Seeing a big stack of printed subscription notices piled on her desk, Lucy busied herself attaching address stickers while Ted read the mail.

"This is amazing," he said, waving a handful of letters. "These are all letters to the editor."

"Don't you usually get that many?"

"Are you kidding? We print them all—maybe three or four a week. And they're usually about John Q. Public's favorite gripe. Like kids playing basketball in the street. Or the no parking sign in front of the library. These are all about Carol Crane."

"What do they say?"

He began reading from the letters. "How heroic she was. How brave. What a wonderful woman she must be. An inspiration to our youth. Courage in action. A true feminist. Our schools are privileged to have her." He slapped them down on the desk and shook his head. "This is really something, Lucy. I've never seen anything like this."

"It's the picture. It's an image people respond to. It's half Jackie Kennedy, half Christa McAuliffe. It's like an icon."

Ted held up the paper and examined the picture. "I see what you mean. She's the teacher-saint."

"I know," said Lucy. "It makes me suspicious. It's too perfect, somehow."

"Go on," said Ted, his interest caught.

"Well, it was a hot day. But here's Carol coming in to work in a little Chanel suit with a jacket and a tight, tight skirt. And high heels. Women who work with kids don't dress like that. Take Sue, for example. She always looks great, but she wears flats and slacks. If it had been Sue in that picture, the whole message would be entirely different. She would have looked competent and strong. Instead of people being all overcome with her bravery and courage for saving the kid, they'd want to know why she didn't defuse the bomb on her way out."

"The perils of being Superwoman," joked Ted.

"Yeah, well think about it. What exactly was Carol Crane dressing for that morning? A normal working day?"

"It was the first day of school. Maybe she wanted to make a good impression."

"I don't know. The whole thing seems pretty fishy to me."

"Oh, Lucy," said Ted, waggling his finger at her. "What a suspicious mind you have."

"I can't help it, it's just the way I am," said Lucy contritely.

"Don't apologize. I like it. Somewhere along the line you must have got some ink in your blood."

Lucy went back to her work, but she couldn't help feeling a warm little glow. It was nice to be appreciated.

CHAPTER TEN

"The thing that gets me," said Bill as he and Lucy drove together to the school committee meeting on Monday evening, "the thing that really ticks me off is the fact that school is compulsory, right? We have to send the kids to school, but the school can't guarantee that they'll be safe while they're there."

Lucy had been looking out the window as they drove along; Bill had taken the long way around on the shore road. She liked passing the old farms with their houses and barns scattered among the golden hay fields. Peeking through the tall firs, she could catch glimpses of gray ocean, with a rocky island poking up here and there.

She turned and looked at Bill. Tonight he'd changed out of his usual working uniform, a plaid flannel shirt and jeans, and was wearing chinos and a blue button-down shirt. Instead of work boots he had slipped on a pair of boat shoes. Tall and bearded, he never seemed to gain a pound; he looked just as he had when they'd married almost twenty years ago. Good old Bill, she thought. He's steady and reliable, you could tell time by him. He left at seven in the morning; he came home at five-thirty and wanted dinner at six. She knew him so well, she could have laid odds on what he would say next. He would bring up Toby's missing backpack.

"It was just last spring, wasn't it," he asked, "that Toby's fancy new Country Cousins backpack was stolen. Did it ever turn up? No. How much was that worth?"

"About twenty dollars. I used my discount."

"What are you smiling at?"

"Nothing," she said with a shake of her head and a little shrug. She didn't know why she felt so defensive when Bill criticized the schools, but she did. "They do the best they can, Bill. The budget is tight, there aren't a lot of frills. But the kids get a good education. Look at the colleges they go to. Sidra went to Bowdoin, that Franklin kid went to Harvard."

"That's all very well and good, Lucy," said Bill, turning the pickup sharply into the high school parking lot, "but nobody's going to college if they all get blown up while they're still in elementary school."

"Tell me what you think," said Lucy, laying her hand on Bill's forearm as he reached to turn off the ignition. "Who do you think set the bomb?"

"It's obvious—it had to be one of the kids. Probably one of those special-needs kids with emotional problems." He turned the key, and the truck shuddered as the engine kicked a few times in protest before shutting off.

"I wish I could be so sure," said Lucy, jumping down from the cab. "It's so much easier when things are black and white."

"What's that supposed to mean?" asked Bill as they fell into step together.

"Admit it," challenged Lucy, waving her arms as she spoke. "You think the school is run by a bunch of liberal wussies who waste our tax dollars, let the kids get away with murder, and don't bother to teach them anything."

Bill turned and stared at her, scratching his bearded chin thoughtfully. "You know, you're right," he said. "And you know what else? I don't think I'm alone."

Looking around, Lucy had to agree. A steady stream of cars was turning into the parking lot, and clumps of people, in pairs and threesomes, were marching toward the school with determination. In the lobby, lines had formed leading into the auditorium.

Finding herself beside Josh Cunningham, Lucy greeted him warmly. "We have to stop meeting like this," she joked.

"Hi, Lucy. Are you here for the meeting?"

"Sure am," said Lucy. Aware that Bill was eyeing Josh rather suspiciously, she hurried to introduce them.

"Josh, this is my husband, Bill Stone. Bill, Josh Cunningham is Toby's teacher. He calls him Mr. C."

"Hi," said Bill, extending his hand. "Nice to meet you."

"Are you coming to the meeting, too?" asked Lucy.

"Not me," said Josh, grinning and shaking his head. "I try to stay as far away from meetings and politics as I can."

"Good idea," agreed Bill.

"No, I just came by to set up a demonstration for my classes tomorrow. It's a model of the atom. For some reason the electrons keep disappearing." He shrugged. "I've got to find them or think of something to replace them."

"Well, good luck," said Lucy.

"You'll need it more than me," he said, indicating the already crowded auditorium. "Atoms can't talk."

As they took their seats, Lucy thought Josh had made a wise choice. School committee meetings were usually poorly attended and took place in the school library. Tonight it looked as if it would be standing room only. Furthermore, this was clearly an anxious crowd. The usual buzz of premeeting conversation was more like a roar tonight as voices bounced off the painted concrete block walls and the uncurtained stage. As people spoke with each other, they made short, choppy gestures with their hands, and nodded sharply, their expressions grim.

Lucy looked for people she knew. There in the front row, of course, was Ted, notebook in his lap and camera at the ready. Also in the front row were an agonized-looking group of teachers from the elementary school, including kindergarten teacher Lydia Volpe, and Sara's teacher, Ms. Kinnear. A few rows behind them sat a contingent from the high school. Sitting uncomfortably on the stage, at a small table set to the side of the larger one reserved for the school committee, were the three school principals: Sophie Applebaum, Frank Todd from the middle school, and Walker Mead, who headed the high school. They looked as if they were about to be charged with crimes against humanity, and Lucy sympathized with them.

The noise level subsided momentarily when one of the school committee members made his way to the stage. It was Stan Eubanks, the chairman. Stan was a round, red-faced man who looked as if he ought to sell insurance, and did. He was joined a few moments later by Caroline Hutton, a retired professor of dance from Winchester College. Lucy smiled to see her; a few years ago they had conspired to protect little Melissa Roderick from an abusive situation.*

Caro and Stan greeted each other with warm smiles and chatted as they began looking through the information packets at their places. A third member, local attorney George Witherspoon, soon appeared and sat down between them. The three became deeply absorbed in conversation, and Lucy wished she could hear what they were saying.

Then the fourth member and newest member of the board, DeWalt Smythe, took his seat. None of them greeted him, but turned instead to their packets, which apparently contained fascinating reading material. DeWalt was the minister of the Revelation Congregation and had been narrowly elected last spring, thanks to the votes of his parishioners, who turned out in record numbers.

Even from a distance, it was obvious that the other committee members were giving DeWalt the cold shoulder; he was clearly the odd man out, separated from the rest by an empty seat. Ruth Winters, a rather nervous woman who ran a gift shop, was absent tonight and Lucy didn't blame her one bit.

Finally, Stan Eubanks banged down his gavel and called the meeting to order. He leaned into the microphone on the table in front of him, and the sound system emitted a piercing screech. Mr. Mopps, the custodian, hurried forward and adjusted the microphone.

When Mr. Eubanks tried again, the shriek was even louder. This was met by the audience with a collective groan.

Mr. Mopps looked anxiously over his shoulder at the crowd, and then bent over the microphone, tapping it hopefully with

*Tippy-Toe Murder

his fingers but achieving little more than brief pauses in the annoying static it was producing. Then, as everyone watched, Carol Crane pranced up the steps to the stage. Taking the mike from Mr. Mopps, she pointed him in the direction of the backstage control box. Seconds later the cackle subsided, and Carol spoke into the mike.

"Testing ... one, two, three." Hearing her voice come through clearly, she smiled and handed the mike to Stan. The audience, recognizing the heroine who had saved Tommy, applauded enthusiastically. Carol gave a little wave and returned to her seat, and Stan called for the first matter of business, an update from the police chief on the status of the bombing investigation.

Chief Crowley got to his feet from his seat in the front row and lumbered toward the microphone set up near the foot of the stairs leading to the stage. He adjusted the metal stand, rocked back on his heels, and began speaking.

"As most of you know if you watch TV or listen to the radio or read the papers, the investigation is continuing." He adjusted the blue tie that matched his uniform with thick, callused fingers. "If you have any questions, I'll do my best to answer them."

"Do you have any suspects?" called out a voice from the audience.

"We got a whole bunch of suspects," said the chief, coolly scanning the crowd.

Stan banged the table with his gavel. "Please don't speak until you are recognized by the chair. And when you are recognized, please identify yourself. You, in the red," he said, pointing to a young mother with an earnest expression.

"I'm Susan Winslow," she said in a voice that could barely

be heard. "I understood you were going to question the children—what happened?"

"I think I'll pass that question along to Mrs. Applebaum," said the chief, grinning smugly. "She went to court and got an injunction."

There was an angry buzz from some of the audience members as Mrs. Applebaum approached a second microphone, located on the opposite side of the auditorium.

"Chief Crowley is correct. As part of the investigation, he requested permission to question all the children and I refused for two reasons. One, the role of the school is to educate the children and I believe the questioning would disrupt the educational process, and two, I believe the children have a right not to be questioned unless there are specific grounds to suspect they are involved. Chief Crowley went to the superintendent of schools." Mrs. Applebaum nodded in the direction of Michael Gaffney, a rather heavy, balding man in a gray suit who was sitting with the committee. "Dr. Gaffney overruled my decision, so I went to Superior Court where I requested, and received, the injunction."

Hands shot up all over the room. Mr. Eubanks recognized Vicki Hughes. Lucy remembered how they had stood together, waiting anxiously, on the day of the explosion.

"I can't believe you would behave so irresponsibly," said Vicki. "Our children's safety is at stake here. I would feel a lot more comfortable if this investigation is allowed to proceed. I certainly don't mind if my child is questioned, if it will help find the person responsible for the bombing."

There was a hum of approval from the crowd as she sat down in her seat. Not everyone joined in, however. A few parents were shaking their heads and looking uneasy. Sophie Applebaum remained placidly in place at the microphone.

"Mrs. Spitzer," said Mr. Eubanks, recognizing little Tommy's mother.

"I just want to say that Tommy is doing fine, thanks to this wonderful woman." With her hand, Mrs. Spitzer indicated Carol Crane, who bobbed up from her seat behind Lydia Volpe. She was answered with a roar of applause from the crowd. Mrs. Spitzer waited for the clapping to subside, and then resumed speaking.

"I am grateful that Tommy suffered no adverse affects, but I do have a question for Mrs. Applebaum and Mrs. Volpe. What happened? Why didn't anyone notice he was missing? It seems to me there was some negligence involved here. I dread to think what could have happened." She sniffed, and fumbled in her pocket for a tissue.

"I understand how upsetting this has been for you and your family," said Mrs. Applebaum.

Everyone was silent, waiting for an explanation.

"Mrs. Volpe is an experienced and capable teacher," Mrs. Applebaum continued.

Lucy nodded in agreement; she knew and liked Lydia.

"I would like to remind you all that this was the first day of school. It takes a few days for the teachers to get to know all their students. I have spoken with Mrs. Volpe and she has told me she did not see Tommy at all that morning. In fact, she marked him absent when she took the roll."

"I brought him to the nurses' office that morning, just as I was instructed," said Mrs. Spitzer with a challenging stare.

"We are continuing to look into it," said Mrs. Applebaum.

"I hope you do," said Mrs. Spitzer angrily. "I think I am entitled to some answers."

The crowd buzzed angrily, and a number of people raised their hands.

"We all want answers," said DeWalt Smythe, rising to his feet from his seat at the table on the stage. He was tall, and his suit with a lapel pin in the shape of a cross was a reminder of his calling. "I promise you, Mrs. Spitzer, that I will make this my personal mission. No stone shall remain unturned, I shall cast light into the darkest corners. Those who are innocent need have no fear; but those who are guilty should be afraid."

He looked directly at Mrs. Applebaum, but she was equally firm in her convictions and did not flinch from his accusatory stare. Caroline Hutton glanced at her fellow board members, who shook their heads in disapproval.

Stan Eubanks banged down his gavel, and Lucy jumped. The tension in the room was terrible; she could not imagine how Sophie could remain so calm in the face of so much hostility.

"I will allow a few more questions," said Stan, "but then I must return the meeting to the committee. We have a heavy agenda tonight."

"This is more important than the agenda," came a voice from the rear, but Stan ignored it and recognized a tall man dressed in a grubby sweatshirt and a pair of yellow fisherman's overalls. The unshaven stubble on his chin indicated he had come to the meeting straight from his boat—he had probably been pulling lobster traps.

"I'm no education expert," he said, "but I do know how to spell . . ." Here he paused and then added, "Pretty much" which got him a laugh from the crowd. "And I got to tell you, I don't understand what they're doing in this school. I know we're all worried about the bombing, but I've been plenty worried about what's been going on here for a long time. My kids come home with papers, they get check-plusses which they tell me means they did very well, and not a word is spelled right. It doesn't seem to me that they're learning English, it looks like some foreign language to me, and what the hell is the matter with a grade you can understand, like an A or a B? That's what I want to know!"

The man remained standing, receiving an enthusiastic round of applause, and waited for his answer.

"I hear this quite often from parents," began Mrs. Applebaum, waiting for the crowd to quiet down. "First of all, I want to assure you that whole language does work. It allows children to learn language by using it, and encourages them to express themselves . . ."

She got no further; quite a few people began booing as soon as she uttered the words "express themselves."

Sensing he was losing control of the meeting, Stan pounded on the table with his gavel. "One more question," he said, pointing at a rather prim-looking woman.

She got to her feet hesitantly. "I'd rather not say my name, and I'm not sure this is the right place, and I don't want to get into specifics, but what is the procedure a parent should follow when a teacher has behaved inappropriately?"

For the first time that evening the room was absolutely quiet.

Stan appealed to Mike Gaffney, the superintendent of schools, who reluctantly got to his feet.

"The usual thing, ahem, is to schedule a meeting with the teacher," he began. Pausing to clear his voice again, he continued. "Uh, to discuss whatever the, uh, problem is. If you're not satisfied after that, you should contact the principal." He sat down.

"I don't think I'd be comfortable doing that," said the woman.

"Well, then, ma'am," said DeWalt Smythe, "the proper procedure is for you to arrange a meeting with me. You can talk to me after the meeting, or you can call me at the Revelation Congregation—the number is in the phone book. And I promise you, together, we will get to the bottom of this!"

Once again the crowd erupted, and Eubanks banged away with his gavel to no avail. It was only when Carol Crane rose and approached a microphone that an expectant hush came over the audience.

"There has been a lot of concern expressed here tonight," she began, speaking in a smooth, professional manner. "I thank you for coming. We all know that our children are our most important resource. It has been said that it takes a village to raise a child—and I think the children of Tinker's Cove are fortunate indeed to live in a village where adults are determined to do what's right for them."

It was amazing, thought Lucy. The woman's voice was magical; already the anger and anxiety that had filled the room was beginning to dissipate.

"I would like to suggest to the school committee that one solution that has worked well in many communities is the establishment of school councils." She paused. "The councils are not like the parent organizations you are familiar with, like the PTA that primarily raises money, but give parents and other concerned citizens a real voice in decisions affecting the school. I would urge the committee to look into this.

"In the meantime . . . I think it's important to let parents know the investigation into the bombing is continuing, engineers have determined that the building is sound, and on behalf of the staff, I want to assure you that we are doing everything we can to ensure that your children are safe and are getting a quality education."

Once again the crowd erupted into enthusiastic applause. Stan Eubanks and the members of the school committee beamed at her in approval. Out of the corner of her eye, Lucy saw Sophie stumping heavily up the side aisle to the nearest door. The principal looked sick, and Lucy jumped to her feet to follow her in case she needed assistance. It took quite a while to make her way out of the crowded row of seats, however, and when Lucy finally reached the lobby, there was no sign of Sophie.

She wandered a little way down the empty hallway, peeking into classrooms and checking the ladies' room, but the principal seemed to have vanished. Lucy turned to go back to the auditorium, but hearing voices as she passed a side corridor leading to the band room and auditorium stage, she decided to investigate.

Lucy didn't exactly tiptoe down the corridor, but she was careful not to make too much noise either. Approaching the band room, she saw the door was ajar, allowing her a clear view of Carol Crane and Mr. Mopps.

"If I've told you once, I've told you a thousand times," scolded Carol. "You have to check the sound system before the meeting. You can't wait until all the people are here to see if the microphone works. Do you understand me?"

"I did check it." Mr. Mopps spoke quietly. "It worked fine this afternoon."

"Don't give me that, Pops," snarled Carol. Lucy was shocked at the venom in her voice. "I know all about people like you. You don't do any more than you have to. You're lazy. You better watch it because I'm keeping my eye on you."

"You can do whatever you want," answered Mr. Mopps. "You're the boss."

"You're damned right I am. And I'm going to make sure you don't get out of line—you know what I mean."

"I don't know what you mean," he insisted. "I just do my job."

"Right." Carol's tone dripped with sarcasm. "And you make sure the little girls' room is especially clean, don't you?"

"Of course. The girls' room, the boys' room, the teachers' room—I haven't had any complaints."

"Play innocent if you want," sneered Carol. "Just remember, I know what you're up to."

Caught up in the little drama she was witnessing, Lucy didn't notice when her purse slipped off her shoulder and landed on the floor with a thud.

The sound caused Carol to whirl around. The anger on her face instantly melted away as she caught sight of Lucy.

"Yes, can I help you?" asked Carol brightly.

"I seem to be lost," said Lucy. "I was looking for the ladies' room."

"Come this way," said Carol, stepping forward and sticking out her hand for a handshake. "I'm Carol Crane, the assistant principal."

"I'm Lucy Stone. My daughter, Sara, is in the second grade."

"Isn't that wonderful?" Carol gave her a dazzling smile. "I know Sara—she's a little peach."

"Well, we think so," said Lucy, following Carol down the corridor. She wondered if Carol really knew who Sara was and tried to think of a question she could ask that would prove it one way or the other, but she couldn't think of anything.

Carol stopped in front of the ladies' room door. "Here it is," she said.

"I don't know how I could have missed it," said Lucy. "Thanks so much."

Pushing the door open, she went inside. Standing in front

of the sink, she washed her hands and face and patted them dry with a rough, brown school paper towel. What was that all about, she wondered, as she left to rejoin Bill. She had never seen anyone change character so completely. In the wink of an eye Carol had switched from nasty to nice.

The crowd was already leaving the meeting, so she waited by the auditorium doorway until she saw him.

"What happened after I left?" she asked, taking his arm.

"Not much. The chairman pretty much told us to get out so they could get on with their business."

"I feel sorry for Sophie," said Lucy. "I think Carol upstaged her on purpose."

"So what?" said Bill. "I think old Sophie got what was coming to her. I think it's about time there were some changes around here. What is it they say—education's too important to leave to the experts."

The fisherman who had spoken earlier was stuck in the crowd next to them, as they slowly shuffled across the lobby to the outside door. Hearing Bill's comment, he turned and slapped him on the back.

"You said it, man. It's about time we—and I mean us parents—took back our schools."

CHAPTER ELEVEN

The next morning, Lucy found herself dragging after she left Zoë at the day-care center. It was Tuesday, deadline was once again approaching, and she knew it would be busy at the paper. Passing Jake's Donut Shack, she decided to get a coffee to go, and one for Ted, too. Falling into line at the counter she found herself behind Lydia Volpe.

"Tough meeting last night," she sympathized.

"Hi, Lucy. You're not kidding. I'm beginning to feel as if I can't show my face in town. A mob will gather, shave my head, and stone me."

"I don't think it's quite that bad," said Lucy. "No one's accused you of witchcraft."

"Not yet," said Lydia. "But it probably won't be long. Black with Nutrasweet," she told the counter girl. Taking the little bag, she stood waiting for Lucy to place her order.

"Two large coffees, one black and one regular," said Lucy. "And two cinnamon crullers." She turned to Lydia. "I know I shouldn't, but some days you just need a sugar-caffeine-cholesterol jolt."

"Tell me about it." Lydia looked terrible. Her usual vivacity was gone, even her black, usually curly hair had lost its bounce and hung in soft waves.

Lucy paid for the coffee and doughnuts, took the bag, and put her free arm around Lydia, drawing her close. Lowering her voice, she asked, "So what did happen with Tommy?"

Lydia shook her head. "Lucy, I never saw him that morning. He never came to class. I marked him absent, just like Sophie said. Then, when we were all standing outside the school, one of the kids said she had seen him. I panicked."

"When they put him on the stretcher, he said he was locked in. Where was he?"

"In the supply closet. You know—it has one of those long, narrow windows in the door. Angela said she saw him in there. At first I was skeptical, but some of the other kids said they saw him, too. I was so busy counting heads that I walked right by and never noticed." She bit her lip. "With the budget cutbacks I have over thirty kids this year—not that that's any excuse. Believe me, not a night goes by that I don't dream about him, trapped in there."

Lydia's enormous brown eyes were starting to overflow with tears, and Lucy gave her arm a squeeze.

"It's not your fault—really. How do you think he got in there? I thought those closets were kept locked."

"It usually is—I don't know. Maybe he chickened out on the way to class, maybe one of the kids shoved him inside as a joke. The school nurse was supposed to bring him to class—on the elevator—but she says she had an emergency. A kid with an asthma attack. When she was finally free to bring Tommy down, he was gone and she assumed one of the aides had taken care of him. I wish she had thought to check with me, that he was safely in my class, but she didn't and I'm not going to bring it up. There's enough finger pointing going on as it is."

"You can say that again," said Lucy. "What was all that about a teacher behaving inappropriately?"

"I don't know, and frankly, I don't believe it. Most of the teachers have been on the job for years. There's never been a problem like this before. Why is all this stuff coming up now? Frankly, it reeks of politics to me."

"Politics?"

"Sure. DeWalt Smythe has an agenda and he doesn't care who he hurts. He's on the side of the angels, of course, so anybody who doesn't agree with him is automatically suspect. Oh, gosh, is that the time?" Lydia shook her wrist in frustration. "I've got to go. But, Lucy, tell Ted what I told you, okay? People need to know what's really going on."

"Do I smell coffee?" Ted lifted his head from the computer screen and sniffed appreciatively. "Bless you. You're an angel."

"Not quite—it's a guilt offering," said Lucy. "I figured it was the least I could do if I was going to be late the day before deadline."

She set the bag on the counter and carefully extracted the hot paper cups of coffee. "I got crullers," she confessed. "I don't know about you but my energy level is zip."

"That's why they invented coffee," said Ted, taking a long slurpy drink.

"So, what did you think of the meeting last night?"

Ted read from his computer screen. "The bomb that detonated in the elementary school last week may not have done much damage to the school building, but the explosion has shattered trust in the school system."

"I think you got that right," said Lucy. "I just saw Lydia in the doughnut shop—she feels there's a witch hunt going on, and she's the witch." Lucy took a bite of cruller. "She says DeWalt Smythe has an agenda."

"Good old DeWalt. You gotta love the guy. He's convinced he's on a mission from God. He wants to pack the school committee with members of the Revelation Congregation. Then they can toss evolution out the window and bring back creationism."

"You're kidding, right?"

"Am not," said Ted with a wry little smile. "DeWalt doesn't believe there's a hole in the ozone—thinks that's a liberal plot to undermine faith in God. He doesn't believe women's brains are as big as men's—somehow their female parts take up the space. And he wants to know why, if all these smarty-pants scientists are so convinced that Darwin was right, well, why are they so worried about a teensy little bit of competition from Holy Scripture?"

"Well," said Lucy, crumpling up the wax paper doughnut wrapping and dusting off her hands, "my brain may be smaller than DeWalt's, but I'm pretty sure it's more efficient."

Ted snorted. "I don't doubt it. But DeWalt has a lot of people convinced he's right. The Revelation Congregation is one of the fastest-growing churches in the state."

"Heaven help us," said Lucy, flicking on her computer.

As she typed, her thoughts inevitably returned to the meeting. She'd never seen anything like it. The bombing had unleashed a tidal wave of parental anger and distrust that had apparently been building for quite a while.

She hadn't realized that so many people were dissatisfied with the schools. She didn't have any complaints herself, but then, she frequently volunteered and was in the classrooms fairly often. She knew firsthand how hard the teachers worked, and how much they cared about the children.

A lot of people didn't have the time or the inclination to volunteer, and they only knew what they heard from others and read in the newspapers. It was true, Lucy admitted, that the Tinker's Cove students had not performed well on standardized tests. And come to think of it, Bill had hired a high school kid to help him this summer but decided to let him go. "He can't seem to use a ruler," Bill had complained.

Maybe there were some problems, thought Lucy, but they could surely be solved if people talked and worked together. That, in effect, was what Carol Crane had proposed. DeWalt Smythe, on the other hand, seemed intent on fanning the flames of discontent for his own purposes.

Lucy's fingers stopped on the keyboard. Could DeWalt have set the bomb, she wondered. He certainly seemed to be gaining the most from it—people who would normally have regarded him skeptically were applauding him enthusiastically last night.

She picked up a pen and chewed on the cap as she considered this new possibility. Could he have done it? As a school committee member, he certainly had access to the school anytime he wanted. If he needed help with the technicalities, he had any number of devoted followers to choose from.

Lucy shook her head. Maybe she didn't agree with DeWalt's ideas, but he was a man of the cloth. Sunday after Sunday he led his congregation in prayer and exhorted them to follow the Ten Commandments. She might not like his style, but she had no reason to doubt his sincerity or his faith.

Leaning back in her chair, Lucy stretched. She realized she

had a headache, and got up to get some aspirin. That's what you get for thinking too hard, she told herself.

That afternoon, Ted let Lucy go a couple of hours early. She was caught up with her work and he was going to be in the office anyway, working on an editorial. She was grateful for the gift of free time—she hadn't finished her reading assignment for class, and it was an opportunity to cook a nice dinner.

Zoë was napping, and she was mixing up Bill's favorite meatloaf, when she heard the school bus brake at the end of the driveway. Minutes later Sarah, Elizabeth, and Toby burst into the kitchen, followed by Lance.

"Elizabeth," protested Lucy. "You're supposed to be at field hockey—and Lance isn't supposed to be here at all."

"He's with me, Mom," said Toby. "We're working on something for the talent show."

"And there wasn't any field hockey," said Elizabeth, self-righteously. "Mr. Cunningham was suspended." She wrinkled her face up in disbelief. "I didn't know they could do that to teachers."

Lucy stopped kneading the meatloaf mixture and rested her gooey hands on the edge of the bowl. "Are you sure?"

"It's true," said Toby, in a serious tone of voice. "We had a substitute for science. I heard it's because of a joke he made about one of the girls on the field hockey team."

"That's not true. He would never do that," said Elizabeth.

"It doesn't seem like his style," agreed Lucy. "There was a woman at the meeting last night who accused a teacher—no name—of inappropriate behavior. Do you think she was talking about Mr. Cunningham?"

"That's crazy, Mom," said Toby. "He's really nice. He treats everybody the same. He doesn't make cracks about the dumb kids like Mr. Swazey does or anything."

"What about at practice, Elizabeth? Does he joke around? Could somebody have misunderstood?"

"Not that I ever heard," said Elizabeth. "Do you think he'll be back tomorrow? We have a game on Friday and we need the practice."

"I wouldn't bet on it," said Lucy. "When a teacher's suspended, there's quite a lengthy process. Do you have much homework?"

"I'll do it later," said Elizabeth. "Come on, Sara. You can drive balls to me so I can practice my stops. You can even use my old field hockey stick if you want."

"No! I don't want to!" Sara was sitting at the table with her arms crossed across her chest. She stuck out her bottom lip.

Lucy couldn't believe her ears. Sara adored Elizabeth and would normally never turn down an opportunity to get some attention from her big sister.

"What's the matter, honey? Don't you feel good?" asked Lucy.

"Come on, Sara. It'll be fun, I promise," coaxed Elizabeth. *"No!"*

Elizabeth shrugged, grabbed her field hockey stick and went on outside. Lucy sat down at the table opposite Sara. From the family room she heard the frantic drumbeats of alternative rock.

"Okay, honey pie. What's going on? I can tell that something is really bothering you."

"Mr. Mopps." Sara kicked her feet.

"What about Mr. Mopps?"

"He's gone."

"That's too bad. Is he sick?"

Sara shook her head. "Ms. Crane told him to get out."

"Really?" said Lucy. "When was this?"

"I went to the bathroom and they were in the hall outside. Ms. Crane was real mad. Mr. Mopps was sad."

"I'm sure he was," said Lucy. "Maybe he broke a rule. Ms. Crane must have had a good reason."

"She doesn't like him. She doesn't like Ms. Kinnear or Mrs. Applebaum either. Will she make them leave?"

"No. She can't do that." Lucy picked up Sara and put her on her knee. "Why do you think she doesn't like Ms. Kinnear and Mrs. Applebaum?"

"It's the way she looks at them." Sara pulled her head back and narrowed her eyes into slits.

Lucy laughed and gave her a squeeze.

"It's not funny, Mom." Sara was solemn. "I'm scared of her. She's mean. She yells."

"Just follow the rules and she won't yell at you. Go on out and play now, okay?"

Lucy could hear Zoë babbling to herself in her crib so she went upstairs and brought her down to the kitchen. She toddled about, pushing her toy lawn mower in circles while Lucy patted the meatloaf into shape and slid it into the oven. She tucked some potatoes in beside it, adding one for Lance. Then, while Zoë investigated the pot cupboard, she finished reading the last few pages of *Sartor Resartus*.

She was just closing the book when the boys appeared, looking for something to eat. Lucy distributed ice cream sandwiches from the freezer.

"Lance, if you'd like to stay for dinner, I can give you a ride home on my way to class tonight."

"Thanks, Mrs. Stone."

"Shouldn't you call your parents and see if it's okay?"

"Oh, that's all right." He punched Toby in the arm and they ran outside. Lucy watched from the window as they joined the girls in an improvised game. The boys practiced their soccer moves, passing the ball with their feet, and Elizabeth and Sara chased them across the yard, trying to regain control of the little white ball with their sticks.

Lucy couldn't quite place Lance. Usually, kids in Tinker's Cove fell into two groups: the kids from nice families, and the ones from not-so-nice families. Although she would never admit it, Lucy tried to make sure her kids only associated with the nice children. The ones they first met at story hour at the library, the ones whose dads coached youth soccer and whose mothers baked for the PTA bake sale and volunteered as class mothers.

Usually it was not difficult to tell which category a new friend belonged to. The nice kids were clean, their clothes might be hand-me-downs but they fit and were appropriate, they had eyeglasses and braces if they needed them. They had nice manners, and they always called home if they came to visit after school. Usually, it was the visitor's parents' responsibility to provide transportation home, but sometimes the host mother would oblige, especially if she happened to need milk, or was transporting another child to Scouts or ballet or swimming lessons. There were rules about these things, unwritten, but understood by everyone.

As she watched Lance race across the grassy yard, Lucy decided she could not place him in either category. His hair and nose ring were not-nice, but his clothes were clean and bore exclusive brand-name logos. His teeth were straight, but Lucy couldn't tell whether they were just naturally that way or had been expensively straightened. He had nice manners, but he hadn't called home. Who were his parents, she wondered, and where did they live? What did they do?

She was tearing up lettuce for a salad when Bill came home.

"What's going on here?" he demanded, his hands resting on his hips and his elbows cocked.

"Hi, to you, too," said Lucy, raising her eyebrows at his abrupt question.

"I thought that kid, Lance or Vance or whatever his name is, isn't supposed to be here. I thought we had a family policy."

"He's here on a technicality," said Lucy. "He isn't supposed to visit Elizabeth, but he came home with Toby."

"That's not acceptable." Bill paced back and forth across the kitchen. "What is he, some kind of wise guy? I don't like that."

"Well, he hasn't paid any attention to Elizabeth all day. He and Toby have been working on a rap song for the talent show. I've been home all afternoon, keeping an eye on things."

"Just look at that, will ya?" Bill snapped.

Lucy looked out the window and saw Lance prancing in front of Elizabeth, agilely bouncing the ball from one knee to the other. Elizabeth was laughing. Toby was watching from a distance. It all seemed pretty innocent.

"I think you're overreacting," said Lucy. "Dinner will be ready in a few minutes. It's meatloaf, your favorite."

"Thanks," Bill grunted, and pulled a bottle of beer from the refrigerator. He twisted off the cap and sat down at the kitchen table. He rolled the bottle in his hand, but didn't take a drink.

"Is something else bothering you?"

"Didn't get a job I bid for."

"There'll be other jobs."

"I thought this was a sure thing. I didn't bother to bid some other work."

"Like I said, something will come along."

"I wish I had your confidence." Bill tilted his head back and took a long swallow of beer.

Despite the fact that meatloaf was usually a family favorite, nobody seemed to enjoy dinner much. Bill kept casting suspicious glances at Lance. Lance and Elizabeth kept making eyes at each other. Toby was morose.

"So, Lance, what does your dad do?" asked Bill.

"I live with my mom. Could I please have more salad?"

"Sure, but you didn't eat your meatloaf. Don't you like it?" asked Lucy.

"I'm sure it's very good," he said politely, "but I'm a vegetarian."

"I didn't know," exclaimed Lucy. "You should have said something. I could have made something else for you."

"This is fine. I mostly eat salad anyway."

"Well, good for you," said Lucy. "Toby and Elizabeth could learn from your example. They never eat their salad, and will probably develop scurvy any minute now."

"Mom!" Elizabeth protested, rolling her eyes.

"Gee, Mom, I'm surprised you're not warning Lance about kwashiorkor," wisecracked Toby. "You get that if you don't get enough protein."

"Don't talk to your mother like that," barked Bill. "Apologize, right now."

"I'm sorry," mumbled Toby. "Could I *please* be excused?"

"Sure," said Lucy, "but there's cherry pie for dessert."

"I don't want any," said Toby, shuffling out of the room.

"Me, either," said Bill, rising and pushing his chair back. "I think I'll watch the news. I understand they're bringing back the statutory rape laws." He glowered at Lance.

"I'm too full for dessert now," said Elizabeth. "Lance, do you want to see my CDs?"

"Sure."

Once they had excused themselves, only Lucy and Sara were left at the table, with Zoë in her high chair between them.

"Pie?" asked Lucy.

"Maybe later," said Sara.

"Help me clear the table?"

"I'd be happy to," said Sara.

"You know you're my favorite," said Lucy, rising and stacking plates.

"I know," said Sara with a conspiratorial little smile.

Lucy was driving Lance home when he surprised her by saying she could drop him anywhere near Smith Heights Road.

"I'd rather take you to your door," said Lucy. Not only did she want to make sure Lance got home safely, but a peek at his house might answer some of her questions about him. Smith Heights was a very exclusive section of town, where many large summer houses belonging to wealthy summer people were located.

"That's all right. You can let me off here."

Lucy braked and Lance climbed out of the car. He waited until she drove off before he turned and headed down a long drive, hidden behind a twelve-foot hedge.

How odd, thought Lucy. It was almost as if Lance was purposefully secretive about his family. Maybe they were just very private people, she rationalized. Maybe they were famous, and didn't want to be bothered. Maybe they were in the witness protection program.

Maybe, she thought as she sped along the road to the college, they had a bomb factory in the basement.

CHAPTER TWELVE

Lucy left for work very early on Wednesday morning. Wednesday was deadline day and she knew Ted expected her to get in as early as she could. As they drove along, the roads made misty by morning sunlight, Zoë complained about the early hour from her safety seat. Lucy hadn't had time to give her breakfast, but had packed it instead for her to eat at the center. Zoë was making it quite clear that she did not approve of this change in her routine.

As she drove along, Lucy's thoughts returned to last night's class. Professor Rea had had them all in stitches, reciting one of Tennyson's lesser efforts.

Pitching his voice in a high falsetto, and fluttering a yellow silk pocket square, the professor had begun by slowly reciting the first line, "Flower in the crannied wall," in a posh British accent. Then he paused and, delicately bringing thumb and forefinger together, continued, "I pluck you out of the crannies," bringing a few giggles from the younger members of the class. Lucy had glanced at the woman next to her and smiled.

The professor held his hand outstretched before him and leaned forward, gazing into it. "I hold you here, root and all, in my hand, / Little flower," he crooned. The giggles turned to guffaws.

Then, he tossed his head back and slowly brought it forward to study the imaginary flower in his hand. "But *if* I could understand / What you are, root in all, and all in all," he recited, giving his head a sad little shake.

Lowering his voice dramatically and giving the handkerchief a little wave, he whispered the final line, "I should know what God and man is." By this time most of the class was in hysterics, and the woman seated next to Lucy was laughing so hard she had to wipe her eyes.

It had been fun, and Lucy had laughed along with the rest, but she couldn't help feeling Professor Rea was being a bit unfair to poor Lord Tennyson. She raised her hand.

"Yes, Mrs. Stone," said the professor, leaning against the blackboard.

"It's easy to criticize Tennyson," she began hesitantly. "After all, he was a very popular poet and critics have tended to hold that against him." Seeing the professor raise his eyebrows, she lost courage and hurried to finish. "But he did write some wonderful poems."

"Like 'The Charge of the Light Brigade?'" asked Professor Rea with a little smirk.

Lucy smiled. "My son used to love that poem."

The professor stared at her in disbelief, and Lucy heard a few giggles coming from the back of the room.

"It was a way to teach him left and right," she hurried to

explain. "You know . . . 'Cannon to right of them, / Cannon to left of them.' It was fun, really," she ended lamely.

"You know the entire poem by heart?" asked the professor.

"Sure," said Lucy. "It's not very long. It's a great poem to recite. People used to memorize poems for entertainment, you know. My great-aunts used to recite 'Hiawatha' and 'The Wreck of the Hesperus' for fun."

"That's very true," said Mr. Irving, the senior member of the class, coming to her rescue. "There was a time when all school children were expected to memorize poetry and to recite it."

"Well, I suspect most of us are happy those days are over," said Professor Rea. "Modern critics dismiss Tennyson as overly sentimental and too willing to pander to popular taste with his gooey rewrites of Arthurian legend."

"But what about *In Memoriam?*" exclaimed Lucy, indignantly letting her enthusiasm get the better of her. Deliberately lowering her voice, and speaking slowly, she repeated a few lines from the poet's tribute to his dead friend. " 'He is not here; but far away / The noise of life begins again, / And ghastly through the drizzling rain / On the bald street breaks the blank day.' "

"Even bad poets have their moments," admitted the professor, studying her curiously. "I suppose you think that good shall come to all and every winter change to spring," he said, sarcastically paraphrasing the poem.

"I guess I do." Their eyes met and Lucy felt her face growing warm. "It's better than the alternative," she said defensively.

Today, however, Lucy wondered if she had gone a bit too far. What had gotten into her? She would never have challenged a professor when she was an undergraduate.

Lucy's musing was interrupted by the blare of a horn. Quickly coming to her senses, she saw the outraged face of a young man driving a small Japanese pickup truck. She realized she must have gone through a stop sign, and resolved to keep her mind on her driving.

She couldn't imagine why she was getting in such a huff over Tennyson. He was long dead, after all. And to give him credit, Professor Rea made the class interesting. The time just flew by. Of course, she'd had the added suspense of wondering if the professor would ask her out again. He hadn't, and she couldn't quite make up her mind if she was relieved or disappointed or perhaps a bit of both.

Leaving Zoë in Sue's care at the center, Lucy pulled into the Quik-Stop to buy a cup of coffee. It was foul stuff, but it was fast and easy. She filled a paper cup from the carafe and set it on the counter along with a roll of breath mints and two dollar bills. Receiving her change, she turned to go, only to meet Mr. Mopps at the doorway.

Seeing that her hands were full with the coffee, he held the door for her.

"Thank you," she said. "I heard about your job—I'm awfully sorry."

He shrugged, a gesture that suggested the Mediterranean rather than Tinker's Cove. "I don't understand—I always try to do a good job."

"My daughter will miss you," said Lucy.

"Who is your daughter?"

"Sara Stone. She's in second grade, with brown hair and a little chubby."

"I know Sara," he said, breaking into a big smile. "She has

a big brother, Toby, no? And a mean older sister, Elizabeth, I think. And a little baby sister she loves very much."

"That's right." Lucy was impressed; she doubted Sara's teacher knew that much about her.

"She likes to talk to me. All the children talk to me. They tell me their little problems. I enjoy the children."

"Last night, I overheard you and Ms. Crane . . ." began Lucy.

"That one—she is evil. I do not like her."

"She's certainly popular . . ."

"Bah!" Mr. Mopps made a gesture of spitting on his hand. "She is a big phony. Always after me. Pops this and Pops that. I tell her I am not Pops, I am Peter, I am Mr. Demopoulos, even Mr. Mopps I do not mind. But I am not Pops. Still, always Pops. And now she makes up these stories about me."

Lucy nodded sympathetically. "I hope things work out for you."

"I can work for my brother—he has a coffee shop in the outlet mall. Better coffee than here." He winked at her.

"I'm sure," agreed Lucy.

"That one at the school," he began, looking into the distant sky as if forecasting the future from the mackeral cloud formations that were building up. "I do not see a long and happy life for her."

"We'll just have to wait and see," said Lucy. "Have a nice day."

"You too, Mrs. Stone. Have a nice day."

It was a few minutes past seven when Lucy arrived at the office. George, she knew, had already been working for hours. He came in at three or four in the morning to lay out the pages by press time. Ted was working the phone, updating the stories he had already written, and checking with the police and fire departments for late developments. He hated to be scooped by the Portland daily and did everything he could to make sure the latest news got into *The Pennysaver*.

"What do you want me to do?" Lucy asked, switching on her computer.

"We've got some last-minute classifieds that need to be typeset—the school is looking for a substitute science teacher and a custodian."

"The kids told me Mr. Cunningham and Mr. Mopps were gone. What's going on?"

"This is a good one," began Ted, only to be interrupted by a ringing phone.

"Thanks for returning my call. Can you tell me exactly what complaints have been brought against Mr. Cunningham? Oh. Suspended until the investigation is complete. I see. Is this the usual procedure? Well, thank you for your time."

Exasperated, he hung up the receiver and shrugged. "Why do they bother to call if they're not going to talk? The superintendent won't confirm or deny anything. I haven't been able to contact Mrs. Wilpers, the woman at the meeting, either. But DeWalt Smythe is reeling off the quotable comments faster than I can write them down. As you may have suspected, he is 'absolutely outraged by Mr. Cunningham's disgusting and appalling behavior.'"

"What does Cunningham say?" asked Lucy, tapping away at the keyboard.

"Poor guy sounds mystified. Says he doesn't know what it's all about, but he's sure the investigation will exonerate him."

"Let's hope so," said Lucy. "What about Mr. Mopps? Why was he fired?"

"That's not exactly clear. All they will say is that he was terminated for cause. I have heard that Ms. Crane doesn't like him, but my source is not terribly reliable." Ted grinned. "She's only seven."

Lucy laughed. "My source has a similar story, and she's pretty upset. She really likes Mr. Mopps."

Ted smiled sympathetically, and snatched up the phone. "A head-on collision? You've got art?" He looked at the clock. "Listen, get over to Capra's photo, tell them you want one-hour processing, okay? Get it here by ten and I can use it."

He began dialing the police station. "George, save some space on page one. Lucy, switch that scanner on. I should have known about this." He spoke into the mouthpiece. "Yeah, I'm calling about an accident out on Bumps River Road, about an hour ago," he began. "What do you mean the report's not filed yet? I've got a deadline!" After a pause, he continued, sarcastically, "Well, can you tell me where I can find Officer Truax?"

Ted slammed down the phone. "Goddamn dispatchers. It wouldn't kill 'em to cooperate—might get 'em a free subscription. Maybe even a box of candy at Christmas. Listen, I've got to track down some cop who is supposedly in a speed trap on Route One. I need you to typeset these." He handed Lucy a stack of papers. "We can use thirty-five inches, okay? And by the way, I think you're looking for the one marked POWER."

He stomped out of the office. Lucy flipped the switch, and the scanner began producing static, punctuated with voices. She listened for a few minutes, but there was no mention of an accident. Eddie Culpepper, however, had forgotten his lunch and his father, Officer Culpepper, was asked to pick it up at home and take it over to the high school.

"Is it just me, or is today crazier than usual?" she asked George.

"About par for the course," said George, without removing his eyes from his computer screen. "This is a newspaper. We don't make widgets."

Lucy nodded. It hadn't taken her long to figure out that the newspaper business wasn't anything like Country Cousins, where she had worked before. At the catalog store, which was open 24 hours a day, 365 days a year, everybody worked by the clock. You punched in when you arrived, and punched out when you left.

At *The Pennysaver*, there was no time clock and the only time that mattered was 10 A.M. Wednesday—deadline. Because of deadline, the weeks tended to fall into a pattern. Monday and Tuesday were increasingly busy as Wednesday approached; activity peaked on Wednesday morning. Ted's temper also grew shorter, Lucy had noticed, the closer it was to deadline.

But once the paper was sent to the press, on a computer disk that George hand-delivered, everything calmed down. Ted usually left the office and Lucy tidied up, enjoying the sudden peace and quiet.

The pace was much slower on Thursday and Friday. Ted didn't care if she came in late and left early, as long as she got her work done.

Compared to Country Cousins, Lucy preferred the newspaper. It was too bad the job was only temporary—she was really enjoying it. Closing out the ads, she shipped the file to George and began leafing through the stack of letters. They were all prompted by Carol Crane's heroism, and they were all remarkably similar. She picked one at random and began typing it.

By the time she had finished, Lucy was heartily sick of Ms. Carol Crane, who apparently embodied the wisdom of Solomon, the patience of Gandhi, and the charity of Mother Teresa. She didn't know why she didn't like the woman; everyone else seemed to adore her. Maybe she just seems too good to be true, Lucy decided, tapping the Alt and Y keys that sent the file to George.

She sat for a minute, ear cocked to the scanner, trying to remember if she had forgotten anything, when the door flew open.

"Hi! I'm Jewel Hendricks—Jewel the Ghoul," said a large, fat, red-faced woman with her hair drawn tightly back into a ponytail. Jewel didn't fuss over her appearance, Lucy noticed. She was dressed in a man's shirt and denim overalls.

"Ted calls me that 'cause I take pictures of accidents. I've got some here. Big crash out on Bumps River Road. You're new, aren't you? He said if I got 'em in by ten he could use 'em, and I did. Just. So you can write me a check. I usually get twenty-five dollars."

"I'm Lucy, filling in for Phyllis." She shook her head apologetically. "Sorry, but you'll have to wait for Ted to pay you. So, who was in the accident? Anybody from town?"

"Nah. Nobody from here. It was just one guy. He flipped over on that curve—you know the one I mean?"

"I do," said Lucy. "Was he hurt?"

"Nope." Jewel seemed disappointed. "Had his seatbelt on. Got a good one of him hanging upside down." She snorted. "Hell of a fix, if you know what I mean. Darned idiot must've been doing seventy or eighty to end up like that." She looked up as Ted came hurrying in. "I got your pictures."

"Good. Did you get any info about the accident?" he asked.

"Actually, I did," said Jewel.

"You're the best! Give it to Lucy and she can write up a caption. So George, where do we stand?"

"Lookin' good, boss. Got an editorial?"

"Yup," said Ted, tossing his notebook on his desk and sitting down. "It's almost finished. Give me a minute." He opened the file and studied it, his hands poised over the keyboard. Then, slowly and tentatively, he began pecking away, his fingers moving more rapidly as he became absorbed in his subject.

Lucy smiled at Jewel. "I don't know how he does it. So, what have you got about the accident?"

Jewel pulled out a grubby, wrinkled envelope. "Driver was Mel Costas of Quivet Neck. Wouldn't tell me his age. Actually, he wasn't too cooperative. I think he was pissed off I wouldn't help him out. Hey, I told him, I'm not risking a lawsuit. Made him wait for the cops. Truck was a Dodge Dakota. You can do something with that, right?"

Lucy studied the photo, and began typing.

"Mel Costas of Quivet Neck found himself in an unusual position on Wednesday, when he lost control of his Dodge Dakota on Bumps River Road. Mr. Costas was not hurt in the accident, but the rescue squad was called to extricate him from his vehicle," she read the caption aloud to Jewel. "That'll have to do."

"The picture really speaks for itself," said Jewel, striding over to Ted's desk. She planted her feet, and put her hands on her hips. "Ted, I want my money."

He didn't look up but continued typing. "Lucy, petty cash is in the top left-hand drawer."

Lucy opened the drawer, found the cash box, and counted it out.

"Thanks. Maybe I'll see ya next week," said Jewel, heading for the door.

"Boss, I've got to get going," said George. "If I don't get it in by eleven, they won't print it until tonight."

"I know, I know," said Ted. "I'm almost done." He stopped typing and read what he had written so far then, in a final burst of inspiration, pounded out a concluding paragraph. "There," he said. "It's awful and we're printing it."

"Got it," said George, moving the mouse around. He quickly flipped through the pages on his screen, making sure he hadn't missed anything, and ejected the disk. "I'm outta here. See you next week, Lucy."

"See you." She looked over at Ted, who was resting his head on his hands. "Are you okay?"

"Yeah. Just tired. I feel like I've put in a full day's work and it's only a little past ten."

"You have," said Lucy sympathetically. "Why don't you go home for a rest? I can take care of the office."

"Can't. I've got an interview with the woman of the hour— Carol Crane. Inquiring minds want to know all about her."

"We sure do," said Lucy. "That's one story I definitely want to read."

"You shall be the first," said Ted. "And I better get going or I'll be late."

"Better wear sunglasses," advised Lucy. "If you look directly at her halo, it might hurt your eyes."

"I'll be careful," said Ted as he exited the office.

❷ Left alone, Lucy poked around under the counter until she found a bottle of spray cleaner. Taking the roll of paper towels from the tiny bathroom, she began tidying the office, beginning with the cluttered counter top. She sorted and stacked the assorted brochures that were displayed there, and then moved to her desk. She cleared everything off and gave it a good wipe, then began neatly replacing the phone books and stapler and pencil mug and all the other necessary items. Realizing there was nothing personal, she decided to bring in a photo of the kids. A photo, and maybe a plant. The office was pretty grim.

The scanner cackled, and she listened as she tackled the sea of papers that flooded Ted's desk. She didn't dare throw anything away, so she scooped them together and set them on his chair so she could dust the handsome old roll top he had inherited from his grandfather, who had been editor of the *Springfield Gazette*.

"One-five," came the dispatcher's voice. "I have a report of an unattended death."

"Copy, one-five," came the response from the patrol officer. "Location?"

"Twenty-three Spring Street, it's a ground-floor apartment. The landlady called in."

"Copy. I'm on my way."

Lucy stopped dusting and considered what to do. There was nothing in the tone of the voices to indicate this was anything but a natural occurrence. People died all the time, as she knew from the obituaries she typed every week. It could be a completely natural death. She started replacing the papers on Ted's desk, moving the phone a bit to the side. She could call him at the elementary school. Then she noticed his camera, sitting on the desk top. If it was a big story, he would need his camera. She might as well take it to him.

Arriving at the elementary school, she parked carefully in the space marked VISITOR. Entering the lobby, she automatically turned right, only to be brought up short by a plywood barrier. Of course. The damaged office was still being repaired. A neatly printed sign told her a temporary office had been set up in the gymnasium, on the opposite side of the lobby.

Pulling open the door, she almost collided with the school secretary, Mrs. Cope.

"You ought to watch where you're going," admonished Mrs. Cope, as if Lucy were one of the children.

"I need to find Ted," said Lucy. "Is he still here?"

"Yes, he's with Mrs. Applebaum. Right over there."

Mrs. Cope pointed to an area partitioned off with temporary screens. Lucy hurried over, and poked her head around the make-shift office wall. Ted and Sophie were standing and chatting; it looked as if Ted was about to leave.

"I'm sorry to interrupt, but I heard something on the scanner that I thought you'd want to know about."

"Yes?"

"It's probably nothing, but I figured you would want to check it out. An unattended death over on Spring Street."

"Spring Street? Where on Spring?" Sophie demanded urgently.

Lucy and Ted turned to her in surprise.

"Twenty-three, I think," said Lucy.

Sophie immediately went quite white, and leaned against her desk for support.

"What's the matter?" asked Ted.

"Should I get some water?" asked Lucy.

"That's where Carol Crane lives," said Sophie, putting her hand to her mouth.

"She wasn't here today," Ted explained to Lucy. "Sophie said she didn't bother to call in sick."

A chill ran down Lucy's spine as she remembered Mr.

Mopps's prediction earlier that morning. It certainly hadn't taken long to come true.

"I'd better get over there," said Ted.

"Here, take this," said Lucy, handing him the camera.

"Maybe you better stay and see that she's all right," said Ted, with a nod toward Sophie.

"Sure," said Lucy, taking the older woman's arm. "I think you ought to sit down."

Suddenly Sophie laughed, almost hysterically. "I'll be fine. In fact," she said, her face cracking into a smile, "I'm feeling better already."

Lucy clucked sympathetically and reached for a water pitcher that stood on a credenza. Pouring a glass of water for Sophie, she commented, "Well, this is a bit of a surprise."

"It couldn't have happened to a more deserving person," volunteered Sophie, still giggling.

"That's what Mr. Mopps said. I ran into him this morning. In fact, he predicted she wouldn't have a long and happy life." Lucy paused thoughtfully and handed the glass of water to Sophie. "You don't think he killed her, do you?"

"Mr. Mopps?" Sophie was incredulous. "He's the nicest, gentlest man alive." She took a sip of water, and added, "But if he did, it would have been justifiable homicide. She was awful to him."

"She wasn't very nice to you either," said Lucy, recalling how Carol had upstaged Sophie at the school committee meeting.

"She was after my job," said Sophie, putting down the glass. "Made no bones about it." She sighed sadly. "I didn't really care for myself. I'm not ambitious, I like it here. Small-town school. Nice kids. And I'm close to retirement anyway. I could go a year or two early, it wouldn't bother me. But I couldn't stand to leave with her in charge. I just couldn't."

"Why not?" asked Lucy.

"I've thought about this," said Sophie. "She wouldn't be good for the school—she didn't have the children's best interests in mind. All she cared about was herself. She would have been here a year or two, and gone on to a bigger and better school someplace else." Sophie gave a little snort. "And then they'd call me back, out of my happy retirement, and I'd have to put things back together again." She nodded, satisfied. "All in all, I think things have worked out for the best."

CHAPTER THIRTEEN

L eaving the school, Lucy knew she ought to go back to the office but she couldn't resist following Ted to Carol's apartment. Twenty-three Spring Street, she knew, was part of a modern apartment complex on the outskirts of town, near the outlet mall.

When she arrived, she saw the police had already sealed off the apartment, and Ted was talking with a small knot of neighbors gathered in the parking lot. Approaching them, she heard Ted introducing himself.

"I'm Ted Stillings, from *The Pennysaver*. Can you tell me what's going on?"

"Oh, I read that," said a young, tired-looking woman holding a baby.

"Was there a robbery or something?" persisted Ted, nodding at the young mother's companions, a middle-aged woman dressed in an aqua pants suit and a white-haired man with glasses.

Lucy recognized the trick. "The best way to start an interview is to play dumb," he had told her. "Few people can resist the temptation to set you straight."

"That was no robbery. She's dead," said the man, as Lucy joined the group.

"Really?" Lucy raised an eyebrow. "Who's dead?"

"That school principal, Carol Crane, that's who," answered the man, keeping his voice quite low, as if death was something to be ashamed of.

"You don't say," said Ted, expressing amazement.

"I do say," said the man.

"What do you think happened?" asked Ted.

"Was she raped?" asked Lucy, earning a disapproving glare from Ted. She decided she had better just listen.

"Was it an accident or something?" asked Ted.

"Not hardly," said the older woman. "She wasn't quite what people thought. She was no better than she ought to be." The woman gave Lucy a knowing little nod. "I used to hear men in there at all hours of the night. I live across from her, you see? Couldn't help hearing."

"Just 'cause she had men friends doesn't mean she wasn't the best thing to happen to the school in a long time," protested the young mother. "This is a real tragedy."

"Do you think one of these male visitors killed her?" asked Ted.

"Wouldn't be surprised," said the woman, narrowing her eyes and pursing her lips. "Used to hear them shouting in there."

"Did this happen a lot?" asked Ted.

"Now and then," said the woman, with a little shrug of her ample shoulders.

"Did you recognize any of them?" Ted addressed his question to the young mother, who was jiggling her baby.

"No. I only saw one guy myself, but it goes to figure she had friends from the school. Colleagues, you know." Her answer seemed directed as much to the woman in the pants suit, as to Ted.

"If you ask me, these young girls ask for it," she said, her double chin quivering with indignation. "Living all alone, entertaining men all night long. We certainly weren't brought up to behave like that."

"No, we certainly weren't," agreed the man. Ted thought he sounded a bit regretful.

"Did you hear anything out of the ordinary last night?" asked Ted.

They all shook their heads.

"Of course, I wasn't home last night—I was visiting my sister and stayed over. I don't like to drive at night anymore," said the woman.

Ted nodded. "When did you get home?"

"Just about an hour ago. When I went in the entry—we share an entry, you see—I saw her door was open. I knew that wasn't right so I called the landlady. A few minutes later I saw the police car come in the parking lot."

"You didn't go in?" asked Ted.

The woman looked insulted at the suggestion. "I mind my own business," she said.

Lucy doubted it, but Ted, she noticed, was hanging on every word like a true believer.

"I can't believe it," said the young mother, biting her lip. She seemed to be near tears. "She saved that little boy's life."

They all nodded.

"But there was no one to save her."

* * *

Ted scribbled down the quote and took their names. Then, giving Lucy a grateful smile, he snapped a photo of the group. Crossing the parking lot together, Lucy watched while he took a few pictures of the exterior of the apartment building.

"You see that cop?" asked Lucy.

"Yeah."

"I think he's one of Dot Kirwan's boys. Maybe he'll talk to us."

"It's worth a shot," agreed Ted.

"He looks so young," said Lucy as they approached the officer.

"They're making them younger and younger."

"Hi," said Lucy, giving Officer Kirwan a big smile. "We're from *The Pennysaver*."

"Can you tell us what's going on?" asked Ted.

"You'll have to check with the chief."

"The neighbors say it's a homicide—name of Carol Crane."

Lucy knew this was another of Ted's tricks. Sometimes he could prompt an official to talk if he seemed to know what had happened.

"Sorry," said the cop as a plain navy blue van pulled into the parking lot.

"That's the state police crime scene investigative unit," Ted told Lucy. "And that's the medical examiner," he added, pointing to a white van.

Ted and Lucy hung around for a few minutes while Ted snapped photos of the technicians as they carried their equipment inside. After a brief flurry of activity, the parking lot was empty again, except for the neighbors. Gradually, they drifted off, returning to their homes. It was quiet, except for the hum of yellow jackets buzzing around the dumpster.

"Might as well get going," said Lucy as they leaned against the fender of her car. "Not much going on here."

"Damn," said Ted, pounding his fist on the hood.

"Hey," protested Lucy. "It's not much, but it's the only car I've got."

"Sorry. It's just so damn frustrating. This is probably the biggest story I'll ever see, and it had to happen right after deadline. It'll be a whole week before the next issue. I've got a scoop and nowhere to print it."

Lucy nodded in agreement. It was just a matter of time before the daily, the TV station, and even the *Boston Globe* would be all over this story.

"Why don't you string it?" asked Lucy. "After all, you're right here on the scene. Why not call the *Globe?* Save them the trouble of sending someone down?"

"Lucy, that's brilliant," exclaimed Ted. "Meet you back at the office."

When Lucy arrived, Ted was already on the phone, chatting up someone named Doreen.

"I'm here in Tinker's Cove, Maine. We met at the newspaper convention last winter.

"Right. That's me. Listen. I've got a story here that I can't use and I thought you might be interested. Remember the principal who saved the kid in the school bombing—you had it on page one last week? Well, she's dead and it looks like murder. So far, nobody else is covering it. I've got an exclusive—for the moment anyway." He fell silent, listening and nodding. "You got it," he said, hanging up.

"Yes!" he exclaimed, making a fist and pulling his elbow in sharply. "We gotta hustle, Lucy. I can use some help. Look in that file for me. Search committee. School committee. July, maybe. See if you can find Carol Crane's résumé."

"Okay," said Lucy, willingly setting aside the paper for her night school class that she had planned to work on that afternoon. Matthew Arnold's view of education and society as presented in "The Scholar Gypsy" couldn't compete with the excitement of working on a breaking news story.

"Do they know how she died?" asked Lucy, pulling out a thick file folder.

"Dunno. Gotta find out. Too soon, I think. Medical examiner won't have anything until tomorrow at the earliest, maybe a couple of days. Right now, we'll work on background."

Taking the folder over to her desk, Lucy sat down and propped her chin on her hand.

"It must have been murder, don't you think?" she mused.

"Lucy, I hate to be insensitive but this is a newspaper office and I really need that résumé. Have you got it?"

"I'll find it," said Lucy, opening the folder and leafing through the papers. "I just can't believe it."

Ted was already writing his story, tapping as fast as he could at the keyboard.

"Why not?" he asked. "You thought there was something fishy about her all along."

"Yeah, but I thought that was just my nasty little mind."

"She made enemies," said Ted.

"You're not kidding," agreed Lucy, thinking of Mr. Mopps and Sophie. They wouldn't miss Carol; they would both be dancing on her grave. "Here's the résumé," she said, pulling out a packet of papers that were stapled together.

"Great. I want you to get some idea of her life before she came to Tinker's Cove. Check the references, call the places she worked before. Okay? I'm going to work the police angle."

Lucy pried the staple open, and pulled Carol's résumé out of the packet. Flipping to the second page she found the first reference, dialed the Harvard Graduate School of Education and asked for Dr. Norton Tredwell.

"I'm sorry, but Dr. Tredwell is on sabbatical," said a pleasant, well-modulated female voice. "He won't be back until January."

"I was given his name as a reference," said Lucy. "Is there any way I can reach him?"

"It would be quite difficult. He's studying the child-rearing practices of several primitive Indonesian tribes. Some are quite isolated."

"How long has he been gone?" Lucy asked.

"Since last January."

"I wonder why this candidate listed him as a reference," mused Lucy, looking back to page one of the résumé. "She doesn't actually seem to have any connection with Harvard at all. Is Dr. Tredwell affiliated with North Megunticook County Community College, or the University of Maine?"

"I rather doubt it," answered the well-modulated voice. "I believe he did his undergraduate work at Brown, and even that's a bit suspect here."

"Perhaps some sort of workshop or continuing credit program? Something like that?"

"This person is from Maine? He does have a summer home there."

"That could explain it. Maybe it's a personal reference."

"Perhaps," agreed the secretary. "It might be perfectly legitimate. People do strike up acquaintances. But when you work at a prestigious institution like Harvard, you can't help becoming a little bit suspicious. Our professors get many requests for references from people they've never heard of. Listing a Harvard professor can add a bit of polish to a lackluster résumé. They take a chance that no one will check. This person was at least enterprising enough to find a professor who is away for a year."

"She does mention that she's a self-starter," said Lucy.

"That's one way of putting it," said the woman with a chuckle.

"Thanks for your time," said Lucy, breaking the connection and looking for the next reference. The letters jumped out at her—Quentin Rea, her professor at Winchester. She dialed the number.

"Professor Rea? This is Lucy Stone, from your evening class . . ."

"Lucy, nice to hear from you." His voice was cheerful and welcoming. "What can I do for you?"

"I'm working on a story for *The Pennysaver* . . ."

"Ah! You're a journalist! I didn't know!"

"I wouldn't quite call it that," said Lucy. "I'm really more of a secretary, but I am doing some research at the moment, about our new assistant principal, Carol Crane."

"Ah, Carol!"

At least he recognized the name, thought Lucy. "You were listed as a reference on her résumé. Could you tell me a little bit about her?"

"Certainly. What do you want to know?"

"Well, how do you know her? Was she a student at Winchester?"

"No, no. I was her faculty adviser at the University of Maine. I worked there until a few years ago, when I came to Winchester."

"As her adviser you must have known her pretty well," suggested Lucy.

"An unforgettable personality. Dynamic. Enterprising. Showed great initiative. Overcame obstacles. Goal oriented. Persevering. Have I missed anything?"

"Honest?" asked Lucy.

"Ah," said the professor, hesitating. "True to herself. How's that?"

"It sounds like you're hedging?"

"You said that, I didn't," chuckled the professor. There was a pause. "Is this for publication?"

"Of course," said Lucy.

"I think I've said enough then."

Lucy wondered what his reaction would be if she told him Carol was dead. She couldn't do that, of course, or the story wouldn't be Ted's scoop for very long.

"How are you finding the course?" he asked, breaking the silence.

"I'm enjoying it," said Lucy. "It's nice to use my brain again. I was worried it might have atrophied."

"You seem to have a very fine brain, indeed."

"Thanks." Lucy was flattered. "I have to get back to work, but it was nice talking to you."

"Oh, the pleasure was mutual," said the professor.

"Goodbye," said Lucy firmly, ending the call. But when she replaced the receiver, her hand lingered. The professor was certainly a ladies man—she wondered if he had been more than an adviser to Carol. If they had been lovers, that could explain his reluctance to say much about her.

"Ted," she called, eager to share her suspicion.

"*Shhh!*" said Ted, waving his hand for silence. "When will the M.E. issue his report? Two weeks? What about a preliminary finding? Against policy? Whaddya mean? Compromise the investigation?" He brightened. "Does that mean there is an investigation?" He looked at the receiver. "Damn. Hung up on me." He quickly redialed. "Sorry, we must have been cut off . . ." he began.

Lucy shook her head. That was a trick she hadn't seen before, she thought, filing it away for future use. She dialed the third reference, the superintendent of schools in Bridgton, where Carol had worked before she came to Tinker's Cove.

"Dr. Franklin has retired," said the secretary, who sounded like a brisk, efficient type. "The new superintendent is Dr. Helen Slavin. Perhaps she can help you."

"I don't think so. Is there any way I can reach Dr. Franklin?"

"You can try him at home," she said, giving the number. "But I doubt you'll find him there. He's been quite involved in the upcoming election—he's been campaigning for Bob Angus, the candidate for the statehouse."

She tried Franklin's home number, and then dialed the Angus for Representative headquarters and left a message on the answering machine. She had little confidence the call would be returned, especially once Carol's death became public. Politicians usually tried to distance themselves from the untimely deaths of young women.

Glancing over the résumé, she typed a precis for Ted. Two years at N.M.C.C.C., two more at the state university, then substitute teaching while working toward her master's degree, again at the state university. A year or two of teaching, then she enrolled in the state university's certificate program for school administrators. A year as an assistant principal in Bridgton, and then she came to Tinker's Cove. Not a dazzling résumé, but local schools were experiencing hard times. As budgets got tighter, there were fewer and fewer administrative jobs. It was probably difficult for a new graduate to get started.

"I've got the info you wanted," she told Ted. "I'm sending it to you right now."

"Print it out instead, easier for me to work from," said Ted, pausing to blow his nose before pushing back his chair and standing up. "Police have called a press conference. I've gotta go now or I'll miss it."

"See you tomorrow, then," said Lucy, glancing at the clock. She had to go, too. She had promised Toby she would watch his soccer game.

Parking the Subaru beside the soccer field behind the high school, Lucy freed Zoë from her safety seat and began walking across the grass to the sidelines. Zoë toddled ahead of her, drawn by the noisy cheers of the bystanders. Home games always drew a healthy crowd of parents and students, who stood along the sidelines because there were no bleachers.

Toby was in goal, she noticed, filling in for Todd Johnson, the team's first-string goalie.

"What's the score?" she asked one of the anxious-looking parents.

"Three-zip."

"We're winning?"

"No. They are."

"Too bad," said Lucy. No wonder Toby was in goal. Todd must be off his game today.

Zoë sat down at her feet and began poking through the grass

with her stubby little fingers. Tired, Lucy sat beside her. Not much was going on; the coach was arguing with a referee about a penalty.

Lucy scanned the faces of the parents watching the game. What would their reaction be, she wondered, when they learned about Carol? She thought of the warm reception she had received at the school committee meeting. A lot of people would be incredibly upset; Carol had become a local hero for saving Tommy from the bomb.

Zoë pressed a handful of grass into her hand.

"Flowers," she said.

"Thank you," said Lucy, pretending to smell the crumpled bouquet. Zoë beamed with pride, and began picking more grass.

The bomb, thought Lucy, wondering if Carol's death was somehow connected to the bombing. What if Carol had figured out who had planted it? That would definitely be a motive for murdering her.

Hearing a groan from the crowd, Lucy looked up. The visiting team was moving the ball down the field toward Toby. The Tinker's Cove team's defense was disorganized, and the Rough Riders forward, a huge kid with bright red hair, was in scoring position. The ball whizzed across the grass, straight to the goal.

Toby was ready. He threw himself across the goal and stopped the ball, then jumped to his feet and threw it to a teammate. Lucy found herself cheering, along with the rest of the Tinker's Cove contingent. The referee blew the whistle and the game was over. Tinker's Cove had lost, but thanks to Toby, they hadn't disgraced themselves.

"Hi, Mom."

"Nice play."

"Coach should have put me in earlier. Todd's got a pulled tendon."

"That's too bad for him, but I'm glad you got a chance to play. Meet you out front."

Lucy picked up Zoë, who seemed to get heavier every day, and carried her back to the car. She strapped her in the safety seat and then drove around to the front of the school, where she switched on the radio and waited for Toby to change out of his uniform.

"Five o'clock news in just a minute," advised the announcer. Lucy hummed along with Natalie Merchant, leaning back against the headrest and shutting her eyes for a few minutes. She began to drift off, and jumped when Toby yanked open the door.

"So, how was school? Didn't you have a math test today?"

"I think I did okay."

"Got much homework?"

"Nah."

The song faded out, and the announcer promised the news after a few messages. They drove along in silence, listening to the commercials, as they followed the familiar route through town and past piney woods to Red Top Hill Road. Finally the throbbing musical theme for the news began.

"Reporter Don Lawson is on location at the Tinker's Cove Police Station at this hour, reporting on a breaking news story. What's going on over there, Don?"

"Police Chief Oswald Crowley has just announced the arrest of Tinker's Cove high school teacher Josh Cunningham for the brutal murder of his colleague, Carol Crane, whose body was discovered in her apartment today. She was apparently smothered to death. Ms. Crane was the elementary school assistant principal who heroically saved a special-needs student when the school was bombed last week. Mr. Cunningham is now in police custody, and will be arraigned tomorrow morning."

Stunned, Lucy turned off the radio and turned to Toby.

"That can't be true," he said, fighting back tears. "Mr. C would never hurt anyone. It's all a mistake. I know it is."

"If it is, it will all get sorted out sooner or later," said Lucy, reaching across the shift console and patting his hand. Privately, she had doubts. The police wouldn't have arrested Josh and called a press conference unless they had some pretty hard evidence.

"I know him, Mom. He couldn't do something like that. I know it."

Lucy studied her son's face. It was still round and boyish, and his teeth seemed too big for his mouth, but the down on his upper lip was already darkening. She wished he could remain her sweet little boy forever. She wished he could always believe that people are good and would never have to lose faith in others, but that wasn't possible. He was growing up; he would soon be an adult.

"Oh, Toby. I know it's hard to accept, but we never really know other people. You knew him as a teacher, but he had a life outside school you know nothing about. I don't think the police would make an arrest so quickly unless they were awfully sure."

Toby set his chin and shook his head. "No matter what they say, I'll never believe it. Mr. C's innocent. I know it."

CHAPTER FOURTEEN

When Lucy got to work on Thursday morning, Ted had an assignment for her.

"I want you to go over to the police station. They're having another press conference this morning."

"Me? Why don't you go?" Lucy was puzzled.

"Two reasons. One, the arraignment is in an hour and I want to be there. Second, I'm not exactly popular with the chief," said Ted. "In fact, it's department policy to ignore *The Pennysaver*. They never tell me about press conferences. I heard about this one from Doreen, my editor at the *Globe*."

"That's crazy," said Lucy. "You'd think they'd want coverage from *The Pennysaver*. It's the hometown paper."

"The chief's got a grudge against me," admitted Ted, with a wry smile. "I printed a story about the use of unnecessary force in an arrest by an especially promising young officer, and he's never forgiven me."

"What was so bad about that?"

"He had to fire the kid."

"So?"

"It was Oswald, Jr."

"Oh," said Lucy, as understanding dawned. "Do you have any special instructions for me?"

"Just get whatever they hand out, write down whatever they say, and try to get a photo."

"Got it."

When Lucy arrived at the police station briefing room, she saw that a crew from the Portland TV station was taping an interview with the chief. This was definitely a step up from the usual local coverage. She picked up one of the press releases that were stacked on a table, and took a seat in the front row and listened.

"Chief Crowley, what evidence led you to arrest Josh Cunningham?" asked Laura Quattrone, Channel Seven's newest rising star.

She wasn't as pretty in person as she was on TV, thought Lucy. Her hair was stiff with spray, and her makeup seemed overdone in daylight.

"Well, Laura," began the chief, and Lucy opened her notebook.

"There are a number of factors that pointed toward Mr. Cunningham." The chief paused and grinned, revealing his huge, yellow teeth. "Mr. Cunningham was suspended from his teaching job at the high school a couple of days ago, and we know that Ms. Crane played an instrumental role in that. We believe he blamed her. Secondly, we found some written evidence in the victim's apartment that implicated Mr. Cunningham. And finally, we have a witness who places him at the apartment at the time of the murder."

"That sounds like circumstantial evidence to me," said Laura, with an apologetic smile. "Do you have any physical evidence?"

"The state police crime investigation unit has examined Ms. Crane's apartment and we will have the results in a couple of weeks."

"Who's the witness?" Lucy turned and saw a young man standing in the row behind her, and decided he was probably from one of the Portland papers.

"I'm not at liberty to reveal that information just now," said the chief, glaring at him.

Lucy suspected the chief's antipathy to the press extended beyond Ted, to anyone who asked questions.

"Why not?" persisted the Portland reporter.

"I'm just not and that's all there is to it," said the chief, going red around the collar.

"Is there any connection between this murder and the bombing?" asked Lucy.

"I can't tell you anything about that," said the chief.

"What about Cunningham's suspension? Was he suspended for making the bomb? After all, he was a science teacher." It was the Portland reporter, following up on Lucy's question.

"This conference is over," said the chief, turning on his heel and leaving the room.

"Sorry," said the Portland reporter, apologizing to the TV crew. "I shouldn't have butted in on your interview."

"No problem. We got what we needed," said Laura, bending down to pack the microphone in a huge equipment bag.

"What did I miss?" asked Lucy.

"Not much. Chief Crowley likes them short and sweet. Take the pictures, but don't ask questions," said the reporter.

"He must be double-jointed," joked the cameraman. "The way he pats himself on the back."

"It's amazing," agreed the reporter. "He oughta join the circus."

They all laughed, left the briefing room, and exited the station together. Spotting DeWalt on the sidewalk, Lucy wondered what he had to say about the murder.

"Hi," she began, approaching him. "I'm Lucy Stone and I work for *The Pennysaver*."

"Nice to meet you," said DeWalt, grabbing her hand.

Face to face, the minister's presence was overpowering. He was tall anyway, and tended to speak every day as if it were Sunday and he was in the pulpit.

"I wondered if you would like to make a comment about Carol Crane's murder."

"I am shocked and saddened that such a foul deed could take place in our town," he said. "Carol was an inspiration to our youth and a positive force for good. I was looking forward to collaborating with her on a number of projects that would have restored family values to the schools."

Lucy wrote it down in her notebook, then raised her head. "Do you think the police have arrested the right man?"

"I do. I've come to compliment Chief Crowley on a fine job. Getting that evil fornicator and vicious murderer off the streets means Tinker's Cove will be a much safer place for our wives and daughters. I'm sure you, as a woman yourself, appreciate that."

"I never felt I was in any danger from Josh Cunningham," said Lucy. "What makes you so sure he's guilty?"

"I have had occasion to look into that man's character," said DeWalt, folding his hands together in front of his stomach and nodding virtuously. "He was not what he seemed to be."

"Few of us are," said Lucy. "Did you have anything particular in mind?"

"Satan glories in unrepented sin," thundered DeWalt. "His disciple, Josh Cunningham, was devious but his sins could not be hidden forever. It only took the voice of one innocent, pure lamb of God to reveal his wickedness and corruption."

Lucy recalled Josh's concern for her in the dark parking lot, and how much Toby admired him. He seemed to her to be a caring person and a committed teacher. He didn't have to coach field hockey, or set up science demonstrations in advance of class, but he did.

"Those are pretty strong words," she said. "What exactly do you mean?"

"He tempted one of the Lord's blessed children and invited her to leave the Good Shepherd's fold. He induced that sweet young handmaiden of the Lord to forsake the teachings of her parents and her church and to fall into sin and degradation."

"He seduced a student?" asked Lucy. "Is that what he was suspended for?"

"Oh, yes. Seduced, indeed. And thanks to Carol Crane, he did not get away with it. She insisted that he be suspended. Staked her job on it when I brought his misdeeds to the attention of Superintendent Eubanks."

"I find this a bit hard to believe," said Lucy. "Are you saying that Josh Cunningham attempted to have sex with a student?"

"Not sex, no. Something worse." DeWalt brought his face down level with Lucy's, and lowered his voice. "He attempted to seduce a student away from the ways of her family and church.

The young woman—you'll understand if I don't use her name—is not allowed to wear slacks or shorts."

"Why not?"

"A number of families in the Revelation Congregation believe in a quite literal interpretation of Holy Gospel, and insist that their daughters wear skirts."

"That's in the Bible?" Lucy was doubtful; she hadn't heard anything about this in Sunday School.

"It's a matter of interpretation. The verse actually forbids one sex to wear the clothing of the other. For that reason, she chose to play field hockey. The players wear kilts. However, Mr. Cunningham advised her to wear shorts for practice."

"You call that inappropriate behavior for a coach?" Lucy couldn't believe it.

"I certainly do. Don't you know the Ten Commandments?" DeWalt pulled himself back to his full height and proclaimed for all the world to hear, "'Thou shalt honor thy father and thy mother.' Mr. Cunningham advised that little girl, that sweet child of God, to stand up in defiance against the very parents who nurtured her and cared for her and raised her from infancy in the ways of the Lord. He urged her to disobey them and borrow practice clothes from her teammates."

"You've got to be kidding," said Lucy, unimpressed with his theatrics.

"It may seem trivial to you," said DeWalt, "but I can assure you that some members of the Revelation Congregation take their Scripture very seriously indeed." With that, he strode off self-righteously and mounted the white granite steps to the police station.

Shaking her head in disbelief, Lucy decided to head over to the courthouse. She wanted to find out how Josh was faring at the arraignment, and she could tell Ted what she had learned about Josh's suspension.

Arriving at the courthouse, Lucy slipped into the crowded courtroom and stood at the back, looking for Ted. Even if she had wanted to sit down, she couldn't have. Every seat was taken, and TV crews and photographers lined the right-hand wall; it was the best position from which to get a good photo of the defendant.

She finally spotted Ted in the second row, but there was no sign of Josh Cunningham. There was a lot of coming and going, however, as court officers, attorneys, and local cops conferred with the clerk, who was scheduling the day's hearings. Finally, all was ready and the bailiff pounded the floor twice with his pike.

"All rise, court now in session, the Honorable Joyce Ryerson presiding."

Lucy sighed in sympathy for Josh Cunningham. Judge Ryerson was known as the dragon lady, and the term was not a reference to her long, carefully lacquered scarlet fingernails. In her court, defendants were always presumed guilty. If they weren't guilty, she was known to argue, why were they there in the first place? She was able to get away with this attitude only because of the New Englander's finely developed sense of original sin. Most of those who came before her knew full well they were guilty of something, even if they happened to be innocent of the precise crime they were charged with.

When the sheriff brought Josh into the courtroom, handcuffed, in rumpled clothes and with a day's growth of beard, Lucy knew the judge would not be lenient. She tended to favor well-groomed defendants, ignoring the fact that few people looked their best after a night in the lockup. Josh's attorney, Bruce Gilmore, could ask for bail until he was blue in the face, Lucy thought, but he wasn't going to get it.

"Your honor, Mr. Cunningham is a respected member of the community, and he has no previous record," argued Gilmore.

Judge Ryerson raised a skeptical eyebrow and glanced at Josh, who looked absolutely miserable. He also looked guilty, even to Lucy.

"What does the prosecution have to say?" asked the judge.

"Well," drawled Fred Carruthers, the assistant district attorney assigned to the case, "we've all heard what a fine, upstanding young man Mr. Cunningham is, and that's all very well and good . . ." Carruthers paused for effect, then continued. "But I'd like to remind the court that he is charged with brutally attacking and murdering a defenseless young woman. I do not think the community would be well served by letting this man run free, where he could be a threat to our most vulnerable citizens.

"Furthermore," he said, holding up a sheaf of papers, "the police have found evidence that Carol Crane had proof in her possession that Josh Cunningham was responsible for the bomb that damaged the Tinker's Cove Elementary School."

Suddenly, the courtroom was in an uproar. A collective gasp was immediately followed by noisy conversation. Flashes of light burst from numerous cameras as photographers disregarded courtroom etiquette and scrambled to capture Josh Cunningham's astonished expression.

"Order! Order!" screamed the judge, bringing down the gavel. "I will not hesitate to clear the courtroom," she warned, glaring balefully at the press photographers. She tapped her fingers on the bench. "I've heard enough. Bail denied. Prisoner to be confined at the county jail until trial. Next case."

Lucy swallowed hard, watching as Gilmore conferred briefly with his client, concluding the chat with an encouraging pat on the shoulder. Then Josh was led away by the sheriff, and Gilmore made his way to the exit, followed by Ted.

When she managed to worm her way past the crowd in the back, she found Ted interviewing him in the lobby.

"Mr. Gilmore, I'm covering this case for the *Globe*. Do you have a minute?" he asked, then broke into a coughing fit.

"Sounds like you're coming down with something," said Gilmore, grinning sympathetically. Unlike some defense lawyers, he welcomed pretrial publicity, especially if it could engender sympathy for his client. "What can I do for you?"

"What's your reaction to the charges made this morning against Josh Cunningham?"

"It's early days, Ted. I haven't really had a chance to go over the evidence. Josh tells me he didn't do it, and you know, I believe him." Gilmore nodded his head for emphasis. "I really do, and that's not always the case, believe me."

"What about this witness the police say they have?" asked Lucy.

Gilmore turned and beamed at her. "I don't know who this person is, but I can say it's pretty rare that a person is absolutely sure of themselves once they're on the witness stand and subject to critical questioning."

"Do you think Josh will be charged with the bombing in addition to the murder?" asked Ted.

"I think we have to be prepared for that. Frankly, I'm looking forward to seeing the evidence myself. Before I see what they've got, I'd rather not comment. I'm sure you understand."

Ted nodded in agreement. "Thanks for your time."

"Anytime," said Gilmore with an affable smile.

Lucy and Ted watched as he made his way across the lobby with an optimistic bounce to his step.

"I don't know what he's so darned optimistic about," observed Ted. "I'm no legal expert, but it doesn't look to me as if Josh's chances are very good."

"It's something they teach them in law school," said Lucy. "Defense Law 101. Always remain upbeat, no matter how poor your client's chances really are."

They began walking to the door, but had to stop when Ted was overtaken by another fit of coughing.

"I know just what you need," said Lucy. "A cup of Jake's chicken soup. It's supposed to be better than Mom's and is guaranteed to cure whatever ails you."

"Sounds good," agreed Ted. "I'll meet you there."

CHAPTER FIFTEEN

When Ted arrived at Jake's, he found Lucy sitting at a table, reading the new issue of *The Pennysaver*.

"If only we could have gone to press a little later," he said. "Then we could have scooped everyone with the story of Carol's murder."

"Well, I think it's a pretty good issue anyway," said Lucy loyally. "I really like Jewel's photo. She'll be pleased it's on page one."

Ted shrugged, and sat down heavily. "You can only do what you can do," he said. "Did you see the *Globe?*"

Lucy shook her head, so he got up and took one from a pile near the donut counter and proudly placed it in front of her.

"This is great," enthused Lucy. "You made the front page. They even used your photo of the neighbors."

"I wish it had been my own paper."

"Oh, well," sympathized Lucy, looking up as Jake came over with two tattered menus.

"We won't need those," said Lucy. "Ted needs chicken soup, and I'll have a bowl as preventive medicine."

"You can't do better," said Jake. "Damned shame," he added, indicating the *Globe* with a tilt of his head. "Still, there's plenty that won't miss that little lady."

"So I'm discovering," said Lucy.

"A lot of the teachers stop in here in the morning for coffee. They couldn't stand her. You know that nice kindergarten teacher? The Italian lady?"

"Lydia Volpe?" offered Lucy.

"Yeah, that's her. She was fit to be tied one day. I heard her talking to the others. Said some parent had a complaint or something. I didn't get the details. Anyway, this Carol Crane musta chewed her out real good. She said she wasn't gonna take that kind of language from anyone, and especially not from her— that's exactly what she said." There was a little twinkle in Jake's eye. "Pretty funny, huh?"

"I guess so," said Ted, not getting the joke.

"Must be the first time in history that somebody over at the school, somebody in charge, I mean, took the parent's side and chewed out a teacher!" Jake grinned.

"You've got a point there," said Lucy, recalling a few teacher conferences she had participated in. Even Sophie Applebaum had made it very clear to her that any problems the children were having were certainly no fault of the school's. The school was always above reproach.

"It's no wonder she got killed," said Jake as he returned to the kitchen. "She broke rule number one."

"What's that?" asked Ted.

"Weren't you in the Navy?" demanded Jake as he ladled out the soup.

"Nope. Not me."

"Well," said Jake as he set the bowls down in front of them. "In the Navy, the first thing they teach you in boot camp is rule number one: Don't make waves."

Lucy picked up her spoon, scooped up some of the rich, golden broth, and then tilting the spoon slightly, let it run back into the bowl.

"What do you think, Ted? Do you think Josh made the bomb and Carol found out and that's why he killed her?"

"No way," said Ted. "Somehow I just can't see him as the bomber."

"Me either," agreed Lucy. "Although he probably would know how to make a bomb. Could it have been a scheme to discredit Carol that backfired?"

"We know she wasn't too popular with her colleagues."

"Sophie thought she was after her job, and she got Mr. Mopps fired. Oh, I spoke with DeWalt this morning. He said Carol insisted that Josh be suspended. And do you know what he was suspended for? Suggesting one of the girls on the field hockey team wear shorts for practice. It's against her religion or something."

"Lucy, go slower. Remember, I have a cold."

"It's not you—it's the craziest thing I ever heard. DeWalt said some people in the Revelation Congregation believe that girls have to wear skirts. By telling this girl to wear shorts to practice, he was supposedly undermining her religious training and encouraging her to defy her parents. You're not supposed to do that. It's in the Ten Commandments. DeWalt told me."

"So I've heard, but I'm not sure God cares an awful lot about what you wear," said Ted, slurping his soup. "What was that you said? Something about Carol insisting that Josh be suspended?"

"That's what DeWalt said." Lucy pulled out her notebook and flipped through it. "I've got it right here. He said Carol put her job on the line and insisted Josh be suspended. He also said he looked forward to 'collaborating with her to restore family values to the schools.'"

"That's interesting," mused Ted. "DeWalt and Carol were in cahoots. With her support, he probably could have picked up another seat or two on the school committee."

"That's a scary thought," said Lucy.

"It would sure change the picture," said Ted. "Up until now, the school committee and the administration, even the teacher's union, usually present a united front. They've got a virtual lock on the system, and anybody who isn't happy with it is at a real disadvantage. Just like Jake said."

"So you think Carol was killed because she was upsetting the educational applecart?" Lucy rolled her eyes.

"You don't realize how much is at stake here, Lucy. The school department is a big employer in this town and it pays very well. We all had to struggle through the recession, I know you and Bill had a pretty hard time, but they had contracts with five and ten percent raises built in. Most of them make thirty or forty thousand a year for ten months' work. Even Mr. Mopps was making twenty dollars an hour, not counting overtime whenever there's a meeting or a basketball game.

"And so far, the unions have had a pretty cozy arrangement with the school committee. That school council Carol was proposing could have brought new people into the process. People who might start asking why the teachers should get another raise when SAT scores have gone down for five straight years."

Lucy put down her spoon. "Are you telling me this whole thing is about SAT scores?"

Ted took another slurp of soup. "You're right," he admitted. "I'm not making much sense. Maybe it's the cold medicine I took. I don't know why Carol got killed, or who did it, but I do know that people were beginning to ask some hard questions about the schools. Then Carol came and all hell broke loose."

Ted didn't stay long after they returned to the office. His cold got the better of him and he decided to head home. Lucy started working on the obituaries, including one for Carol Crane. The standard form from the funeral home gave only the sparsest details, and no survivors were listed. Lucy padded it out with material from the story about the bombing, and included information from Carol's résumé. There were no visiting hours, she noticed, and no funeral was planned either. There would be, however, a memorial service at the school.

Absorbed in her work, she didn't see Sophie approaching through the plate glass window, and looked up, surprised, when the door opened.

"I have two letters to the editor," began Sophie, placing two envelopes on the counter in front of Lucy's desk. "One from the teacher's union, and one from the administrator's association. They both state our faith in Josh Cunningham."

"I was at the arraignment this morning," said Lucy. "He looked terrible—he must be in shock."

"Of course he is," said Sophie. "This is absolutely unbelievable."

"The police seem to think they have a pretty solid case."

"Well, I know Josh, and I know he didn't do any of this. If you think about it, all the evidence against him comes from Carol."

"You think she was scheming against him, before she was killed?" asked Lucy. "Why would she do that?"

"I don't know," admitted Sophie, the frustration evident in her voice. "But I do know she was a schemer. She had plots within plots. People like that usually end up in trouble, one way or the other."

"She sure got trouble," said Lucy. "Smothered. In her own bed." She chewed thoughtfully on the cap of her pen. "Were she and Josh seeing each other?"

"Not that I know of," said Sophie. "But then again, she didn't confide in me."

"She has no family?" asked Lucy.

"Never mentioned anyone. Mr. McCoul told me that nobody has contacted him about her remains. The union is paying for cremation, and we're having a memorial service." Sophie smoothed the lace collar to her print dress. "It's only decent."

"It's kind of sad, really," said Lucy. "Everybody loved her and nobody loved her."

Sophie snorted. "You could put that on her gravestone, if she were going to have one. Unfortunately, the union's funds are limited." She leaned across the counter toward Lucy, and lowered her voice to a whisper. "Just between you and me, this vote was very close. It took some convincing to get them to ante up enough for the cremation." She raised her eyebrows above her silvery plastic eyeglass frames, and gave a grim little nod.

"Maybe DeWalt would like to make a contribution," suggested Lucy.

"Now there's an idea," crowed Sophie. "Of course, I've never heard of him actually making a contribution himself, at all. He's much better at collecting them." With that, she marched out the door, letting it bang behind her.

*   *   *

That evening, as Lucy sat in class waiting for Professor Rea to arrive, she thought about Carol Crane. Right from the start she had sensed something phony about her; she was certainly not the person she was pretending to be. But why? What was it all for?

She looked up as Professor Rea hurried into the room a good ten minutes late. He wasn't quite himself, she thought. He hadn't bothered to style his hair and it hung in flat clumps around his face. He didn't seem to have his usual energy either. Instead of pacing back and forth in the front of the room as he usually did, he sat down at the big wooden desk and, leaning his head on his hand, apologized for failing to finish grading the Matthew Arnold papers.

"I'll try to have them for you next time," he said. "Tonight we're going to talk about the force of convention in Victorian society. By way of example, I'm going to tell you about Professor Wilfred Owen Herbert Hewson, an extremely distinguished mathematician at Oxford.

"To all appearances he was the typical bachelor academic. Absentminded. Head in the clouds. Lived by himself in a comfortable house with one servant, his maid. When he died, his colleagues were astounded to learn that he left his entire fortune, which was quite considerable due to the family coal mine, to the maid.

"The only explanation for his unexpected generosity to the domestic that his colleagues could come up with was to assume that she had been his mistress. They were very shocked indeed to learn that she had actually been his wife. This was even more upsetting to them than a possible illicit affair. Why?"

He scanned the class with dull eyes. When Mr. Irving raised his hand, he nodded at him.

"Class differences were very marked at that time," offered

Mr. Irving. "Chances are the woman didn't even know how to read. She couldn't have filled the role of a gentleman's wife—think of Shaw's *Pygmalion*."

"Maybe she wasn't like Eliza Doolittle—maybe she didn't want to change," offered the pretty blond girl who always sat in the front row.

"Maybe he didn't want her to change," said Lucy. "Maybe he loved her the way she was."

"Exactly," said Professor Rea. "Mrs. Stone has it. The really shocking thing about Professor Hewson was that he loved his wife because she wasn't a lady. She was coarse, and vulgar, and uninhibited and very passionate. The professor's diary reveals he was both madly in love with her and deeply ashamed of it."

Shame, thought Lucy, thinking of Carol. It was true that some people had no relations whatsoever, but it was very unusual. Carol must have a family somewhere; she didn't spring up in a cabbage patch. Whoever they were, and wherever they were, there had certainly been some sort of rift.

But if Carol had maintained any sort of contact, the police would certainly have found it. An old address book, insurance forms, it wasn't that difficult for an investigator to find surviving relatives in order to notify them of a death. The only way that Carol could be so completely alone, thought Lucy, was if she had cut herself off entirely. Chances were, she guessed, that Carol had a past but she was ashamed of it.

After class, as the students filed out of the room, Professor Rea drew Lucy aside.

"I had no idea Carol was dead—why didn't you tell me?" he demanded. Lucy noticed that his hands were trembling.

"I'm sorry," she said, feeling guilty for taking advantage of him. "We were trying to keep the story from breaking as long as we could."

"Just doing your job," he said bitterly.

"I didn't realize you were that close to her, or I wouldn't have done it," said Lucy. She was shocked to discover that as much as she felt absolutely terrible about tricking him, she was still hoping he would tell her about his relationship with Carol. She looked up at him, her eyes brimming with empathy.

"Well, it's over now," he said, giving an abrupt little shrug and snapping his briefcase shut. "I don't know why Carol's death came as such a shock. She lived close to the edge. She played games. Sooner or later she was bound to push somebody too far."

"The police think that person was Josh Cunningham. Do you?"

"All I know is what I saw on the news." He picked up his briefcase and turned to go. "It's ironic, really. This poor devil thought he was getting rid of Carol by killing her. All he's done is get himself in more trouble. That's Carol for you. Always having the last laugh."

With that, he strode out the door.

Lucy gathered up her books, and walked slowly down the hall. She thought about the Oxford mathematician with the secret life, and she thought about Carol Crane. Who was she really? How much did anyone in Tinker's Cove know about her?

Taken at face value, she was a heroine who risked her own life to save a crippled little boy. She was a dedicated educator, with innovative ideas.

But then there was the business of the phony references on her résumé. The confrontations with other staff members. That pink suit. Something didn't ring true.

She lived close to the edge. She liked to play games. Quentin obviously knew a lot more about her than he was willing to tell. Lucy wondered what their connection really was; she was willing to bet it went a lot deeper than the usual student-advisor relationship.

Tomorrow, she decided, as she exited the building and headed for the parking lot, she was going to take another look at that résumé. Carol Crane wasn't dropped into Tinker's Cove from Mars. There had to be a way to find out about her past. Hadn't she heard somewhere that you could find anyone in the United States with a few phone calls?

Reaching the parking lot, Lucy took her keys out of her pocket and held them ready in her hand. She had parked under the streetlight, as Josh had advised, and was soon safely inside her car and heading home.

As she drove along the dark roads, her mind jumped from image to image. She thought of Mr. Mopps's prediction, and how it was soon followed with the gruesome discovery of Carol's body, lying in tangled sheets with a pillow over her face. She thought of DeWalt Smythe's self-righteousness, and his eagerness to condemn Josh. She pictured Lydia, writhing at the stake as she was burned alive for practicing witchcraft. She thought of Sophie, arranging a memorial service for a woman she detested. She remembered Josh Cunningham's bewildered expression, and Toby's insistence that he must be innocent.

At last, she saw the familiar outline of her house, dark except for the porch light Bill had left burning for her. She turned into the driveway and braked, parking in her usual spot. She yawned, and got out of the car, mounting the porch steps slowly. She was tired, and needed some sleep. Tomorrow was going to be a busy day.

CHAPTER SIXTEEN

Ted was hunched over his desk when Lucy arrived on Friday morning, his body wracked with deep, chesty coughs.

"You sound terrible. Why don't you go home?"

"Can't," said Ted. "Got to cover that candidate's coffee."

"With all due respect, I think I can handle it. Why not let me go?" said Lucy.

"Do you really think you could manage?" Ted was doubtful.

"Why not? I'll write down what they say, take whatever they hand out, and snap a few pictures. What else is there to do?"

"It's not that easy," said Ted, remembering interns who forgot to get names, and rookie reporters who were incapable of holding the camera straight for a simple grip and grin—the posed shot of two people shaking hands and smiling.

"I'm not a kid, Ted. I can take pictures—I've got an album full at home. I can listen and write at the same time—I have kids. As for names, I'll probably know everybody there."

"I give up. I'm going home," said Ted, snuffling and searching his pockets for a handkerchief.

"I think you should, in the interest of public health," said Lucy, handing him a fresh box of tissues.

"The microbe is mightier than the man," he said, handing her the invitation to the coffee. "If you run into trouble, give me a call. Promise?"

"Promise," said Lucy. "And remember, drink plenty of fluids."

When Lucy arrived at the address Ted had given her, a newish house with an elaborate arrangement of windows surrounding the front door, she knew she was in the right place. The sides of the road were lined with cars, many of them with ANGUS FOR STATE REP bumper stickers.

I'm not here to judge or argue, even if I am a lifelong Democrat, she reminded herself as she approached the door. I'm just here to report whatever ideas Bob Angus is running on. She rang the doorbell.

The door was opened by Mrs. Spitzer, Tommy's mother, who greeted her warmly. "Come in, come in. Our candidate isn't here yet, but I expect him shortly."

"I'm Lucy Stone," said Lucy, extending her hand. "I'm from *The Pennysaver*."

Mrs. Spitzer leaned forward conspiratorially. "Are you a reporter?"

"Yes. Is that all right?"

"Are you going to write about this for the paper?" Mrs. Spitzer's eyes widened.

"That's the idea," said Lucy.

"How wonderful!" exclaimed Mrs. Spitzer, hugging herself

with excitement. "Let me introduce you to the others. Girls! Look who's here! A reporter from the newspaper!"

Instead of blending into the background as she had planned, Lucy found herself the center of attention.

"Are you going to take pictures?" asked a pretty young woman in a flowered pink dress.

"I hope to," said Lucy with a friendly smile. Looking about the room, she searched for a familiar face.

She soon discovered that while the faces were familiar enough, none belonged to anyone she knew well. These were women she had seen around town, in the grocery store, or at soccer games, but with whom she had never had occasion to exchange more than a few words.

"Can I get you some coffee?" asked Mrs. Spitzer, fluttering nervously beside her.

"I'd love some," said Lucy. "Tell me, how is Tommy?"

"Fine, just fine. He wasn't hurt at all, thanks to Carol. What a tragedy. I just can't believe anyone would do a thing like that." She dabbed at her eye with a hankie she took from the sleeve of her dress.

"I think everyone's in a state of shock," said Lucy. "First the bombing, and now this."

"It's terrible," agreed Mrs. Spitzer, leading Lucy to a table covered with assorted baked goods. "Who would think these things could happen in our little town?" she said, filling a cup for her.

"Thank you," said Lucy. "Are you active in politics? Have you hosted a candidate's coffee before?"

"Oh, no," she said. "I would never have thought to do it, but DeWalt asked me and I didn't want to refuse. He was so nice after the bombing. So concerned about Tommy."

"That's nice," said Lucy, choosing a cookie and putting it on her saucer.

"Excuse me, I see some more guests are arriving," said Mrs. Spitzer, hurrying to open the door and welcome the newcomers.

Lucy leaned against the wall and nibbled her cookie. Always curious about her neighbors, she studied the room. It was a big L-shaped space, what builders called a great room, which combined living and dining areas. The kitchen was really part of the room, too, set off from the rest by only a low counter.

Lucy wondered if the Spitzers had chosen the house because they liked the floor plan, or because it was practical for a family with a handicapped child. The hallway leading to the bedrooms was equipped with a railing, but there were no other modifications that Lucy could see. The open plan offered few barriers to little Tommy; it would be easy for him to get around on his crutches.

There was beige contractor-quality carpeting on the floor, and beige wallpaper with tiny flowers. A smattering of pictures that were too small for the room hung from the walls. The furniture was new, too, probably bought from Sears for the house. Everything was very clean, much cleaner than Lucy's own house. Mrs. Spitzer must spend all her time waxing, scrubbing, and polishing windows, she decided.

The women who had come to the coffee were youngish. Like Mrs. Spitzer, they were mostly in their early thirties. They had fresh-scrubbed faces and soft, feminine hairdos and they were all dressed in their Sunday best. Lucy hadn't seen so many pastels since her last roll of Necco wafers.

The quiet hum of conversation was broken suddenly when the door flew open and DeWalt blew in, followed by two others, both men. All three were dressed in business suits. The women all sat up a bit straighter and smiled in welcome. Lucy put down her coffee cup and reached for her notebook.

"Where's our hostess?" demanded DeWalt, looking around the room. "Ah, there you are! Sorry we're late, but Bob wanted to meet a few voters at the Quik Stop."

"That's all right," trilled Mrs. Spitzer. "I'm so honored to have you all here. Would you like some coffee?"

"You couldn't keep us from your fine coffee," cooed DeWalt, oozing charisma. "But first, I'd like to make some introductions. Is that all right with you?"

"Of course," said Mrs. Spitzer, stepping aside.

"Ladies," began DeWalt, pausing to make eye contact with every woman in the room. "I'm thrilled to be here with you this morning to have you meet my good friend, Bob Angus, who hopes to be the Republican candidate for state rep from this district. Also with us is his campaign manager, Bill Franklin."

The women clapped politely, and Bob Angus stepped forward.

"I'm Bob Angus, and I'm running for state rep because I want to represent you. I'm not just saying that, I really mean it. There's something wrong in our country. You know it and I know it. The Christian values upon which this great country was founded have been lost."

The women nodded and murmured agreement. Lucy scrawled down his speech in her notebook, looking up from time to time to study Bill Franklin. Franklin. Where had she heard that name?

"Families, families like yours and mine are under attack," continued Bob Angus, warming to his theme. "By the media, which offers lewd and promiscuous entertainment. By the government, which encourages irresponsible behavior and financially rewards young women who have children out of wedlock. Even by our own schools which promote immoral behavior in so-called 'sex education' classes."

The women nodded more vigorously; Angus had hit a chord.

"Now, if I'm elected, I'm going to work hard to bring back those family values you and I cherish. One way I'm going to do that is by filing a parental notification bill. This bill will require the schools to let you know, in advance, when they are going to teach some controversial subject, say homosexuality, for example. That way, you can make sure that your child does not attend those classes."

The women began clapping enthusiastically, and Angus beamed genially at them.

"Thank you. Thank you all. I hope I can count on your votes in November. Now, do I smell coffee?"

While Bob Angus worked the room, Lucy approached his campaign manager.

"Mr. Franklin?"

"Actually, I'm Dr. Franklin," he said, smiling genially at her. "We educators love our honorifics, you know, especially once we're retired. I was the superintendent of schools in Bridgton until last year."

"Of course. I knew I'd seen your name. Carol Crane listed you as a reference on her résumé."

"Oh, yes. That's a very sad business." He shook his gray-haired head. "Carol was so full of life. She touched many people in Bridgton."

"The same here, in Tinker's Cove," said Lucy. "Do you know where she grew up, anything like that? The paper would like to print a tribute, but we haven't been able to find out much about her."

"I wish I could help you. She was only with us for a short time. We hired her when our assistant principal was disabled in an auto accident. We needed someone fast, we were really quite desperate, and Carol was available. She turned out much better than any of us could have anticipated. In fact, when there was a fire in the school, she saved the day. . . ."

"A fire?" Lucy's heart started racing. "Can you tell me more about it?"

"Thanks to Carol's quick thinking, no one was hurt. We were very grateful and we were very sorry we didn't have a permanent position to offer her. I was very happy when I heard she got the job here."

Seeing that DeWalt and the candidate were heading toward the door, Lucy remembered that she needed to get a picture before they left. "Just one more question—why are you campaigning for Bob Angus?"

"Bob's the best man for the job, it's as simple as that, and you can quote me."

"I will," said Lucy, scribbling it all into her notebook. "I'd like a photo of Mr. Angus, perhaps with Mrs. Spitzer?"

"Come with me," said Dr. Franklin. "Bob! This young lady would like a photo for the newspaper."

The candidate was more than happy to cooperate, and Lucy snapped what she hoped was an original variation of the grip and grin in which he posed accepting a cup of coffee from Mrs. Spitzer.

Before the men could depart for their next engagement, however, DeWalt was stopped by a pale woman whose light brown hair was drawn tightly back into a bun. She reached out and tugged at his sleeve, and he turned toward her.

"We had a murderer in our school, teaching our children," she said, anxiously pressing her hands together in front of her stomach.

"I understand your concern," DeWalt assured her. "He should never have been hired. We have to begin requiring a higher moral standard of our teachers. After all, we are entrusting them with our children."

The pale woman's face contorted in anger. "It could have been my daughter, instead of poor Carol Crane! It could have been any of our daughters!"

DeWalt nodded solemnly. "There is only one way to change things. You have to elect good people, like Bob Angus. You have to elect folks like yourselves, like me, to the school board. That's the only way we'll get rid of those hopeless liberals like Sophie Applebaum. That's the only way we'll get Christian values back into the schools."

"But not everybody's Christian." Lucy blurted it out without thinking.

The room suddenly fell silent, and once again, all eyes were on her. Lucy squirmed.

"I mean," she explained, "there are people of many faiths, even here in a little town like Tinker's Cove. Jews, Buddhists, Muslims, all kinds of people."

Nobody said a thing. They just looked at her. She was no longer the friendly reporter from *The Pennysaver;* she had become the personification of the liberal media establishment. It was definitely time to go, before they brought out the hanging noose and formed a lynch party.

"Well, I'll be on my way," she said, spotting Mrs. Spitzer. "Thank you so much."

She didn't extend her hand in farewell; she was afraid Mrs. Spitzer wouldn't have taken it. Instead, she gave a little wave and hurried out the door. Why, she asked herself, couldn't she just take her notes and pictures without butting in? Why did she have to open her big mouth? She was supposed to report the news, not make it.

CHAPTER SEVENTEEN

Back in the Subaru, Lucy wasted no time getting back to the office. Once there, she immediately called the *Bridgton Gazette* and spoke to the editor. He obligingly agreed to fax her a copy of the story he had printed about the elementary school fire last spring. It would take a while, however, so Lucy busied herself with the obituaries.

She was halfway through an account of Susan Peters Thompson's life—she enjoyed sewing and was a member of the Ladies' Aid Society—when she heard the door open. Looking up, she was surprised to see Quentin Rea.

Today, Lucy was a bit surprised to notice, he was no longer the grief-stricken figure of the night before. He was grinning broadly, casually holding his jacket over his shoulder with one finger. He gave his sandy hair a toss and cocked his head, waiting for her to speak.

"What brings you here?" she asked, swallowing hard.

"I want to place a want ad," he said as his eyes met hers.

Lucy quickly ducked beneath the counter, reaching for a blank form. She slid it across the counter to him, and he picked up a pencil. His hands were nice, she thought, with thick fingers that looked as if they did more than turn pages.

She felt awkward, standing there while he filled out the form, so she sat back down at her desk and resumed typing the obituary. Interestingly enough, she discovered, Mrs. Thompson also raised Airedales.

"I'm all set," he said. "I'm only asking thirty-five dollars, so it's a free ad."

"That's right," said Lucy, glancing curiously at the form. "You're giving up rollerblading?"

He grinned and shrugged. "Too hard on my knees—I have an old ski injury."

"I'm sure someone will snap them up," said Lucy, giving him the carbon and filing the rest of the form.

It was a signal for him to go, but he didn't turn to leave. Instead, he looked around the office.

"So this is the famous *Pennysaver?* You know, this place has got a lot of atmosphere. Look at this floor—it's black with ink."

"Yeah," said Lucy. "Notice the smell? Ted swears it's hot lead, from the old linotype machine."

"I don't doubt him," said Quentin, coming around the counter to Lucy's desk. "What are you working on? A piece of investigative journalism?"

He stood behind her chair, and Lucy got a faint whiff of his spicy cologne. It was nice, she thought to herself. Of course, Bill would never wear cologne.

"It's an obituary—my work here is pretty much confined to

obits and legals and classifieds. I was just helping Ted the day I called you about Carol Crane."

"Poor Carol," he said, adding a sad little sigh. "Listen, are you hungry? I'm starving. Why don't we go out to lunch?"

"I don't usually . . ." Lucy began.

"There's a great place not far from here—the Queen Victoria Inn. It's a bed and breakfast, but they serve lunch and tea. I bet you'd love it."

Lucy felt her resistance crumbling. She'd heard so much about the Queen Vic, as her friends called it, but hadn't been there yet herself. Everyone loved the place, and, she rationalized, a leisurely lunch would give her an opportunity to question the professor about Carol Crane. "I've always wanted to try it," she said.

"Let us delay no longer," he said, gallantly offering her his arm.

Lucy took it, feeling for a moment as if she were wearing silk and a bustle instead of her usual jeans and polo shirt. When they got to the door, however, she took the opportunity of removing her hand from his arm. She was uncomfortable with the implied intimacy.

"Tinker's Cove is a real treasure trove of antique houses," he said as they strolled down Main Street, past a row of stately old nineteenth-century mansions, "but there aren't many grand old Victorians, are there?"

"Most of the houses are older," agreed Lucy. "They were built by sea captains in the days of sailing. The village went into a slump after the Civil War and not much was built. Only the Ezekiel Hallett house, which burned down a few years ago, and the Queen Vic. It was built as a guest house by a rather famous actress when she retired. Her name was, believe it or not, June Summers."

"Really," Quentin stated, raising an eyebrow. "How do you know all this?"

"My husband's a restoration carpenter," said Lucy, glad to find a way of working Bill into the conversation. "He knows all about most of these buildings."

"He knows their secrets, eh?"

"A lot of them do have stories to tell," said Lucy, beginning to relax. "Some of them were stops on the Underground Railroad, others had tunnels to the sea—for smuggling. Even the Queen Victoria has a hidden door that connects two bedrooms."

"I'm not surprised," said Quentin, bounding up the steps to the gingerbread-encrusted porch. "The Victorians had the same passions we do—they just kept them covered up." He held the door open for her.

Stepping into the dim hallway, Lucy felt as if she had stepped a hundred years into the past. Thick Oriental carpets covered the floor, a round table holding a bell jar filled with stuffed tropical birds stood in the center of the room. The walls were covered with a luscious rose-patterned paper.

A young woman in an old-fashioned maid's outfit, complete with lace cap and apron, greeted them and led them to the conservatory. There she seated them on cushioned wicker arm-chairs drawn up to a little round table. Although there were several other tables in the room, all filled with people, each table was quite private thanks to the lavish distribution of potted palms and ferns.

A waitress soon brought a tray containing a teapot and cups, and a silver cake stand featuring plates of tiny sandwiches, pastries, and scones.

"Shall I pour?" asked Lucy, mindful of her feminine responsibility.

"Thank you," said Quentin, settling himself comfortably. "Do you know what Henry James once wrote? 'There are few hours in life more agreeable than the hour dedicated to the ceremony known as afternoon tea.' Of course, this is lunch so we'll have to pretend it's teatime."

"It is pleasant," said Lucy, taking up the teapot. "It's a shame that we're all in such a rush these days that we rarely take time for relaxation. Sugar? Cream?"

Quentin shook his head and took the cup from Lucy, his fingers brushing hers in the process. Lucy tried not to notice.

"Delicious," he said, gazing steadily at her over the gold rim of his teacup.

"Would you like a sandwich?" asked Lucy, ignoring his stare and studying the arrangement of food.

"Good idea," he said, piling several onto his plate. "I'm famished. The academic life isn't quite as leisurely as people think."

"I have a confession to make," said Lucy, nibbling on a tiny, crustless sandwich. "I accepted your invitation because I wanted to ask you about Carol Crane."

"Why?" he asked with a defensive little shrug. "I told you everything I know."

"I don't believe that," said Lucy. Her voice was soft, and she tilted her head, inviting him to confide in her.

"Okay," he said slowly. "What do you want to know?"

"Anything you can tell me," said Lucy. "I just can't figure her out."

"Well, as you've guessed, we were once quite close. I don't mind admitting that her death has really shaken me up. She was so young." His voice broke and he took a swallow of tea. "I'll tell you what I know—and you can even print it. But I don't want you to use my name."

"That's fine with me. You can be a source close to the deceased," said Lucy, leaning forward eagerly.

"Well ..." Quentin paused, collecting his thoughts. "She grew up in Quivet Neck, on the coast. It's one of those places where there's a lot of old money. Big seaside mansions. Yachts. Tennis. The Club. All for the summer people. Old money. The people who live there year round form what used to be called the servant class. They work in the big houses, or the club. There's a huge social gulf between those who summer on Quivet Neck and those who just happen to live there.

"Carol's mother died when she was quite young and she lived with her father, who was a janitor in the local school. College was out of the question—never even thought of. The best Carol could have hoped for, really, was to find a husband with a good year-round job—an auto mechanic, maybe."

Lucy nodded. She knew all about the economic realities of life in coastal Maine.

"All that changed, however, when Carol got a job as a lifeguard at the club and saved a little boy who fell into the deep end of the pool while his mother was busy sipping her fifth gin and tonic. His very grateful parents offered to pay her way at the local community college. So, off Carol went to North Megunticook County Community College. After two years there she went on to the state university, where I met her." He paused, and picked up his cup. "I say," he said, adopting an upper-class British accent, "is there any more tea in that pot? This reminiscin' is thirsty work, don't you know."

"I'm sorry," said Lucy, feeling a bit as if she'd strayed into a Dorothy Sayers novel as she lifted the pot. "I've been neglecting my duties."

Quentin drained the cup and, refreshed, resumed his narrative.

"I don't think Carol really liked the state university very much. Too big, too many people. It was easy to get lost in the crowd. Of course, she soon remedied that. There was a shuttle bus that provided transportation on the campus. Most of the drivers were older men, retirees from the railroad. One day Carol was on a bus when the driver suddenly collapsed. The bus happened to be at the top of a very steep hill, and Carol managed to get it under control, saving the lives of all aboard. Everyone knew her after that."

"Are you saying she staged that accident somehow?" asked Lucy.

"I'm sure she did," said Quentin. "She used to give the driver homemade fudge now and then—she could easily have poisoned him."

"But why?" asked Lucy. "What was she after?"

"Adulation. Admiration. Attention. She had to have it."

"And she didn't care who she hurt to get it?"

"Not a bit," Quentin said. "To Carol, people were just there for her to use. She was ambitious and manipulative, and she could be quite cruel."

Raising her eyes to meet his, Lucy saw the hurt revealed there. She knew without being told that Quentin had been one of those Carol had taken advantage of and then discarded. Impulsively, she reached across the table and covered his hand with hers.

"I hope you won't abuse my trust," he said, his voice thick with emotion.

"I would never do that," promised Lucy.

"I believe you." He withdrew his hand and placed it over hers. She felt his warmth as he began gently stroking her fingers. He slowly smiled, and she noticed his lips were generous and full. What would it be like to kiss him, she wondered, realizing he was leaning across the table, drawing closer to her.

"Oh, my goodness," she exclaimed, pulling her hand away and checking her watch. "Look at the time. After one. I have got to go."

"Do you?" A teasing smile flitted across his face.

"Oh, yes," said Lucy, jumping to her feet and jostling the table. "Let me give you something toward the check."

"Never mind. Please, let it be my treat."

"But I was interviewing you."

"It was my pleasure. I hope we can do it again soon," he said, taking her hand and bending down to kiss it.

"I doubt it—I'm awfully busy," said Lucy, snatching her hand away as if she had been stung.

"Then I'll see you in class," said Quentin.

"In class," agreed Lucy, tossing the words over her shoulder. It wasn't until she was outside the inn, back on the sidewalk, that she began to relax. Still breathing heavily, she struggled to catch her breath as she hurried along.

Feeling rather ridiculous—after all, she was hardly a blushing maiden—Lucy refused to deal with her jumbled and confused feelings toward Quentin. She resolved to deal with them later and firmly shoved them into a back corner of her mind, while she considered this new picture of Carol.

A poor, motherless girl with no prospects. A girl whose father was a janitor, who no doubt yearned to be like the girls at the club. They enjoyed an endless summer, with no responsibilities. They were free to sun themselves, free to play tennis and go sailing, free to go to dances and flirt with the boys. Carol, on the other hand, had to work all summer and still couldn't afford clothes like the girls at the club wore.

Their fathers were lawyers and doctors and businessmen. Men who wore suits and told other people what to do. Her father was a janitor, who cleaned up after other people.

No wonder she seemed phony, Lucy thought, as she crossed the street to *The Pennysaver*. She was inventing herself as she went along. She thought of an interview she had read in which a famous TV star recalled her humble origins as the daughter of sharecroppers. "I'm always afraid I'll wake up and find myself back in that shack," she had confessed.

Carol had probably felt the same way, thought Lucy, opening the door to *The Pennysaver* office. She had come a long way from Quivet Neck, and she wasn't planning on going back.

Entering the office, Lucy checked the phone messages—an address change and a missing paper—and the fax machine, flipping through the accumulated papers until she found the *Bridgton Gazette* story.

What she read confirmed her worst suspicions. The fire was eerily similar to the Tinker's Cove bombing, right down to the front page photo of a soot-smudged Carol Crane holding a rescued child in her arms.

CHILD SAVED BY PRINCIPAL, proclaimed the headline. The fire, like the bombing, had not been as serious as originally thought. While there had been plenty of smoke, actual damage had been limited. And just like little Tommy Spitzer in Tinker's Cove, Jeremiah Holden had been trapped in a supply room. And even though he insisted he had been locked in, his claims were discounted by investigators. The boy was deaf, after all, and it was difficult to communicate with him. It was generally agreed that he had panicked and locked himself in.

Reading the description of the fire, Lucy felt sick. Two such similar incidents couldn't be coincidences, especially when you added in that trick with the bus. They all had to have been staged by Carol herself.

What sort of person could trick two little boys—handicapped children, no less—and lock them up only to pretend to save them? And what about the poor bus driver?

Lucy put her head in her hands and rubbed her eyes. Carol had certainly fooled everybody in Tinker's Cove. She wasn't a heroine; she was a monster who manipulated people and events. She didn't care whom she hurt, thought Lucy, growing angry.

What if she'd miscalculated? What if Tommy had been injured, or even killed? Had Carol even considered that? She probably had, and figured she'd come out ahead no matter what happened.

It's no wonder she was killed, thought Lucy, growing quite cold. A person who messes around with other people's lives is bound to make a lot of enemies. She rubbed her arms and then switched on the computer. This was one story that had to be told.

CHAPTER EIGHTEEN

When Lucy had finished, it was after four o'clock. She knew she ought to hurry home and get dinner started, but lately, she admitted sadly to herself, family suppers hardly seemed worth the effort. Furthermore, she knew a memorial tree-planting service for Carol Crane was scheduled for four-thirty at the school. Ted was too sick to go—she could stop by and snap a few photos on the way home. After all, Elizabeth and Toby were certainly old enough to get supper started. It was about time they learned a little responsibility, she decided, as she called to give them instructions.

A few minutes later, Lucy turned in the drive to the elementary school and parked the Subaru behind a white TV van. Tinker's Cove was certainly in the news these days. Grabbing her camera and notebook, she hurried across the lawn to the memorial grove, begun only a few years ago when the parents of a first grader who died of leukemia donated a flowering crab apple tree in her memory. Now, the grove had grown to a half-dozen ornamental trees. There, teachers and administrators and a number of parents had gathered, along with the TV camera crew.

Rather than arranging themselves in a single group, however, Lucy noticed that they had split into two camps. Mrs. Applebaum, Ms. Kinnear, Lydia Volpe, and most of the teachers were standing on one side. The other group contained the superintendent of schools, one or two school committee members, and a number of parents. DeWalt Smythe detached himself from that group and stepped forward, opening his worn copy of the Revised Standard Version.

"Let us pray," he began. "Lord, we are gathered here today to remember your servant Carol." He paused, and raised his face, eyes closed, in what Lucy thought was a rather ostentatious display of piety for the benefit of the TV camera. "Carol was a shining example of Christian womanhood, an educator who taught by heroic example."

Just wait 'til you read *The Pennysaver* this week, thought Lucy, raising her camera and clicking away.

In the group from which DeWalt had stepped sniffles could be heard as people fumbled for handkerchiefs and wiped their eyes. In the other group there was an obvious lack of grief. In fact, Lucy sensed a certain air of impatience as DeWalt continued his lengthy prayer.

"And so, dear Lord, it is with great sadness that we dedicate this little tree to your faithful servant Carol, whose death at the hand of a colleague can only remind us that so long as we are willing to tolerate wickedness and Godlessness in our community, the truly good shall fall as lambs before wolves. It is only when we decide to choose the path of righteousness, and accept your holy laws, that goodness and virtue will once again flourish upon the earth. Amen."

As soon as the final word was pronounced, the group of teachers broke up and went their separate ways. The other group, however, lingered to admire the tree and console each other. Lucy considered interviewing some of the mourners, but figured DeWalt had really said it all. Furthermore, the TV crew was monopolizing his attention. Instead, she followed the teachers who had regrouped in the parking lot.

"I'm so sick of that guy, I could throw up," she overheard Lydia Volpe say.

"I just wish people knew what the real Saint Carol was like," muttered Ms. Kinnear. "Hasn't it occurred to anybody that it's a little odd nobody has claimed her body? Sandy McCoul at the funeral home told me they don't know what to do with it."

"Even if you tried to tell them, they wouldn't believe it," said Sophie, in a resigned voice, glancing at the weeping mourners. "And now they've got Josh as a scapegoat. I'm so worried for him."

Lydia shook her head. "Did you hear the news? The DA has granted immunity to some informer who says Josh hired him to set the bomb to get back at Carol. Can you believe it?" Her dark eyes flashed with anger.

Lucy was tempted to join in the gossip, but reminded herself that she was there to get information, not share it. They could read all about it when the paper came out. "What informant?" she asked.

"I'm not sure. I only heard a snatch on the radio on my way over here. I didn't get his name."

"Mel something," said Ms. Kinnear.

"Mel Costas?" asked Lucy, remembering the accident report Jewel had filed just before deadline.

"That's it," said Ms. Kinnear. "Mel Costas. He seems like a pretty good candidate for the murder, if you ask me, but they say he has an ironclad alibi. He's coming clean about the bombing because he's so upset about Carol." She sniffed. "Sounds pretty suspicious to me."

"Me, too," said Lydia. "No one will ever convince me that Josh Cunningham would do a thing like that."

"It's as if she's reaching out from the morgue—as if she didn't cause enough grief when she was alive," said Ms. Kinnear, with a little shudder.

"I don't suppose you want to go on the record with any of this," said Lucy. "I'm filling in for Ted."

"Good Lord, no," said Sophie. "As far as *The Pennysaver* is concerned, we're shocked and grieved by Ms. Crane's tragic death."

Lucy dutifully wrote down the quote in her notebook. "What about this parental notification bill that DeWalt is sponsoring?" she asked.

Sophie rolled her eyes in exasperation. "Completely impractical. Expensive, too. Can you imagine the work involved in notifying parents whenever a teacher plans to include a 'sensitive topic' in a lesson plan? And who decides what's sensitive and what isn't? Most teachers will end up avoiding anything they think might be controversial."

"It will stifle free expression in the classroom," said Ms. Kinnear. "Say we were talking about families and a child said he had two mothers or two fathers. Well, we couldn't talk about that unless I'd warned the parents in advance, so I would have to cut off discussion."

"Do topics like that really come up in second grade?" asked Lucy, a bit surprised.

"Oh, sure," said Ms. Kinnear. "The kids see TV news, they hear their parents talking. Gosh, the kids whose families attend the Revelation Congregation are always talking about the poor murdered babies."

"It's true," agreed Lydia. "One of my kindergarteners was in tears the other day—she was convinced an 'evil 'bortion doctor' would kill her brand new baby sister."

"That's horrible," said Lucy.

"The poor things hear all this rhetoric and don't know what to think, and if you try to tell them the truth, you get in trouble." Lydia sounded bitter.

"Teachers have to be very careful even now, without the law. Can you imagine how restricted they would feel if it went into effect?" said Sophie. "Especially since it could be used to punish teachers who hold liberal views."

"Punish? What do you mean?"

"Nowadays, thanks to tenure, teachers can't lose their jobs simply because they're unpopular with a certain segment of the community. But if this law is adopted, it will give those people a tool. They can complain that a teacher violated the parental notification law, and it could be grounds for dismissal."

"And it will be almost impossible to comply with it—there are bound to be slipups," said Lydia.

"It almost seems like it was designed to entrap teachers," Lucy said slowly.

"It sure does," said Lydia, dark eyes flashing. "I'm beginning to feel like an endangered species."

"Look what they're doing to Josh," said Ms. Kinnear. "DeWalt is demonizing him; he isn't even waiting for the trial to find out if he's guilty or not. If they can do that to him, they can do it to any of us."

The others nodded silently in agreement.

Lucy thanked Sophie for her comment and hurried off, mulling over what the teachers had said. She was shocked at how vulnerable they felt, and couldn't decide if their fears were justified or not. These days, everyone seemed to be paranoid when it came to their jobs.

The little clock in her car told her she was running late, and the day-care center was due to close in just a few minutes. Zoë was the only child left when she arrived, which made her feel terribly guilty.

Finally turning into her own driveway, she was relieved to see that Bill's pickup truck was not there, which meant he wasn't home yet. He must have had to work late, too. At least she wouldn't have to deal with his foot-tapping impatience as she prepared dinner.

She had no sooner got out of her car than the kitchen door flew open, and she heard Toby's call for help. Running up the steps, with Zoë clutched to her chest and her purse and diaper bag swinging from her arms, she flew into the kitchen. There she found Elizabeth unable to catch her breath.

"I can't breathe," the girl gasped, her chest heaving with effort. Her eyes were wide with panic as she broke into a high, barking cough. Tears streamed down her cheeks, and the floor around her was littered with crumpled tissues, proof that her nose wouldn't stop running.

Lucy handed the baby to Toby and dropped her bags, kneeling on the floor beside Elizabeth. Checking the beds of her finger-nails, she saw they were a healthy shade of pink.

"You're going to be fine," she said, looking directly into her daughter's frightened eyes. "You're panicking and it's making things worse. Try to breathe slowly and evenly, okay?"

Elizabeth nodded, and tried to gain control of her rapid, shallow breaths, but succombed instead to a fit of coughing.

Making a quick decision, Lucy turned to Toby. "I'm going to take her to the emergency room—I want you to take charge here, okay?"

"Do you still want me to make supper?" he asked.

"I don't know," said Lucy, flustered. "You must be starving. How about some soup and sandwiches? Something like that—do what you think best. Come on, Elizabeth." She pulled the girl to her feet and supported her by wrapping an arm around her waist. "Time to see the doctor."

During the drive to the cottage hospital, Lucy kept a nervous eye on her daughter. Her eyes were still streaming, and her breaths were ragged gasps in between fits of coughing and wheezing. Lucy did her best to hide her concern from Elizabeth, but she was frantic by the time they pulled up at the emergency room entrance.

A nurse took one look at Elizabeth when they entered and led them immediately to a curtained cubicle. She quickly checked her pulse and blood pressure and within minutes they were joined by a doctor.

"We need you to fill out some papers," said the nurse, leading Lucy back to the front desk. "She's in good hands."

By the time Lucy had finished filling out a health history, signed a consent form, and handed over her insurance card, Elizabeth was much improved. Her breathing was still rough and choppy when Lucy returned to the cubicle, but she was no longer gasping frantically for air.

"This was a pretty typical asthma attack," said the doctor. "Has Elizabeth been treated for allergies?"

"Not really," said Lucy. "I noticed she was allergic to our cat so we gave it away."

"People tend not to take allergies very seriously, but that's a mistake," said the doctor. "Allergies are very dangerous. She really needs to see a specialist to get this under control. I wouldn't delay if I were you—I'd make an appointment right away. In the meantime, here are some antihistamines and an inhaler, in case she has another attack. I showed her how to use it. You did the right thing, bringing her in. I mean it," he nodded seriously. "You can't afford to ignore asthma. Children die from it every year."

Back in the car, Lucy tried to make sense of the episode.

"Has that ever happened before?"

"No, Mom. Honest."

"Do you have any idea what brought it on?"

"No. Toby and I were fooling around, and he threw a pillow at me. I threw it back and we had a little pillow fight. Next thing I knew, I couldn't breathe. It was scary."

"Sure was," said Lucy, reaching for Elizabeth's hand. She attempted a joke. "I can think of something scarier."

"Yeah? What?"

"Not having supper ready when your father comes home."

"Nothing's scarier than that," agreed Elizabeth, but she didn't join Lucy in a restorative laugh, as she normally would have.

She's afraid, thought Lucy, with a painful little stab of insight. She's afraid to laugh because it might set off another attack.

* * *

They had no sooner pulled in the driveway than the kitchen door popped open and Bill hurried out to meet them.

"How's Elizabeth?" he demanded anxiously.

"She had an asthma attack—they gave her some medications and said we ought to see a specialist."

"Asthma?" He looked at Elizabeth suspiciously. "Nobody in my family has asthma."

Lucy shrugged. "A lot of kids have it nowadays—maybe it's something to do with air pollution. That's my theory, anyway." She put her arm around Elizabeth's shoulder for a quick hug but Elizabeth shook it off and made a point of bounding up the porch steps. They heard the familiar sound of the door to her room slamming as they entered the kitchen. Soon the sound of Road Kill, Elizabeth's favorite band, drifted down the stairs.

"I don't think she's too thrilled about this," said Lucy, spreading the inhalers and medications out on the kitchen table. "She has to take all this every day."

"Just say no," said Bill, attempting a joke at the impressive assortment of drugs that included blue, orange, and pink inhalers, nasal spray, and several bottles of pills.

"Don't you dare tease her about this," warned Lucy. "Promise?"

"Promise," agreed Bill.

"Has everybody eaten?" Lucy asked hopefully.

"Yup. Zoë's had a bath and is in bed. Toby's doing homework and Sara is watching TV. Everything's under control."

"That's a relief," said Lucy, collapsing into a chair and propping her elbows on the kitchen table.

"Can I fix something for you?" Bill was hovering over her,

unwilling to leave her alone. Lucy could tell he was upset, too. Normally he would have been in his usual after-dinner spot, the recliner chair in the family room, flipping through the channels with the remote control.

"Peanut butter and jelly would be fine, with a big glass of milk. Comfort food."

"You got it," said Bill, setting to work. "How about Elizabeth?"

"You can try, but I don't think she'll eat anything."

Bill yelled up the stairs, trying to be heard over Elizabeth's CD player. "Do you want some supper?"

"No!" came the unequivocal answer.

Lucy gave Bill an "I told you so" sort of shrug as he set her sandwich before her. He gave her shoulder a squeeze and sat down beside her.

"Don't worry. It'll be okay," he said.

"I hope so," said Lucy, taking a big bite of peanut butter and jelly. "I hope so."

CHAPTER NINETEEN

On Monday morning Ted was back at work.

"You did a good job on that story about the parental notification bill," he told her.

"What about my Carol Crane story?" asked Lucy.

"It's great stuff," said Ted, "but I can't use it."

"Why not?" asked Lucy, crestfallen.

"Well . . . you make some pretty serious allegations and you don't back them up."

"It's just common sense," sputtered Lucy. "The fire and the bombing couldn't be coincidences."

"I agree," said Ted. "But nobody official filed any charges against her. There isn't a hint of suspicion about the Bridgton affair."

"Well, what about the stuff Professor Rea told me?"

Ted smiled slowly. "I think he told you what he wanted you to know. He gave you his perspective. What politicians call spin control. If Carol is even half as manipulative as you suspect—well, I bet the story he didn't tell you is a lot more interesting than the one he did."

"I can't believe I was so stupid," said Lucy, recognizing the truth in what Ted said. "I let him lead me by the nose. I didn't question a thing he said."

Lucy started on the pile of press releases that had accumulated on her desk, but her mind wasn't really on the next meeting of the Village Garden Club or the fact that the Broadbrooks Free Library was switching to winter hours and would no longer be open on Tuesday evenings. Instead, she kept thinking of her conversation with Dr. Franklin. Had he been holding something back, she wondered. After all, Carol had upset a lot of people in the Tinker's Cove schools—she must have had a similar effect in Bridgton.

Checking Carol's résumé, which was beginning to get a bit worn about the edges, she gave him a call. This time, he was home, apparently taking a break from the campaign trail.

"Dr. Franklin? This is Lucy Stone, from *The Pennysaver*. I spoke to you at the coffee for Bob Angus."

"I remember."

"Well, I wonder if you're aware that Carol Crane was involved in an incident here in Tinker's Cove that was very similar to the fire in Bridgton? Instead of a fire, we had a bomb in the school, and Carol saved a little boy who was locked in a supply closet."

"That's an amazing coincidence." Dr. Franklin's voice seemed to waver a bit.

"I don't think it's a coincidence at all," said Lucy. "I suspect Carol planned them both."

"Why would she do that?"

"I've done some research and it seems to be part of a pattern. She used these crisis situations to become a hero and to gain power. Does that sound at all plausible to you?"

"I don't know." He sighed. "There were rumors about her but I put them down to jealousy. When Carol got so much attention it seemed to put a lot of people's noses out of joint." He paused. "This is all off the record, of course. A lot of folks here will simply not hear anything negative about Carol."

"But you've heard negative things?"

"Actually, yes. Our police chief advised me that Carol had been involved in a police call. Neighbors complained about a woman screaming in the night. It was Carol, fighting with a man. He said he was her husband, but Carol insisted he was an unwanted guest. It was never repeated, and Carol left soon after." He paused. "I have to admit, I was relieved when she left. I was beginning to suspect she was something of a troublemaker."

"And that's why you gave her such a glowing recommendation?" Lucy was shocked.

"That's the way it's done, my dear. That's the way it's done." Dr. Franklin suddenly sounded like a very old man. "You just pass the problem along, and then it becomes somebody else's problem."

Saying goodbye then replacing the receiver, Lucy decided to give Sophie a call. She just couldn't believe what Dr. Franklin had told her.

"Sophie, Lucy Stone. I just had the oddest phone conversation with Dr. Franklin, the Bridgton superintendent. He told me he gave Carol a good recommendation to get rid of her. Could that be true?"

"It wouldn't surprise me at all," admitted Sophie after she had digested Lucy's question. "In fact, it's getting so bad that the better a teacher's credentials are, the more suspicious I am."

"I don't understand."

"Well," explained Sophie patiently, "because of tenure and union contracts and all that, it's very expensive for a school system to fire a bad teacher. There has to be a hearing and the teacher is entitled to a lawyer and the whole thing drags on for months and even then the teacher isn't fired. Usually they're just required to take a remedial classroom management course or something. In truth, the only way you can get rid of them is to get somebody else to hire them."

"But if everyone knows this, how come it works?" asked Lucy.

"Sometimes it doesn't," said Sophie. "But Carol was hired by a search committee made up of parents and school committee members, DeWalt included. They were awfully impressed with her credentials." Sophie sniffed. "I knew she'd be trouble from the get-go. She started after Mr. Mopps her very first day."

"Why was that?"

"I don't know. It was almost as if she just couldn't stand the man. I never understood it."

"Now that she's no longer on the scene, couldn't you hire him back?"

"I tried," said Sophie. "His brother told me he left town, went back to Brooklyn."

"That's interesting," began Lucy.

"Lucy!" roared Ted, from across the room. "I need those town news items and those obits *Now!*"

"Gotta go. Thanks, Sophie," said Lucy, hanging up the receiver and reaching for the keypad.

Lucy typed steadily for the rest of Monday and all day Tuesday, working her way through the huge stack of press releases and classified ad forms she had neglected in favor of her investigative reporting the week before. Finally, at three on Tuesday afternoon, she left to take Elizabeth to the allergist.

"You can let asthma control you," the doctor told Elizabeth, "or you can control it. The way you do that is by taking your medication every day."

Elizabeth nodded meekly as he explained her daily regimen of pills and nasal spray and inhalers, but exploded after they had left the office and reached the car.

"I'm not gonna do it! I'm not gonna fill my body with all that stuff," she declared as she fumbled with her seat belt.

"It does seem like a lot," sympathized Lucy. "But he said he'd review it at your next appointment. I think you have to give it a try."

"It's ridiculous! I don't see how all those chemicals could be good for me. And I am not going to carry an inhaler wherever I go like some sort of geek." She finally snapped the buckle into place.

"I know how you feel—I think natural is better, too. But sometimes our bodies don't quite do what we want. Remember how scared you were? Wouldn't it be better to try and avoid that happening again?"

"It won't happen again," said Elizabeth. "I won't let it."

"You can't control it," said Lucy, her voice rising. "When he gave you those patch tests, could you stop the reaction? It's the same thing, only it's your breathing. Don't be stupid. It's not fair to put me through another attack—"

Elizabeth looked at her, her eyes widening in surprise.

"It's not just about you. A lot of people love you." Lucy smiled slowly. "You're my favorite, you know."

"No, I didn't know," said Elizabeth, surprised.

"Well, you are. All the time I was pregnant with Toby I wished for a girl. When he was born, well, I loved him, of course. I was really happy that he was healthy and had all his toes and fingers, but I couldn't help feeling a tiny bit disappointed. Then you came and I was so excited to finally have a little girl."

"But Mom, we're always fighting."

"That's okay. I fought with my mother, too. In fact, you remind me of myself more than any of the others."

"If you say so," said Elizabeth, looking rather doubtful.

"So, do me a favor and at least try the medication 'til your next appointment, okay?" Lucy started the car.

"Okay," grumbled Elizabeth. "If it makes you happy."

Lucy started the engine, heading for home. As they drove along, she remembered Elizabeth's arrival in the family. All through her pregnancy, Lucy had worried about Toby's reaction. After being the center of attention for two and a half years, she was worried that he would resent the new baby.

When Lucy and Bill brought the tiny baby Elizabeth home from the cottage hospital, Toby had seemed uninterested. He busied himself playing with his trucks, and his Legos, and ignored both the baby and his mother. After a day or two, Lucy realized what was going on.

One afternoon, when Elizabeth was napping, Lucy scooped Toby up and planted him on the sofa beside her. He tried to squirm away, but she wrapped an arm around him and hugged him.

"Today," she said, opening the family album, "I have a very special story for you. It's the story of baby Toby."

She pointed to a picture of herself, her belly swollen with pregnancy. "That's Mommy with baby Toby inside."

Toby was interested, and studied the picture. When he was ready, she turned the page.

"That's brand new baby Toby."

Toby shook his head. "Baby 'Lizbet."

"Nope," insisted Lucy. "That's you. Once, you were just as small as Elizabeth. You couldn't talk. You couldn't walk."

Lucy pointed to another picture. "You're bigger here. Six months. See, you're sitting up."

She turned a few pages. "Now, baby Toby's standing. And here, baby Toby's playing with his big, red fire engine."

"Truck!" said Toby, pointing with a chubby finger.

"And here's a picture of Toby now. What a big boy!" said Lucy, giving him a squeeze. "You're my favorite big boy!"

"Big Boy!" agreed Toby, snuggling close.

Ever since then, Lucy had made a point of letting each of her children know how special they were to her. She often told each child he or she was her favorite. She didn't know if they compared notes, but she didn't think it mattered. Whenever she said it, that child was, for the moment, her very dearest child.

They arrived home with time to spare. Now that Lucy had been working for three weeks, a system had finally begun to evolve. While Lucy put dinner together, Sara played with Zoë, Elizabeth set the table, and Toby ran a load of wash. When Bill came home, the house was peaceful and orderly and dinner was ready to go on the table.

"Smells great," he said, lifting the lid of the pot and sniffing appreciatively.

"Beef stew. With red wine and mushrooms."

"You haven't made that in ages."

"I know. I found some old recipes on Saturday, while you were out fishing with Toby." In fact, following up on a tip from Sue, Lucy had searched high and low until she found her crock pot, long forgotten on the top shelf of the pantry.

They both turned as Zoë toddled into the kitchen. "Daddy!" she exclaimed, holding out her arms.

Bill scooped her up and lifted her high above his head, making her squeal.

After dinner, Bill settled in his favorite chair to watch the news with Zoë in his lap. Sara cleared the table and Elizabeth and Toby loaded the dishwasher. When Lucy left for her class, she had the distinctly odd but pleasant sensation of knowing that everything was under control.

In class, Lucy tried to concentrate on Professor Rea's lecture, but her mind kept wandering. Thinking back over their luncheon, she realized how artfully he had directed the conversation. She had been so thrilled to be getting the inside scoop that she had swallowed not only his line, but the hook and sinker, too.

A burst of laughter from the class brought her attention back to the professor. He was a consummate actor, she realized. With impeccable timing he was able to lead the class through a daunting amount of material, much of it tedious and boring. After all, the Victorians weren't known for concise expression. But whenever the pace slowed, whenever the students' attention wandered, he was able to get them back on track with a joke and a laugh. It was easy to underestimate him because he made it look so easy.

Confident, charming, sophisticated, good-looking—was he perhaps a bit too good to be true? Why had he never married, Lucy wondered. It seemed a bit odd. Perhaps he wasn't quite the well-adjusted bachelor that he seemed.

What exactly had his relationship with Carol been? At lunch, he had given Lucy the impression that Carol had injured him, but he didn't offer any specifics. What really happened? And was it all long in the past, as she had assumed, or had they been seeing each other recently?

What had he said? *Carol lived close to the edge. She liked to play games. She was bound to push somebody too far.* Had Carol pushed him too far? What would his reaction have been?

Lucy pushed the unbidden thought away. Besides, he had seemed genuinely grief-stricken the other night, when he had first learned of Carol's death. You couldn't fake something like that, could you?

He stopped her after class, waiting until the others had left the room before speaking.

"I really enjoyed lunch the other day," he began, slowly running his tongue over his bottom lip.

"I had a nice time, too," said Lucy. The memory of him licking a dab of cream filling off his lip popped into her mind, and she tried to suppress it.

"Is something the matter? You seem anxious," he said, flicking off the light as they passed through the doorway into the hallway.

"Oh, no. Well, actually I am a little distracted." Lucy wasn't about to admit her real thoughts during class. Instead, she said, "I just learned that my daughter has asthma. I'm worried about her."

"Always the good mother," he said, in a teasing tone.

Lucy felt defensive. "What do you expect? I am a mother. I have four kids. It's a lot of responsibility."

"Of course," he agreed as they walked down the corridor. "I can't imagine how you do it. I think of my own mother, always worrying about us, never thinking of herself. It's like that for you, isn't it?"

"I don't know," said Lucy, honestly confused. "Sometimes I think I've been putting them first for too long. Maybe it's time for me to concentrate on myself a little bit. But that's not easy to do. In a way, having a family has allowed me to put things off. Maybe it's time for me to decide what I want to be when I grow up."

He bent his head, as if to kiss her, but she whirled away.

"Growing up is never easy," he said, making a smooth recovery. "What do you think you would like to be?"

"A teacher, I guess. Then I could have a career that wouldn't conflict with the family too much. I'd have the same hours as the kids, summers off."

"Always the kids." He grinned. "Do you think you'd like teaching?"

"I'm not sure," admitted Lucy. "I'm not sure of anything."

"It sounds as if you need some intensive counseling from an experienced advisor," said Quentin, keeping his voice light and teasing. "Why don't you come over to my place? It's not far from here."

"Oh . . ." Lucy felt the blood rise to her cheeks, and she took a step backward. "It's so late, I really have to get home."

"I understand." He sounded disappointed.

"Besides," said Lucy, arching an eyebrow and holding her notebook up to her face as if it were a fan. "You know perfectly well that a proper Victorian lady would never visit a gentleman's quarters unchaperoned."

"Forgive me," he said, snapping his heels together and bowing.

They parted, and as Lucy made her way to the parking lot, she wondered if she had made the right choice. In Victorian novels, women who fell from virtue were inevitably punished. But she wasn't wearing long skirts and petticoats; she was a thoroughly modern woman and she was entitled to express herself and seek fulfillment, wasn't she?

CHAPTER TWENTY

"He what?" exclaimed Sue. Lucy hadn't been able to resist pausing for a confessional chat when she dropped Zoë at the day-care center bright and early on Wednesday morning.

"Invited me to his apartment for a career counseling session."

"But you didn't go?"

"Of course not. I wouldn't do a thing like that."

Sue looked at her skeptically. "You don't sound very sure."

"I keep having thoughts," admitted Lucy.

"About him?"

Lucy nodded.

"What kind of thoughts?"

"Oh, about his tongue. And his lips. The way he smiles. His hair. His hands."

"Ohhh," groaned Sue. "Can't you think of something else?"

"Oh, sure. I try. But then I'll be doing something and they'll pop up. Mostly I try to substitute Bill. Think of him."

"Does that work?"

"Not really."

"This is awful, Lucy. You've got so much with Bill. Home, kids . . ."

"Mortgage, Visa bill," countered Lucy. "Not to mention fights and awkward silences and tiptoeing around sensitive subjects. I mean, I love this course, but has he shown any interest at all? Has he even asked me if it's interesting . . ."

"Stop it!" interrupted Sue. "Look at Deb Altman. She had a perfectly nice marriage and gave it all up for a fling with the plumber. Now she's living in a crummy duplex with three kids and no man in sight."

"You're right. You're absolutely right. But, you know, it's great to discover that somebody finds you attractive," said Lucy, remembering how wonderful she'd felt when Quentin looked at her. She'd felt warm and glowing, graceful and desirable.

"Bill doesn't even look at me anymore," she admitted bitterly. "It's like I'm part of the furniture, something he reaches for automatically when he's in the mood. Like a cold beer in the fridge." Lucy paused, and added slowly, "And it's nice to know that I can still get interested myself. Sex with Bill is something I'm supposed to do. There's never any flirtation, he never courts me. It's just something he expects. It's part of being married. But the times I really want to do it are few and far between. Know what I mean?"

"I know," said Sue, letting out a big sigh.

At the office, Ted was rushing to finish up a summary of the new septic regulations before deadline and asked Lucy to proofread the stories he had completed. Switching on the computer, Lucy read his account of the case against Josh Cunningham.

Straightening out Ted's garbled typing—he knew perfectly well how to spell but sometimes hit the keys so rapidly that the letters got reversed, producing *nad* instead of *and, ihs* instead of *his*—she learned that the police had indeed produced Mel Costas, the man Jewel the Ghoul had photographed in the accident on Bumps River Road, as a witness.

According to Mr. Costas, who described himself as an "old family friend" of Carol's, he had spent the night at her apartment. He had only meant to spend the day visiting, but had been having some problems with his truck and decided to spend the night rather than risk driving home. When he left, at a little past eight, he saw Josh pulling into the parking area at the apartment complex.

Police had cleared Costas of any suspicion in the murder. Carol's watch, broken in the struggle with her assailant, had stopped at eight-thirty, the time of Costas's accident.

Costas also told police that Josh Cunningham had approached him some months before about placing a bomb in the school, but Costas maintained he had refused and passed the information along to Carol.

"Howzit comin', Lucy?" George's voice broke into her thoughts. "I need that story toot sweet."

"I'm almost through," she said, finishing up and shipping it to him.

Leaving *The Pennysaver*'s office with another issue safely put to bed, Lucy had the whole afternoon stretching before her. Convinced that the key to Carol's death lay in her life, she wondered how she could get the information she needed so Ted would print her story.

Starting up the car, she drove to the apartment complex on Spring Street. Thinking she might be able to chat up some of the tenants, she pulled into a parking space marked VISITOR. Only a handful of cars were in the lot, the play area was deserted, and the benches scattered about on the lawn were empty. Noticing a sign pointing to the manager's apartment, Lucy impulsively followed the arrow and rang the bell.

The door was opened by a doughy-faced woman with a faded dye job wearing polyester pants.

"I'm looking for an apartment," said Lucy. "I wonder if you have a vacancy."

"Sorry," said the woman, starting to close the door.

"That's too bad," said Lucy. "These apartments look so attractive and I really want to get out of the place I'm living in now." She leaned forward as if including the manager in a secret. "I've got a one-bedroom in one of those big old captain's houses on Main Street. It's charming, all right, but the plumbing is barely adequate and I'm a little nervous about the wiring. I'd love to get into something newer."

"You're single? No kids?"

"Oh, yes," said Lucy. "It would just be me, myself and I."

"Pets?"

"Oh, no. Too dirty."

"Well . . . I might have something. Strictly speaking, I'm not supposed to show the apartment. The previous tenant's stuff is still there. But for you, I'll make an exception."

"I don't want you to do anything you shouldn't," said Lucy.

"It's okay. Believe me, she's not gonna be complaining."

Trotting across the grassy courtyard and into the dim vestibule, she unlocked the door to Carol's apartment. C.CRANE was still affixed under the tiny brass knocker.

"The rent is five-eighty a month. Utilities are separate," she said, opening the door.

Lucy followed her into a spacious combination living-dining room, waiting while the manager hurried over to the large window and opened the drapes.

"Does it come furnished?"

"No, like I said, these things belong to the previous tenant. Just haven't had a chance to get them out yet."

Lucy saw a white leather couch, with an enormous print of a Georgia O'Keeffe flower hanging on the wall above it. A glass-topped coffee table sat in front of the couch, bare except for a silk flower arrangement. Two matching easy chairs, also covered in leather, and a large-screen TV completed the arrangement. A stereo system was neatly placed on shiny gray shelves, but there were no books or magazines.

In the dining area another, larger glass table was placed beneath a modern chrome lighting fixture. It was surrounded by four chairs, covered in pink and gray material. A second silk flower arrangement occupied the center of the table.

The kitchen was separated from the dining area by a half-wall that formed a counter. It was neat as a pin, and Lucy guessed Carol hadn't cooked much.

"Didn't I hear that somebody died over here? I think it was a murder, wasn't it?" asked Lucy, trying the tap to check the water pressure.

"Don't you worry. These apartments are very safe. Top-quality locks on windows and doors. Whoever killed her, she must have let him in. And the police have got him anyway."

"That's a relief," said Lucy, pulling open a drawer and examining the neatly stacked stainless steel flatware inside it. The kitchen was fully equipped with new appliances including a stove, refrigerator, and dishwasher. There was even a garbage grinder in the sink.

"It's very nice," said Lucy. "You should see what I'm coping with now. Could I see the rest?"

"The bedroom's here," said the manager. Her mules flapped against her cracked heels as she led the way down the carpeted hall.

The bedroom contained a king-size bed, covered with a sateen bedspread printed in a swirling art nouveau design. Another gigantic O'Keeffe flower hung above the bed.

"Is this where . . ." asked Lucy.

The landlady nodded. "There was hardly any mess, you would have thought she was sleeping."

Lucy quickly scanned the room. She knew she shouldn't linger; it would appear unnatural. The dresser was clear except for a Japanese lacquered jewelry box and a watch. There were no clothes lying about. She opened the closet and peered in. Everything was neatly hung up. As she knew, Carol favored pink and pastel suits and dresses. Rows of high-heeled pumps were arranged on the floor, standing in pairs.

The bathroom was just as neat. The vanity sink held a large assortment of cosmetics, but they were carefully arranged in a lucite organizer. The pink towels hung on the rack, carefully folded in thirds. Even the wastebasket was empty, except for a folded sheet of paper. Instinctively, Lucy reached for it. It was the Revelation Congregation's monthly newsletter.

"I'll have to think it over," Lucy told the landlady, who was waiting impatiently by the apartment door. "The rent is quite a bit more than I'm paying now."

"Better not wait too long," she advised, locking the door behind them. "These apartments never stay vacant very long."

Heading back to her car, Lucy wondered if it had been worth the bother to see the apartment. It revealed very little about its occupant—it had looked more like a furniture store than a home. And what, she asked herself, was Carol doing with the Revelation Congregation newsletter? Was she a member? She decided to head over to the old Bijou theater and pay DeWalt a visit.

The Revelation Congregation had bought the abandoned Bijou when the membership outgrew the town hall basement. Now the marquee no longer advertised film classics, but the big black letters were used to spell out brief Bible verses. Today, Lucy noticed as she parked the car, the message was "God have mercy on me, a sinner (Luke 18:13)."

She doubted, as she pulled open the ornately carved door, that DeWalt had himself in mind when he chose the verse. He did not seem like one who considered himself a sinner. No, he was a crusader for truth attempting to save evildoers from themselves and their wicked ways.

Once in the former lobby, Lucy waited a moment for her eyes to adjust to the dimness. Hearing the hum of a vacuum cleaner, she opened the doors to the theater, finding to her surprise that it had been converted quite tastefully into a sanctuary. A large cross hung where the movie screen used to be, and the once solid walls had been pierced with windows boasting Gothic arches. It didn't look that much different from the Tinker's Cove Community Church that Lucy attended now and then.

"Can I help you?" asked the man who had been pushing the vacuum cleaner.

"I'm looking for DeWalt Smythe."

"His office is upstairs, where the balcony used to be. Just take those stairs."

Lucy thanked him and climbed the single flight, finding a neatly carpeted hallway at the top. A table with a bowl of chrysanthemums stood under a window on one side: three doorways were on the opposite wall. One was ajar, and had the word PASTOR painted on it. Lucy tapped gently.

"Come in," boomed DeWalt's voice.

Lucy pushed the door open and entered. It wasn't quite the booklined study of Dr. Howes, her minister, but looked instead like the office of a small business with a metal desk and file cabinets. A fax machine sat on a stand to one side, and a graph charting the growth of the church hung on the wall. The line climbed steadily upward, seeming to indicate that as more members joined the church, the closer they would all be to heaven.

"I'm sorry to bother you," began Lucy.

"Not at all. That's what I'm here for." He chuckled paternally and spread out his open palms. "To be bothered. To care. To help. I always try to remember the words of our Saviour Lord Jesus Christ, 'Inasmuch as ye have done it unto one of the least of these my brethren, ye have done it unto me.' That's the twentyfifth chapter of Luke, verse forty. But of course, you are not the least of anything, Mrs. Stone, and I am always happy to see you. Won't you sit down?"

He offered her a steel chair, with a rigid plastic seat. Lucy sat down.

"Well, DeWalt, I'm trying to write a tribute to Carol Crane for *The Pennysaver* and I've been running into a lot of dead ends. I was hoping you could help me."

DeWalt shifted in his seat, which was one of those expensive new types designed especially for executives. It sprouted knobs everywhere, making it infinitely adjustable to comfortably support the contours of almost any corporate body.

"What did you want to know?" he asked.

"Well, I know you were on the search committee that hired Carol. In fact," continued Lucy, making a small leap of faith, "I heard that you lobbied strongly for her with the other committee members."

"Indeed I did," said DeWalt, puffing out his chest. "Carol was an outstanding candidate. She was highly qualified and came with very positive references."

"I've discovered that her references weren't genuine," said Lucy. "In fact, it seems she planted the bomb herself, in order to get attention. It's part of a pattern—she set a fire in Bridgton, and staged accidents when she was in college."

DeWalt stared at her, open-mouthed. "I had no idea," he sputtered. "I thought she was . . ."

"A shining example of Christian womanhood," supplied Lucy. "At least that's what you called her at the memorial service."

He rolled his heavy head from side to side. "My wife warned me about her, but I didn't listen."

"Your wife?" Lucy was surprised.

"When Carol came to be interviewed—this was in July, I think—she stayed with us. It's not unusual. Rather than spend school district dollars on motels, the committee members put up the candidates.

"As I got to know her, I discovered that we shared similar views on education. Carol seemed just as interested as I am in restoring Christian family values to the schools."

"You mean you helped her get the job, because she would

become an administration voice for the Revelation Congregation?" challenged Lucy.

"There's absolutely nothing wrong with people who share the same values working together," insisted DeWalt. "There was no formal agreement or anything, no deal. I just got an impression that she would be cooperative, that's all."

"But your wife was not so sure?"

"Zephirah is more perceptive than I am," admitted DeWalt. "She says I'm always preaching, and it's probably true. She was struck by something that occurred during dinner. I was explaining the beliefs of the Revelation Congregation, and I told Carol we believe in a literal interpretation of the Bible. For example, wives should be submissive to their husbands. For some reason, Carol really took exception to that. Zephirah said I must have touched a nerve—those were exactly her words. Touched a nerve."

"Well, she was a modern working woman," said Lucy. "That's not such an odd reaction."

"No," agreed DeWalt. "I wouldn't have thought twice about it, except for what Zephirah said."

"So, once Carol was hired, did she cooperate with you?"

"She surely did. In fact, she was always running to me with reports about this one or that one. Especially Sophie. Sophie lost the room assignments. Sophie was spending too much on school supplies. Sophie was too old. I began to think she was trying to get Sophie fired."

"What did you do?"

"I confronted her and counseled patience. After all, Sophie is due to retire in a few years, and there was no reason why the job wouldn't go to Carol. I told her that I'm a minority on the committee, and even if I wanted to get rid of Sophie, I could never get the other members to go along with it. Not to mention Superintendent Eubanks."

"How did Carol react?"

DeWalt scratched his chin thoughtfully. "She seemed angry. In fact, I remember telling her that she should let go of her anger. I tried to get her to come to Sunday service."

"Did she?"

"No." He folded his hands in front of him. "If she had, it all might have ended differently. Very few people who accept the Lord Jesus Christ as their Savior get themselves murdered— at least that's been my experience."

To Lucy, this seemed a bit self-serving. "But even though you knew Carol was no angel, you practically raised her to sainthood at the memorial service. How could you do that?"

"We have to use the tools the good Lord gives us. I don't think Moses stopped to pull the Egyptian soldiers out of the Red Sea, do you?"

Lucy's eyes were round with shock. "It seems to me that Carol is worth a lot more to you dead, than she ever was alive," she blurted out.

"Are you suggesting that I killed her?" Something in DeWalt's tone turned her spine to ice.

"Oh, not at all," Lucy hastened to reassure him. This was not where she wanted the conversation to go. Next thing she knew, she'd be battling for her life in the baptismal tank.

"I feel the need to seek the Lord," said DeWalt, falling to his knees and pressing his hands together. "Will you join me in prayer?" he asked, as he bowed his huge head.

"No, but thanks for asking," said Lucy, getting to her feet and heading for the door. "I'll just leave you to your prayers."

Lucy was exiting the renovated theater when she was startled to hear her name called. Looking up, she saw Miss Tilley glaring at her.

"What were you doing in there?" the old woman demanded.

"Interviewing DeWalt," said Lucy. "For *The Pennysaver*."

"It doesn't seem to me that the paper ought to be giving him any free publicity," she said, with a little sniff.

"You need have no fears on that account," said Lucy with a smile. "I was just asking him about Carol Crane."

"You're investigating her murder, aren't you?" Miss Tilley narrowed her eyes shrewdly.

"I'm trying," said Lucy, "but I don't seem to be getting very far."

"My dear old poppa used to say that success was five percent inspiration and ninety-five percent perspiration."

"That's good advice," said Lucy. "I'll have to tell the kids that." She took the old woman's arm. "Can I give you a ride somewhere?"

"I was just headed home, from the library. I have to keep an eye on that new woman—she's a bit shaky on the Dewey decimal system." Miss Tilley had officially retired as librarian several years ago, but she still felt a certain responsibility toward the Broadbrooks Free Library.

Once Lucy had gotten her settled in the front seat, with the seatbelt fastened, she started the car. "Tell me," she began as they pulled away from the curb, "what do you think of DeWalt?"

"He's a fake. They all are, all these newfangled religions. I learned all about it by watching Norah."

"The talk show?" Lucy was surprised. "I didn't know you watch TV."

"It fills the time," said Miss Tilley, causing Lucy to look

closely at her elderly friend. Filling time had never been a problem for her before.

"Don't look at me that way!" she snapped. "I'm not getting feeble or anything. It's an interesting show, that's all. Norah is a very intelligent woman."

"She must be—she's the highest paid woman in America, after all. So tell me, what did Norah have to say about churches like the Revelation Congregation?"

"They take advantage of people who are unhappy, or stupid. They pressure the members to make large contributions. Some of them even dole out punishment to the members who aren't up to snuff. It's nothing at all like being a Unitarian, though even that isn't quite what it used to be. You never hear Emerson or Thoreau mentioned these days." She rolled her watery blue eyes in disgust.

"DeWalt seems so certain that he's doing the work of God," mused Lucy. "How can he be so sure?"

"Because he's an egomaniac," said Miss Tilley flatly as Lucy pulled up in front of her antique Cape Cod–style house.

She sat smoothing her gloves while Lucy climbed out of the car and opened the door for her. Taking her by the elbow, Lucy helped her out of the car and walked her to the door.

"I can manage perfectly well on my own," Miss Tilley informed her.

"Of course you can. I'm just trying to show you how polite I am."

"Poppa always said to judge people by their actions, not what they say. In that regard, Reverend Smythe comes up a bit short."

"Oh?" asked Lucy.

"I've heard"—Miss Tilley leaned forward and whispered in

her ear— "he has *prolonged* prayer sessions with some of the women in his congregation."

"Wouldn't surprise me a bit," said Lucy, patting the old woman's hand. "Take care now."

"I will," said Miss Tilley, opening her door and disappearing inside.

Checking her watch, Lucy saw it was later than she'd thought, and the day-care center would soon be closing. Pressing her foot to the gas, and hoping the police were too busy with Carol's murder to set any speed traps, she raced across town. As she drove, she thought about her talk with DeWalt.

Miss Tilley was right about him, she decided. The old woman had confirmed her own doubts. DeWalt had been hiding something, and Lucy suspected he was a lot closer to Carol than he admitted. Why else would he make a point of bringing his wife into the conversation?

If DeWalt had been involved with Carol, thought Lucy, he certainly got more than he'd bargained for. Had Carol made demands? Had she threatened to expose him? If she had, he would have had a motive to murder her. And from what she knew of him, he would probably have convinced himself that he was just doing God's will. There was nothing more dangerous, she decided, than an egomaniac with a direct pipeline to the Almighty.

Lucy pulled up at the day-care center and braked. Pressing her hand to her forehead and rubbing hard, she tried to push all thought of the murder from her mind. She and Zoë had been separated so much since she began working, she thought, with a sharp stab of guilt and longing. The little toddler deserved her complete attention. They were really overdue for some special mommy-daughter time.

CHAPTER TWENTY-ONE

Arriving at the office on Thursday, Lucy plucked a fresh *Pennysaver* off the pile on the counter. She winced to see Josh Cunningham's picture, prominently placed above the fold. The unkempt, hounded figure in the grainy black and white photo bore little resemblance to the cheerful, confident coach she'd chatted with only a few weeks ago.

She read the story through one more time, looking for some discrepancy, some flaw in the DA's argument that would prove his innocence. She didn't find anything and, sighing, turned the page.

She took in her breath sharply when she spotted, right there on page three, her story about the parental notification bill. "By Lucy Stone" was printed in bold black letters beneath the headline. She was sitting there, grinning like an idiot, when Ted came in.

"Hi, Lucy." He paused and studied her. "First time?"

Lucy nodded. "I can't believe that something that's this much fun is actually legal."

"I know," agreed Ted. "That's how I feel, too. If I actually made any money at this, I'd have to feel guilty. Fortunately, that's not a problem."

"There's more to life than money," said Lucy, absentmindedly stroking the paper.

"That's for sure, 'cause so far I've seen damn little money but plenty of life." He paused and said slowly. "I got a call from Phyllis last night."

"How's her mother?"

"Much better. The chemo is going very well, and Phyllis said her mother doesn't really need her. She's coming back."

"That's wonderful," said Lucy, wishing she meant it. Happy as she was for Phyllis, and her mother, she dreaded losing the job. "When will she be back?"

"Tomorrow," said Ted with a little shrug. "Lucy, you've been great. I wish I could keep you on, but I really can't afford it. I was up half the night crunching numbers."

"I knew it was only temporary," said Lucy, thinking that you have to be careful what you wish for. Only yesterday she had been wishing for more time to spend with Zoë. Now she'd have it in spades. She gave a weak little smile. "It sure was fun."

"If you want to try your hand at freelancing, I can always use features."

"I might just do that." Lucy tried to sound enthusiastic, but it was difficult. Features meant interviews with prize-winning gladiola growers, and gabby old men who collected antique matchbooks.

"That's terrific," said Ted, pulling out his chair and sitting down at his desk, spreading the paper out before him. "Damn," he muttered.

"What's the matter?"

"Typo. In an ad, no less."

"Oops," said Lucy, but instead of her usual squeak, her voice was flat.

That afternoon, her final paycheck safely deposited in the bank, Lucy and Zoë were home well ahead of the school bus. Zoë was upstairs napping, and Lucy was catching up on the reading for her course when the three older children arrived.

"How come you're home?" asked Toby, lifting the top off the cookie jar.

"Phyllis is back. Ted doesn't need me anymore." Lucy swallowed down the lump that had formed in her throat.

"Does that mean you're going to be home all the time now?" asked Elizabeth suspiciously.

"I guess so," said Lucy, sitting down at the kitchen table, ready for a companionable after-school chat. "I'm going to miss working. It was fun."

"Yeah," said Elizabeth, dropping her book bag on the floor and heading for the stairs.

"Do you want a snack?" Lucy asked Sara.

"I'm full. We had cupcakes. It was Jared's birthday. His mom made them."

"Wasn't that nice?" enthused Lucy, thinking that perhaps she could volunteer at the school now that she had more time.

"Do we have any shoe boxes?"

"Probably. Why?"

"I need to make a diorama."

"Of what?"

"Life at the North Pole. I'm going to use my plastic penguin."

"Better make it life at the South Pole, then. There aren't any penguins at the North Pole."

"There aren't?" Sara was doubtful.

"No."

"Shit," said Sara.

"What did you say?" Lucy was about to lecture her second-grade daughter on the evils of profanity when a loud crash was heard upstairs.

"Get out of my room, you dork!"

"What's going on?" Lucy charged up the stairs.

"Toby was in my room!"

"I only wanted to borrow a CD," explained Toby.

"Well, then you should ask. Shouldn't he, Mom? I mean, it's bad enough that I have absolutely no privacy and have to share my room with a baby—"

"I'm not a baby!" exclaimed Sara, who had followed her mother up the stairs.

"You all better quiet down, or you will wake up the baby," advised Lucy. "Toby, how about getting started on your homework. Sara, check the hall closet. I think there are some empty shoe boxes in there." Lucy put her arm around Elizabeth's shoulder and led her to her bed. "How are you doing?" she asked.

"What do you mean?"

"Just wondering. Things have been kind of rough lately, with the asthma and all."

"I'm okay."

"Are you taking your medicine?"

"Sure, Mom."

"How come you didn't go to field hockey practice?"

"The new coach doesn't know anything about the game."

"Don't be silly."

"It's true, Mom. She was calling corners when they should have been long shots!"

"So, she has a lot to learn. You're the one missing out if you don't go."

"Yeah, you're right. I'll go tomorrow."

"How's Lance? You haven't mentioned him lately."

"He hasn't been in school all week. Probably sick or something."

"Did you call?"

"Yeah. No answer."

"That's odd."

"God, you make such a big thing about everything. He doesn't have to answer the phone if he doesn't want to. There's no law or anything."

"That's true," said Lucy, smiling agreeably. She wasn't going to let Elizabeth irritate her. Besides, Zoë was beginning to stir.

Scooping the baby up for a hug, Lucy changed her diapers and carried her downstairs. She was busily exploring the pot cupboard, and Lucy was making the salad, when Bill came home.

"Hi! How was your day?" she asked brightly.

"Okay." He pulled a beer out of the fridge. "How about you?"

"I've had better. Ted told me he doesn't need me anymore." It wasn't any easier to say the second time.

"Just as well," said Bill. "There's plenty for you to do here at home."

"I know, but I really liked working."

"You knew it was only temporary," said Bill, belaboring the obvious.

"It's still hard to take. I thought that once Ted learned how good I am, he'd want to keep me."

"Humph," snorted Bill. "Nobody's indispensable."

When the whole family was seated at the table, Lucy made her big announcement.

"Guess what? I have a story in *The Pennysaver!* With my name and everything!"

"Cool," said Toby. "Could I have some more potatoes?"

"That's great, honey," said Bill, handing her an empty salt shaker. "Would you mind filling this?"

"If you're getting up, I'd like some more milk, please," said Toby.

"Me, too," said Sara.

"Me!" exclaimed Zoë, mimicking her.

"How about you, Elizabeth?"

"No, thanks. I don't want to be fat like Toby."

"Elizabeth!" said Bill sharply as Lucy turned and went into the kitchen.

Alone, she heard the voices of her children, squabbling at the table. She reached up into the cupboard, got the salt, and refilled the shaker. Replacing the package, she closed the cabinet door and leaned her head against it. It was ridiculous to feel so upset. After all, moms were appreciated only on Mother's Day. That's why they invented it. So they could treat you like a household appliance the rest of the year.

Lifting her head, she opened the fridge and reached for the gallon container of milk.

*   *   *

"You look a little down."

Lucy turned and faced Professor Rea. "I guess I am."

"Want to talk about it?"

"No," said Lucy.

Quentin began gathering up his lecture notes. "Well, then, let me see if I can't cheer you up." He studied her, adopting the attitude of a doctor making a diagnosis. "I have just the thing. How would you like to see my photographs of the Brownings' flat in Florence? How can you resist a peek at their private life together?"

"I can't," said Lucy, smiling slowly. After all, she told herself, she was only going to his apartment to look at some photos. There was nothing the matter with that, was there?

Quentin Rea's apartment was on Main Street, above the Carriage Trade, a rather expensive dress shop. As they climbed the stairs, carpeted with an Oriental runner, Lucy wondered what to expect. Her experience of bachelor apartments was limited— she had met Bill when they were both in college, living in dorms. After graduation they had lived together for a year or two, and then got married. She had never before visited a man alone in his apartment, she realized, thinking it was about time. She was forty years old, after all.

Smoothly unlocking the paneled door, Quentin opened it with a flourish. "My humble abode," he said, stepping aside for her to enter.

Humble was not the word Lucy would have chosen to describe

Quentin's living room. He had left a lamp burning, and Lucy stepped into a generously proportioned room with two large windows overlooking the street. It was filled with gleaming antique furniture, the floors were covered with intricately patterned Persian rugs, and low bookcases lined the walls.

Lucy studiously avoided meeting his eyes, studying instead his collection of paintings by some of the better local artists. Lucy recognized the distinctive abstract style of Liv Caldecott, and the whimsical primitives of Ric Dreyfus. Tucked away in a corner in a special little cabinet she spotted a Chinese water pipe.

"Shades of Coleridge," she exclaimed. "May I see it?"

"I'd be honored," said Quentin, gently opening the glass door. He lifted out the pipe and handed it to her, his fingers brushing hers in the process. Her hands shook as she took it, and she concentrated on trying not to tangle the chains that dangled from the mouthpiece.

"Where did you ever find this?" she asked, making a great show of admiring the cloisonné design of water lilies and the assorted brass fittings. She was beginning to think it was a mistake to come. In such an intimate setting every word seemed heavy with meaning, every gesture sensual.

"It was my grandfather's."

"Your grandfather smoked opium?" asked Lucy, finally raising her eyes to meet his.

"No," said Quentin, smiling and revealing his whiter than white teeth. "He smoked Prince Albert pipe tobacco. My aunt brought it back from India for him. She was in the Army there during the Second World War."

"It's very lovely. Is it valuable?"

"Not really. A couple of hundred dollars, maybe. It's precious to me," he said, replacing it in the cabinet. "My grandfather was very proud of it—he even made this little case for it."

"Where you close to him?"

"He taught me to love books—he started me off on Dickens and Sir Walter Scott."

"You know, they don't teach those books in school anymore. Not even *Ivanhoe*." This was a topic close to Lucy's heart, and a safe detour from the one-way road to intimacy they seemed to be following.

"Your expression just then . . ." began Quentin.

"What about it?" Lucy was suddenly self-conscious.

"You looked so, oh, I don't know. Engaged, I guess. Interested. Alive. You don't know how rare that is. I've been teaching for a long time now, and most of my students look like cows. You're different. I enjoy watching you—you react to everything."

"It's a curse," said Lucy, warming to his flattery and beginning to relax. "I can never keep a secret."

"Do you have secrets?" He tossed off the question as he squatted in front of one of the bookcases, looking for a volume.

"No," said Lucy, standing beside him and resting her hips on the top shelf. She sighed, and added, "And even if I did, I don't think anybody would bother to try to find them out."

"What do you mean?" asked Quentin, pulling a book and turning to casually settle himself beside her.

"I started out as a person," said Lucy, putting her growing sense of discontent into words. "But that all ended when I became Mom. I stopped being a person and became a role."

"You have your job at the paper. Isn't that fulfilling?" His voice was gentle, concerned.

"I was only filling in for someone. They don't need me

anymore." This time, with him, she couldn't stop the tears from flowing.

He drew her to him and she sobbed into his shoulder. He folded his arms around her and patted her back. "There, there," he murmured.

All the tension and anxiety of the last few weeks, all the fears she had resolutely pushed deep into her subconscious, came welling to the surface and overflowed. She indulged her emotions and abandoned herself to her tears. Finally, she drew a deep, shuddering breath and he pressed a fresh handkerchief into her hand. She wiped her eyes, and then looked up at him.

He bent down and kissed her. She knew she should resist, but she didn't. Feeling his tongue brush her lips, she parted them. He held her more tightly, pressing her to him and she felt herself melting against him.

At that moment, she wanted to stay in the comfort of his arms forever. She wanted to taste him and smell him, and feel his warmth deep within her. He slipped his tongue deeper into her mouth and she wrapped her fingers in his soft, springy hair. She felt his hand on her breast and she leaned into it, feeling a surge of desire run through her body.

"Oh, Lucy," he moaned, grasping her hips and pressing himself against her.

This is insane, she thought, kissing him so hard that their teeth struck. Summoning every bit of willpower she possessed, she pulled away.

"I can't," she said. "I don't think I'm doing this for the right reason. I'm just feeling particularly unappreciated today. My mother used to tell me I had an unpleasant habit of feeling sorry for myself."

"Does there have to be a reason?" he asked, lightly stroking her chin.

"There's always a reason," she said as his fingers slipped down to her neck. They remained there, gently but persistently massaging her. As much as she wanted to stay, she knew she could never go home if she did. She pressed her hands against his chest and pushed him away.

"If you're afraid that you might be taking advantage of me, don't worry," he said. "I'm perfectly willing to be abused in this manner."

"Oh, I couldn't live with myself if I did that," said Lucy, attempting to make a joke of it as she started for the door.

"You must have really loved that job," he said, causing her to break her stride.

"I really did."

"Lucy Stone, Investigative Reporter," he teased.

"You can laugh," she said. "I deserve it. I wasn't very good at the investigating part. My editor said I was too gullible."

"Is that so?" he asked, smoothing his hair. Casually, he added, "How did that piece about Carol Crane come out?"

"I didn't get very far," admitted Lucy, wondering what he was after.

"Oh, well," he said, "I guess it doesn't matter now."

"Not anymore," agreed Lucy, cautiously deciding it might not be wise to tell him she was planning on pursuing the story on her own. "I really have to go. Thanks for letting me cry on your shoulder."

"Anytime," he said, opening the door for her.

Hurrying along the dark and empty streets to her car, Lucy was suddenly overwhelmed with the enormity of what she had almost done. A shoulder to cry on, a kiss or two, and she was ready to toss her whole family away.

She thought of Zoë, who still depended on her for so much. Not quite a baby, but always ready for a cuddle. Zoë still thought the world began and ended with Mommy—how could she ever have considered putting her little one's security in jeopardy?

And Sara. Sweet, dependable, helpful Sara. Once Sara made a friend, she had a friend for life. Look how she had stuck up for Mr. Mopps. Lucy thought sadly how she had almost let little Sara down.

And then there were Elizabeth and Toby. Oh, sure, they were difficult teenagers, but that just made them more vulnerable. They were engaged in the difficult task of finding themselves and their places in the world and they needed the security of their mother's love more than ever, even if they didn't know it.

Worst of all, how could she have even considered hurting Bill like this? Maybe he wasn't the most sensitive man in the world, but he had never let her down. He had given her a house, he put food on the table, he had been there by her side when their children were born. He was reliable and steady and she could always depend on him. He would never do a thing like this to her.

The realization stung. How could she have been so selfish? Reaching the car, she jumped in and started the engine. She couldn't wait to get home. But as she sped along the deserted nighttime roads, she wasn't sure whether she was rushing to the safety of Bill's arms, or away from something she didn't want to face.

CHAPTER TWENTY-TWO

In the wee hours of the morning, Lucy woke and heard one of the children moving around. She got out of bed and met Toby in the hallway. His hair was mussed from sleep and he was pale and shaky.

"What's the matter?" she asked, feeling his forehead.

"I threw up," he said.

"Maybe you've got a touch of flu," she said, taking him back to bed. He let her tuck him in, and didn't brush her hand away when she smoothed his tousled hair.

"Can I get you some ginger ale?"

"I'm fine, Mom."

"Well, call me if you need anything. I'll hear you."

"Okay, Mom."

Lucy visited the bathroom and returned to bed. Lying beside Bill, who was snoring gently, she was unable to go back to sleep but remained alert, listening for sounds of distress from Toby's room. Sometimes she wished she could be more like Bill, who could sleep through an earthquake. Instead, she knew she would worry and fret for the rest of the night, watching the minutes pass on the digital clock.

Toby didn't get up again. After about an hour, she went to check on him and found him sleeping peacefully. She went back to bed, but doubted she would sleep. Back in the security of her home, surrounded by husband and family, her visit to Quentin's apartment seemed like madness.

If she were DeWalt Smythe, she thought, she would blame it all on the devil. She had been tempted. It would be nice to be able to shift the blame, but Lucy believed that evil and goodness came from within people themselves, not from external forces. If she had been tempted by the devil, it was a devil of her own making.

Finally, a minute before the alarm was set to go off, she reached out and switched it off. Then she padded downstairs to start the coffee.

An hour later, she woke the rest of the family, except for Toby, and got them started on their day. She planned to keep Toby home from school, but when he woke, around nine-thirty, he was quite upset with her.

"Mom, you should have woke me," he said as she fixed him a cup of tea.

"Don't be ridiculous. You were sick last night."

"I feel fine now."

"That's because I let you sleep," she said, setting his meager breakfast on the table. "Drink this and we'll see what happens."

"I don't like tea."

"How about some ginger ale?" she asked.

"I told you—I'm not sick. Could you drive me to school?"

"Not until you've taken something and kept it down," she said. "Why do you want to go to school so much? Are you afraid you'll miss a test or something?"

"I don't have any tests today."

"Well, what is it?" she demanded, exasperated. "You're behaving very oddly."

"It's nothing," he said, and went back upstairs.

Picking up Zoë, who had been industriously emptying the pot cupboard, Lucy followed him. She found him in his room, sitting on the side of his bed, holding a pile of handwritten letters and notes.

"What are those?" she asked, sitting down beside him with Zoë on her lap.

"They're letters of support for Mr. C. Eddie said his dad could deliver them."

"The kids did this?" asked Lucy, unfolding one of the notes. Written in a round script it read, "Dear Mr. Cunningham, we really, really miss you. I hope jail's not too bad and you get out soon. The substitute thinks the periodic table is in the cafeteria!"

"Yeah. Everybody thinks it's real unfair, the way they're keeping him in jail. Especially since he didn't do it."

"You really believe that, don't you?"

"Everybody does. There's a demonstration today and everything."

"A demonstration?"

"Yeah. We were all going to bring signs and parade in front of the school during lunch."

"So that's why you wanted to go to school."

Toby nodded.

"I'll make a deal with you. If you stay in bed and rest, I'll take those letters over to the jail myself."

"You will?" Toby's eyes widened in surprise.

"Yeah. I'll go after lunch, when Zoë takes her nap. You have to promise to keep an eye on her, though."

"You're the greatest, Mom."

"Well, I wouldn't do this for just anybody, but you're kind of special. You're my favorite, you know."

"I bet you say that to all the kids," said Toby with a flash of humor.

"Maybe I do," she said, putting an arm around his shoulders and giving him a hug. "You're still one terrific kid. Now, how about that ginger ale?"

"Okay," he said, settling himself under the covers and opening up a comic book.

Lucy checked in on Toby periodically, and decided that he seemed to be on the road to recovery. He napped for an hour or so around eleven, but woke up refreshed at noon and announced that he was hungry. He grimaced when she offered dry toast and chicken broth, but ate it all.

Zoë spent a busy morning rediscovering her toys, after spending so much time at the day-care center. She didn't show any signs of coming down with Toby's illness and polished off her lunch of leftover beef stew. Lucy snuggled beside her and read *Blueberries for Sal* to her and she settled down happily for her nap.

When it was time to go, Lucy gave Toby detailed instructions of what to do in case of any conceivable emergency, and set out in the Subaru. The county jail was located in Gilead, about twenty miles away, but it was a pleasant drive along windy roads over rolling hills. Lucy rolled down the window and sped along;

the wind felt good as it ruffled her hair, and she sang along with the radio.

She was about halfway there, and had just crested a little hill and was heading down the other side, when she noticed a car stopped at an intersecting road. She tapped the brakes; her little wagon was accelerating as it rolled down the hill and she didn't want to go too fast. The hill was steeper than she'd thought, however, and the car picked up speed anyway.

She checked the car at the intersection; it was a little white economy model. As she approached, it suddenly pulled out right in front of her.

Her mouth opened in an O and she stamped down on the brake. Realizing she was going to hit the white car, and seeing that the road was clear, she pulled out into the opposite lane. Just then a car appeared from around the curve ahead, coming straight toward her. She flicked on her lights and honked her horn. The white car that had been blocking her lane suddenly jerked forward and sped ahead.

Gripping the steering wheel with shaking hands, Lucy pulled back into her own lane, and proceeded slowly. The oncoming car came abreast of her and slowed to a stop; the driver glared at her angrily.

He thought I was trying to pass the white car, Lucy realized. She signaled for him to roll down the window, anxious to explain the situation, but the driver shook a finger at her and then drove off.

I can't believe it, she thought angrily. How could he think it was her fault? If she hadn't been driving carefully, and paying attention, she wouldn't have been able to avoid that white car. She would never even think of passing on a hill, with a curve ahead. What kind of driver did he think she was? And whatever possessed the driver of the white car to pull onto the road in front of her?

Lucy drove the rest of the way extra carefully, and was still fuming about the near-accident when she turned into the parking lot at the county jail. It sat solidly at the top of a hill in the county complex, just as it had years before when she'd visited Franny Small.* She didn't like it then, and she liked it even less today. Franny had been confined in the women's wing, which wasn't quite as forbidding as the men's section. As Lucy walked along the wire mesh fence that surrounded the brick building, she looked up and winced, seeing the coils of razor wire gleaming in the sunlight.

Pushing open a heavy door, she found herself in a tiny lobby. It needed to be aired out and smelled unpleasantly of cigarettes. A uniformed guard stood behind a counter topped with a thick sheet of Plexiglas. She leaned forward and spoke into the little round opening.

"I'd like to see Josh Cunningham," she said.

"Name?" asked the guard. He had white hair and a ruddy complexion, and looked as if he enjoyed spending time with the grandkids.

"Lucy Stone."

He studied a sheaf of papers attached to a clipboard. "Sorry." He shook his head sadly. "You're not on the list."

"Oh. How do I get on the list?"

"Here—you fill out this application." He slid an official-looking form through the slot, and nodded encouragingly. "If you're approved, you'll be notified in three weeks."

"Three weeks?" Lucy's face fell. "Oh, well, I guess it can't

*Tippy-Toe Murder

be helped. Can I leave these? Will you see that he gets them?"
She raised the shopping bag of letters so the guard could see
them.

"What's in there?"

"Letters from his students."

"Yeah?" The guard leaned forward and peered in the bag.
He stuck his tongue in his cheek and considered. "Listen, lady,
are you related to the prisoner?"

"Oh, no—I'm just the mother of one of his students."

"Are you sure you're not his sister? Or maybe his cousin?"

"Oh," said Lucy, catching the guard's drift. "It just so happens
that I am a cousin. Unfortunately, our families were never close
and I sometimes forget."

The guard nodded sympathetically and produced a sign-in
sheet. He then instructed her to push open the door next to his
window when the buzzer sounded. She did, and found herself in
a bare room with a table in the center. The guard met her there
and went through her purse, and the bag of letters. He then
returned the purse but kept the letters and told her to proceed
through another door, into the waiting room. There, she was
shocked to see a makeshift nursery, with cribs and toys, set up
by a window. It was an oddly human touch in such a stark setting,
but it made sense. The prisoner's wives would naturally bring
their children on visiting day. She swallowed hard, and sat down
to wait.

Before long, a door opened and she was told she could enter
the visiting room. There, she found a row of cubicles containing
plastic chairs. The sides were solid metal, painted gray, but the
front wall was scratched Plexiglas with a few parallel slits cut
into it. A Xeroxed sign was taped to it, warning that there could
be absolutely no physical contact with the prisoners.

She chose a cubicle and sat down. A few minutes later Josh Cunningham appeared on the other side of the divider. He didn't recognize her.

"Who are you?" he asked. He looked thinner than Lucy remembered, and the easy-going attitude was gone. He was tense and anxious, and narrowed his eyes suspiciously.

"I'm Lucy Stone—Toby's mother. He's in your science class, and you coached my daughter, Elizabeth."

"Oh." He sat down. "Lizzy's Mom. I remember you now. Why are you here?"

"The kids organized a letter-writing campaign. I volunteered to be the postman. The guard took the letters. I think they're checking them for knives."

A grin flitted across his face, and vanished. Deep lines had set in around his mouth.

"The kids really miss you," she said, casting about for something encouraging to say. "They can't wait for you to come back."

He snorted. "That's not very likely, I'm afraid."

"What do you mean?"

"Even if I get off, which will take some kind of miracle, after all the stuff DeWalt's been saying about me, I don't think I'll have a job. Not for long, anyway." He looked down at the little counter in front of him.

"You really love teaching, don't you?"

"It's been my life." He looked up at her and she saw that his eyes were brightening. "I know that's corny, but I love it. When you can give a kid some bit of knowledge, or some skill, you're empowering them. It's a great feeling."

"I know." She remembered teaching Toby to ride a bicycle, how exhilarated he had been when he could finally pedal all by himself. "It's scary, too. You've got to trust them, that they'll be responsible."

"You said it—the DeWalts of this world don't really trust kids to make their own decisions. That's why they want the controversial books out of the library, and they don't want me to teach anything that contradicts the Bible." He smiled. "And they actually believe that if we don't have sex education, somehow the kids won't figure it out themselves."

Lucy laughed, and Josh joined in.

"You don't have any alibi or anything?" Lucy asked.

"No. Normally I would have been in school, but thanks to Carol and DeWalt, I was suspended. I had breakfast at Jake's around seven-thirty, and then I went home. I was alone, but I can't prove it. And then they found all this phony evidence that I made the bomb. It's all kind of unbelievable to me. I really don't get it." He scratched his head. "The worst part is knowing that I'm innocent, but everybody thinks I'm guilty."

Lucy remembered the angry driver earlier that morning, and how much she had wanted to tell him that the near-accident wasn't her fault.

"I know how you feel, a little bit," she said, wishing she could squeeze his hand or pat his shoulder. "A lot of people know you're innocent—they believe in you. Really." She nodded encouragingly. "Don't give up."

"I'm not giving up—I'm just trying to be realistic. Based on my experience so far, I don't have a lot of faith in the criminal justice system."

"I don't blame you. But it's all made-up evidence Carol slapped together." Lucy paused for a moment. "Why did she choose you?"

"I guess because I'm a science teacher. I have the knowledge to make a bomb, if I wanted to." He paused and added, "Plus the fact that DeWalt was just waiting for an excuse to get rid of me."

Lucy nodded. "I'd like to help you. If there's anything I can do . . ."

"You've done a lot, just by visiting and bringing those letters. I'm going to enjoy reading them." He got up, and the guard who had been observing them opened the door for him. He stepped through, and it clanged shut behind him.

Lucy got up and went to the door. She reached for the knob, only to discover that there wasn't any. She pushed against the door, assuming it was the swinging kind, but it did not yield. She was locked in, she realized.

She knocked on the door, but nothing happened. She glanced at her watch. It was nearly two, Zoë would be waking up. She tapped her foot impatiently, and banged on the door. Nothing happened. They must have forgotten her. She banged louder, and called out. This wasn't funny. She wanted to get out of here.

"Hey!" she screamed. "Let me out!"

The door opened.

"It's about time!" she exclaimed angrily.

"Sorry. Had a little problem in cell block ten," said the grandfatherly guard. "Did you have a nice visit?"

"Yes, I did. Thank you for letting me in."

"Now, that's something I don't hear too often," said the guard, giving her a friendly grin.

"I guess it isn't," agreed Lucy, waiting for him to buzz open the final door. When it sounded, she yanked it open. She couldn't wait to get out into the open and breathe the fresh air.

                              *   *   *

When Lucy got home, she found Toby stretched out on the family room sofa. Bill was sitting in the recliner, with Zoë on his lap. They were all watching cartoons.

Lucy sat down with them, propping her feet on the coffee table.

"How's Mr. C?" asked Toby.

"He's okay," said Lucy. "He was really happy to get the letters."

"I wish you'd told me," said Bill, giving Zoë a little bounce. "I could've gone. The jail is no place for a woman like you."

Lucy thought of the cribs and toys. "I didn't mind," she said. "How come you're home so early?"

"Finished up the job."

"That's nice." Lucy felt a little stab of guilt. She wondered if he had something else lined up. If not, they would have to tighten their belts for a while. The money she had paid for the course would have come in handy.

"Any word about that Widemeyer bankruptcy?" she asked.

"I don't think I'll ever see that money," he said.

"Do you want something? I'm going to make some coffee." Lucy got up.

In the kitchen, she put the kettle on and filled a glass with ginger ale for Toby. Remembering Zoë, she put a little apple juice in a plastic cup for her. Turning to carry them into the family room, she bumped into Bill. He took the drinks out to the kids and returned.

"I thought I'd keep you company," he said.

Here it comes, she thought, sitting down at the table. He's out of work, we don't have any money, and why the hell have I been carrying on with that professor. She looked up at him, expecting the worst.

He was grinning.

"What are you so happy about?"

"I got a call this morning—you know that old farm on Bumps River Road?"

Lucy knew the farm he was talking about. It included an old house plus a barn and assorted outbuildings, all ready to tumble down in the first strong wind.

"Well, some Hollywood movie producer has bought it and wants me to restore it." Bill's eyes were bright with excitement.

"Really?" Lucy could hardly believe it.

"Really. He's going to turn the barn into a screening room."

"That's great. When do you start?"

"Yesterday, according to this guy. He wants it to be ready for next summer." The whistle on the kettle screamed and Bill turned off the stove.

"Wow," said Lucy, watching as he spooned instant coffee into two cups. "I hope you're overcharging him shamefully."

"I'm not working cheap, that's for sure." He set the cup down in front of her and sat down beside her at the table.

"I'm so relieved," confessed Lucy. "I've been having second thoughts about spending all that money on my course."

"Aw, don't worry about money," he said, covering her hand with his. "You should leave that to me."

"I was worried because I thought you were worried." Lucy looked at her coffee.

"I was worried," he admitted, "but then I figured there wasn't much I could do about it. Either there's work, or there isn't. Worrying doesn't change a thing, and it was keeping me from enjoying all the stuff I've got. Like you, and the kids."

"I know I've been kind of self-centered lately," began Lucy.

"I wasn't very understanding," admitted Bill, lifting his cup and taking a swallow. "I can see that you're ready for a change. You need more than the house and the kids. My mom went squirrelly for a few years there, when I went to college. She should have got a job or something but Dad wouldn't let her. I don't want to do that to you."

Lucy leaned her head on his shoulder. "You're a good man, Charlie Brown," she said.

"How many times do I have to tell you?" asked Bill, gently stroking her cheek. "The name's Bill. Bill, not Charlie."

"Okay, you're a good man, Bill Stone."

"That's better," he said, bending down to kiss her.

CHAPTER TWENTY-THREE

Monday morning found Lucy bouncing along in the school bus, wondering what dark masochistic tendency had prompted her to agree to chaperone the eighth-grade field trip to the state university library. Now that she wasn't working, she had plenty of time to serve as a parent volunteer, just as she used to when Elizabeth was in grade school. But this time she didn't think Elizabeth was thrilled about having her mother along. Not that it mattered. Lucy had a motive of her own for coming along—she planned to do some research of her own on Carol Crane's college career.

"Thanks so much for helping out today," said Mrs. Crowley, the middle school librarian, falling into the seat beside her as the bus turned a corner. "I can't tell you how much I dread this trip."

"Why is that?"

"It's too long—it's nearly a two-hour drive. The kids are cuckoo by the time we get there."

"Why do they keep doing it—they go on this trip every year, don't they?"

"That's exactly right—it's a tradition." Mrs. Crowley rolled her bright blue eyes, which peered at the world over her half-glasses. She wasn't the sort of woman who bothered much about her appearance. Today she was wearing her usual denim skirt and print blouse, with a cotton sweater thrown over her shoulders. She had put lipstick on her top lip but, distracted, had forgotten the bottom. "It was started back in the forties or fifties by Miss Tilley. Do you know who she is?"

"Of course. Miss Tilley was one of the first people I met when we first moved to Tinker's Cove. I went to the library, looking for books on remodeling, and she got me hooked on mysteries. But Miss Tilley was never part of the school system," said Lucy.

"True. But she has a lot of influence and it was her belief that all Tinker's Cove students should be exposed to a real reference library. So, every year, the entire eighth grade makes this trip to do research for their term papers. At least, that's what they're supposed to do—mostly they sneak off and visit friends or older siblings at the college, or hang out at the student union."

"Why don't they just go to the Winchester College library? It's a lot closer."

"Winchester has a good library, for a small liberal arts college, but it's simply not in the same league as the state university," said Mrs. Crowley. "But if there ever was a year to postpone the trip, this was it."

"You got off to a rough start," said Lucy.

"You can say that again," agreed Mrs. Crowley. "It's taking longer than usual for the kids to settle down and get focused."

Lucy nodded thoughtfully. "What did you think of Carol Crane?"

"I didn't have too much contact with her."

"How did Josh get involved with her? Was she over at the high school a lot?"

"Not that I know of. The only time I saw her there was the day the superintendent brought her around and introduced her." Mrs. Crowley leaned closer to Lucy. "That was odd, if you ask me. Josh's class was in the library, doing research. He didn't pay much attention to her, he was busy helping a student and just gave her a little nod, but I definitely got the impression that she knew him. She didn't say anything, though, so maybe I was wrong."

"That's funny, isn't it? I mean, usually if you recognize someone, you reintroduce yourself, don't you?"

"Well, I do," said Mrs. Crowley with a little snort. "But Carol seemed to play the game by her own rules." She paused, and gave Lucy a little smile. "It made me curious, so I did a little research. I discovered they grew up in the same town—Quivet Neck."

"How did you find that out?"

"Oh, simple. It was in the town report."

Lucy felt a bit chagrined. Why hadn't she thought of that? "Did you find anything else out?" she asked.

"Not much. She was making forty-two thousand a year, you know."

"That's what I heard," said Lucy, trying to cross her legs, but finding the space between the seats too narrow. "Can't they make these buses more comfortable?" she asked as the driver made another turn and she was thrown against Mrs. Crowley. "Sorry," she apologized as she regained her balance.

"Only ninety more minutes," said Mrs. Crowley, ducking as a notebook whizzed past her ear. "Okay, guys!" she yelled, jumping to her feet and facing the students. "Settle down. We'll all be a lot more comfortable if everyone is considerate. I don't want to issue any detentions, so don't make me. Okay?"

This was apparently an effective threat—the kids quieted down. Lucy looked for Elizabeth, and found her sitting with two girlfriends, Melissa Burke and Emily Anderson. Lance was several rows away, sitting with Noah Lenk. Lucy was surprised—even a newcomer couldn't help but be aware that the Lenks were a disreputable clan known for their run-down houses, fierce dogs, and family squabbles that often erupted into violence, landing the participants in jail.

"What do you know about Lance?" Lucy asked Mrs. Crowley.

"Not much. He's a good student—well behaved. I don't have any complaints about him."

"He and Elizabeth seemed to be something of an item when school opened, but now things seem to have cooled."

"That's typical—these kids switch partners so fast that I never know who's going with whom."

"It's just as well," said Lucy. "They don't have time to get into trouble."

"Well, I didn't say that," said Mrs. Crowley, pulling a book catalog out of her bag.

Lucy turned and looked out the window. The leaves were still green, autumn was still a few weeks away, but they had a worn and tired look. Asters were blooming along the road, and spikes of goldenrod added a bit of color. The route to the college was taking them inland, away from the coast, and they passed farms and long stretches of woods.

She massaged her temples, trying to ease the headache that

was developing. She didn't think it was simply the result of the noisy kids and the rattling old bus—this was a stress headache and she deserved it. Why had she let herself go so far with Quentin, she asked herself, feeling her cheeks warm as she remembered her visit to his apartment.

Her mind might know what she did was wrong, but her body didn't agree. Feeling the first stirrings of arousal, she shifted in her seat. This was ridiculous—she wasn't a teenager at the mercy of her hormones.

It was more than simple sexual attraction, she told herself. She had been feeling sorry for herself over losing her job. Bill hadn't been very supportive; he had resented her new independence. Even the kids had been especially difficult. Toby was in the throes of adolescence, his voice was changing and he was shaving a couple of times a week, and on top of all that he was upset about Josh Cunningham. And Elizabeth was a worry, especially now that she had been diagnosed with asthma.

Lucy turned again to check on her, and was relieved to find her laughing with her friends. She seemed to be doing fine, but Lucy wasn't convinced she would continue to take her medicine now that her symptoms had disappeared.

"You have to control asthma, or it will control you," the doctor had warned them, but Lucy doubted that Elizabeth believed it. Well, she'd just have to learn for herself, decided Lucy, thinking wistfully of the days when she had controlled every aspect of her children's lives. At least she had Sara and Zoë, who still thought Mom had all the answers.

Was that it, she asked herself. Was she already suffering from some sort of empty nest syndrome? Is that why she had turned to Quentin?

She could come up with any number of reasons why she was

attracted to Quentin, but if she was honest with herself, it was a bit more difficult to understand what he saw in her. She wasn't young anymore and she was preoccupied with her family. Why had he picked her when he could have his pick of hundreds of beautiful young coeds?

He had told her she looked alive and interested, she recalled, smiling at the memory. That's how she liked to think of herself, and she had appreciated the compliment. But come to think of it, how alive and interested did she really look after an hour or so of evening school? It was a line, she realized, embarrassed at her stupidity. He probably told that to all the older students he succeeded in luring to his apartment. A way to flatter them, overcome their resistance, and reel 'em in. How could she have been so gullible?

Arriving in front of the library, the bus braked and came to a stop. Absorbed in her thoughts, Lucy hadn't noticed, and was thrown forward. Mrs. Crowley jumped to her feet.

"Stay in your seats for a moment—I have a few instructions." She glanced at her watch. "It's almost ten o'clock. That gives us a little more than two hours for research. That's not much time so I advise you not to waste it." She gave the students a meaningful glance.

"I want you all back here at this exact spot no later than twelve-thirty. That is when we must leave if we are going to be back at the school in time for the buses home. Got that?" She leveled her gaze, moving from face to face.

"Remember—this is a library—I expect you to behave like ladies and gentlemen." This time she positively glared at them, attempting to etch her instructions on their brains. "All right, we will file off the bus single file and gather on the sidewalk."

Mrs. Crowley turned and stepped off the bus. The aisle

immediately filled with pushing and shoving adolescents who blocked Lucy's exit. She was the last one off and saw that, while most of the students were following Mrs. Crowley, a few renegades were already heading out in different directions. Elizabeth, she saw with some relief, was sticking with the main group, and she followed them into the library.

They were welcomed there by the university librarian, Mr. Plunkett, a rather short, chubby gentlemen with very thick eyeglasses. He explained the function of a reference library in rather more detail than Lucy wanted to know, so she studied the elaborate ceiling murals which depicted various myths, including the rape of Leda by the swan. When the students scattered to pursue their own research, she asked if the library contained copies of the college newspaper.

Mr. Plunkett assured her it did, and gave her directions to the periodicals desk, where she requested issues from the years when Carol Crane was an undergraduate. Knowing her interest for self-promotion, Lucy thought it highly unlikely she had slipped through the university unnoticed.

Lucy was given several boxes containing rolls of microfilm and took them to a reading machine, where she followed the instructions and threaded the film through the mechanism. She was then able to flip through the old issues quite rapidly.

All colleges are the same, she thought, scanning accounts of football triumphs, protests about the food service and lack of parking, and administrative disciplinary actions against unruly fraternities. Campus feminists were also making their views known, and demanding equal opportunities for female students.

There was no mention of Carol Crane, but Lucy thought she might have seen her in a photograph of a "Take Back the Night" march. When she spotted an article detailing a sexual harassment complaint against an instructor, Lucy read closely, sensing an issue tailor-made for Carol.

Sure enough, she was one of four students who had filed a complaint alleging the instructor had behaved in a "sexist manner" in class by presenting "offensive material" and making "inappropriate jokes." Reading the instructor's name, Lucy gave a little gasp. It was none other than Quentin Rea.

Reading the complaints, Lucy didn't know whether to laugh or cry. The students were reluctant to provide specifics at first, insisting it would be humiliating, but gradually revealed that they objected to the content of an Elizabethan literature course.

"It was terribly embarrassing," said one student.

"I couldn't believe the four-letter words," said another.

"I dreaded going to class," stated a wide-eyed Carol Crane. "It was very stressful."

At first, Quentin brushed off the complaints, suggesting the students drop Elizabethan literature in favor of something more refined, like Victorian poetry. "The Elizabethans had a very different lifestyle from ours. They emptied their chamber pots out the window, into the street. They nursed their babies, or hired a wetnurse. They lived very public lives in large extended families; everyone in the household shared the same bed," said Rea. "All this is reflected in their literature."

His argument made sense to Lucy, but the issue escalated when Carol Crane accused Rea of attempting to seduce her. The case went to a faculty jury, and although Rea was acquitted, his contract was not renewed for the following year.

Suddenly, the letters seemed to jump out at her. This is it, thought Lucy excitedly. This was the connection she'd been looking for. She knew there had to be something more than Quentin was willing to admit between him and Carol. Lucy had suspected an affair, but this, she realized, was worse. Sexual harassment had become a modern witch hunt on some campuses. Hadn't she read recently about a Nobel laureate who had been suspended from his professorship for using language some of his students found offensive?

Carol was looking more and more like the little boy who cried wolf, thought Lucy. Whenever things got a little dull, she got somebody in trouble. It didn't matter who got hurt, as long as she gained some sort of advantage.

It was no wonder she was murdered, thought Lucy. The wonder was that it hadn't happened sooner.

Checking her watch, Lucy realized she would have to hurry if she wanted to get something to eat before the bus left. She reluctantly returned the boxes of film to the reference librarian, wishing she had time for more research, and hurried across the campus to the student union.

Entering the crowded snack bar, she kept an eye peeled for Elizabeth, but didn't see her. Come to think of it, she hadn't seen her in the library either. She did see Elizabeth's buddies, Emily and Melissa, and made her way over to them.

"Do you know where Elizabeth is?" she shouted over the lunchtime din.

They exchanged a conspiratorial glance and shook their heads.

"I'm worried that she'll miss the bus," persisted Lucy.

"Oh, she'll be back in time," volunteered Melissa.

"So you know where she went?" accused Lucy.

"Not really—but she's real responsible," added Emily.

"Was she alone?" Lucy was beginning to feel like Elliot Ness. The girls exchanged another look.

"Listen, this is no joke," advised Lucy. "I'm worried about her."

"She went with Lance and some professor guy. He came into the reference room all excited and said he was a friend of Miss Tilley's . . ." began Melissa.

"And how great it is that we come to the university every year . . ." added Emily.

"And how he had this plant that blooms only once every hundred years and that anybody who wanted to see it should go with him," concluded Melissa.

"A century plant?" asked Lucy.

"That's it!"

"And where is this century plant? In a greenhouse or something?"

"I didn't listen to that part," confessed Emily.

"Me either," added Melissa. "But Lance was real interested and convinced Elizabeth they should go."

Great, thought Lucy, turning and marching across the lobby to study the campus map. Elizabeth discovers she's allergic to practically every plant on earth and promptly becomes an amateur botanist. Studying the confused jumble of buildings that constituted the campus, Lucy wished she were back at little Winchester College, where she knew her way around. The state university was much bigger and all the buildings looked similar, constructed of brick in the same utilitarian style.

Lucy finally found the Arbuthnot Conservatory—a conservatory for plants, she fervently hoped, and not music. It was tucked behind the admissions office and next to the gym so it shouldn't be too hard to find. It was already a quarter to twelve, and if she couldn't find them by ten past or so, she would have to head back to the bus herself. What then? She brushed the thought from her mind; she'd simply have to cross that bridge when and if.

A sign obligingly placed opposite the student union pointed the way to both the gym and the admissions office. Lucy hurried off at a brisk pace. She hoped Elizabeth had remembered her inhaler—they could be growing any variety of plants in the conservatory and she was bound to be allergic to some of them.

She had been doing much better, Lucy reminded herself, and hadn't had any more attacks since seeing the allergist. That probably meant she was taking her medicine, but Elizabeth bristled so much whenever Lucy brought the subject up that she couldn't be sure.

The conservatory was farther than she'd thought. Lucy checked her watch and saw it was already nearly twelve. A steady stream of students was pouring from the buildings, and Lucy was headed against the flow of traffic. She began studying the faces of the oncoming students, hoping to spot Lance and Elizabeth.

Finally she stopped a young fellow in a plaid shirt and asked for directions.

"Sorry," he said with an apologetic smile. "I'm a poli sci major."

"Just behind that brick building," said his companion. "You can't miss it."

Great directions, fumed Lucy, considering all the buildings were brick. She headed in what she hoped was the direction of the girl's wave. This was ridiculous, she realized. Even if she found the right building, how would she ever find Lance and Elizabeth? How could her daughter be so irresponsible? She'd like to wring their necks. And if anything had happened to Elizabeth, that Lance would get a piece of her mind.

"Mom—what are you doing? You're going in the wrong direction!" Lucy looked up from the asphalt path, straight into Elizabeth's puzzled face.

"Are you okay?" she demanded.

"Sure, Mom. But we've got to get back or we'll miss the bus."

"I know that. Why do you think I was looking for you?"

"Calm down, Mrs. Stone. Everything's under control," volunteered Lance.

"Don't you tell me to calm down!" Lucy exploded angrily. "What were you doing taking Elizabeth to a greenhouse? Don't you know she's allergic to plants?"

"Mrs. Stone, there are plants everywhere." Lance's tone was extremely reasonable. "This place is covered with trees."

"Well, that's different," insisted Lucy, who was in no mood to be rational. "You gave me a terrible fright. Are you sure you're okay?"

"I'm sure," sighed Elizabeth. "But I'm not so sure about you. You look awfully pale. Have you eaten?"

"No—I was looking for you."

"Don't you think you're overreacting?" asked Elizabeth, reaching into her backpack and producing a packet of cheese and peanut butter crackers. "Here. Eat these. You'll feel better."

How did this happen, wondered Lucy, as she meekly followed Lance and Elizabeth back to the bus. She was supposed to be the mother; she was supposed to be in charge. She had every right to be angry with Elizabeth. But somehow Elizabeth had managed to turn the tables on her. Suddenly she was the rational caretaker, and Lucy was the one who needed to be taken care of.

She opened the packet of crackers and ate one as she walked along, a step or two behind the kids. They made a cute couple, she had to admit it. Lance was taller than Elizabeth and tilted his head attentively toward her. They seemed comfortable with each other and were obviously having a good time. Probably laughing at her expense, she thought with a flash of paranoia, then shrugged the idea away. When she was a teenager, her mother was the last person she thought about.

Back on the bus, Lucy wondered if Elizabeth was right. Was she overreacting? Why was she making such a big deal out of things? So she'd lost her job—so what? It happened to people all the time. She would pick up and go on. And so she'd nearly slipped into an affair—these things happened. She should be grateful that they had stopped in time. After all, if she had gone ahead and Bill had found out, it would have been a disaster. For her, and for the kids. She shuddered.

Something had held her back, she realized, and it wasn't her own sense of virtue. She had been ripe for an affair, but somehow she had never quite trusted Quentin. She found him attractive, all right, but she never felt as if their relationship was developing naturally, at a normal pace. Quentin always seemed to be pushing things, trying to manipulate her. Sometimes, it was almost as if a third person kept coming between them—Carol Crane.

Why, just the night before he had taken her in his arms and kissed her, and then instead of murmuring sweet nothings into her ear, he had asked her about Carol! He hadn't really been interested in her at all, she realized, he just wanted to know how her investigation was going. Well, now she knew what he had been trying to hide, she thought, nodding grimly to herself. Carol had already forced him out of one job; he must have been terrified of her. Was she blackmailing him, wondered Lucy. Had she threatened to tell Winchester College authorities about the sexual harassment incident?

Lucy suddenly felt cold despite the warm weather and wrapped her arms across her chest and rubbed her arms. The one person who had an overwhelming reason to kill Carol Crane, she realized, was Quentin Rea.

CHAPTER TWENTY-FOUR

When Lucy picked up Zoë from the day-care center, after returning from the state university, Sue had bad news for her.

"I think she's coming down with something. Has anybody in the family been sick?" she asked, wrinkling her forehead in concern.

"Toby had the flu last week."

"Well, I wouldn't be surprised if Zoë's the next victim. Poor baby."

Zoë was indeed a poor baby, up most of the night with an upset stomach. Lucy changed the bedding in the crib twice, tossing the soiled linens into the washing machine in the wee hours of the morning. Sleep was impossible; all Zoë wanted was to be held and rocked. She finally went to sleep around five-thirty, giving Lucy a scant hour of sleep before she had to get the family up at a quarter to seven.

When Bill left for work, and the older kids left for school, she fell exhausted into bed. She slept until eleven when Zoë's cries woke her.

"How's my girl?" she asked, lifting Zoë out of her crib. Her hair was damp with fever, but she was no longer fretful. Lucy changed a very messy diaper and carried her downstairs. Clear fluids were definitely the order of the day. Fortunately, she still had plenty of ginger ale and chicken broth from Toby's bout the previous week.

Lucy's energy level was low, so she was content to lie on the couch with Zoë on top of her stomach and watch cartoons. Occasionally she would flip the channels to something a bit more interesting, like a soap opera or a talk show, but Zoë had no interest whatsoever in Erica Kane's problems, and she absolutely refused to watch a rerun of Norah's talk show. Norah might be a household name with millions, but Zoë much preferred Casper.

Giving up, Lucy flipped back to the cartoon station. Picking up the *TV Guide*, she discovered Mr. Magoo was next. Things could be worse, she thought, stuffing a pillow behind her head. She stroked Zoë's silky hair and nuzzled the top of her head with her chin. The medication she had given her seemed to be working; the fever had definitely come down.

When the kids came home from school, Lucy handed the baby off to Toby and took a long, hot shower. Alone in the bedroom, she took her time dressing and spritzed on some cologne. After nursing four children through assorted childhood ailments, she had learned that she could take better care of them if she took a little extra care of herself.

She picked up her watch to strap it on, and realized it had stopped. She would have to get a new battery. She opened up her jewelry box and took out her good watch, a delicate gold and diamond affair her mother had given her for Christmas. It was similar to the one Carol Crane wore.

She checked the gold watch to see that it was still running, and was surprised to see that the time was off. It was an hour behind. She gave it a little shake and adjusted the hands, then went downstairs to see how Zoë was doing.

The little toddler was just fine, apparently feeling more like herself. By the time they sat down to dinner, she had also regained her appetite and demanded something solid to eat. Lucy gave her some toast fingers and she polished them off, getting quite a bit of grape jelly on her face in the process. When it was time for Lucy to leave for class, she was apparently fully recovered and enjoying a game of patty-cake with her father.

Lucy started the Subaru and checked her watch; it was running fine. She hadn't worn it in quite a while, not since New Year's Eve, she realized. Now they were on daylight saving time, but she hadn't had any occasion to reset the watch until today. It wasn't slow; it had just been running on standard time.

Driving to the college, her thoughts turned to Quentin. She hoped he wouldn't be angry with her for bailing out the other night. While she was hardly experienced in affairs of the heart, especially illicit ones, she did know that thwarted lovers usually harbor a certain resentment toward uncooperative partners—at least they did when she was in high school. Then she had spurned the affections of a football player and he had refused to speak to her for most of senior year.

Pulling up at a stop sign, Lucy hoped Quentin would not have a similar reaction. If he was angry with her, he could make things very awkward for her. He could embarrass her in class, he could give her low grades, he could even fail her. The thought made her stomach whirl—she had invested too much money and effort to risk failing. Especially since her newspaper career was going nowhere, and she was thinking even more seriously of getting her teaching credentials. If she failed this course, she might as well give up the idea of getting certified.

As she parked the car in the student lot, Lucy wished she'd worked a little harder on that Carlyle paper. If it had been a really solid piece of work, she could appeal a low grade, but she knew she had slapped it together at the last minute.

Lucy mounted the stairs slowly, and walking down the corridor to the classroom, she almost turned around and went home. Why bother, she asked herself. Why expose herself to Quentin's scorn? She had a perfectly good husband who really didn't want her to work. There was more than enough at home to keep her occupied—the last few days had shown her that—and Zoë deserved a full-time mother. She had been there for Toby and Elizabeth and Sara, and Zoë should have the same attention.

Reaching the classroom doorway, Lucy swallowed hard. This was silly. If she was going to give up, she had to have a reason. It was stupid to surrender before the battle had even begun. She squared her shoulders and marched into the room, eyes straight ahead, to her usual seat.

She sat down without even glancing at Quentin, and began rummaging in her bag for a pen and notebook. Not until she had arranged everything to her satisfaction did she risk taking a quick look his way. To her surprise, he gave her a big smile.

Reflexively, she smiled back, but she was puzzled. This was not what she had expected.

"The Victorians invented the houseplant—true or false?" he asked the class, opening the discussion.

"I never thought about it before, but I think it's probably

true," said Mr. Irving. "Every Victorian parlor had an aspidistra, I know my Aunt Edith was tremendously proud of hers."

"You're right," said the professor, once again beaming a big smile toward Lucy. "They collected plants from all over the world and built greenhouses and conservatories to house them. Why?"

Lucy didn't have the faintest idea and she was too distracted to give the question much thought. In fact, after Elizabeth's excursion to see the century plant last week, Lucy didn't want to think about vegetative themes in Victorian literature at all. More interesting to her was the professor's unexpected friendliness. Puzzled, she furrowed the forehead she had carefully applied alpha-hydroxy lotion to just an hour before, and chewed her pen.

"You're looking very thoughtful, Mrs. Stone," said Quentin. "Any ideas?"

Lucy started. "Not really—I guess their houses must have been, uh, heated enough that the plants wouldn't die," she said, hoping she didn't sound too stupid.

"Very true . . ." he said, smiling broadly and nodding encouragingly to her. "Thanks to technology, such as the replacement of open fireplaces with more efficient stoves, houses were warmer than they had ever been."

What's going on here, she wondered. Instead of being angry with her, Quentin seemed to be going out of his way to be friendly. This wasn't what she had expected. When she was in college, it was assumed that a girl who got more than she'd bargained for had simply given the wrong signals. And even at Country Cousins, the women who had worked there for a while warned new employees never to go to the storeroom alone. George, the night-shift supervisor, was always leaning over their shoulders to adjust their computer screens, and often his hands would stray from the brightness knob.

The women at Country Cousins never made an issue of George's behavior—they needed the jobs. But things had changed, Lucy realized, especially on college campuses. The student newspaper accounts of the accusations against Quentin were proof of that.

Of course, thought Lucy. No wonder he was being so nice. He was probably terrified that she would complain to the dean. After all, even though he had been acquitted, he had lost his job, and it had taken him a long time to climb back onto the tenure track. A second accusation would mean the end of his teaching career. She remembered her suspicions on the bus yesterday, when she had realized the danger Carol Crane posed to him. Carol's presence in Tinker's Cove had threatened him and Carol had died.

The pen slipped from Lucy's fingers, and she stooped to retrieve it. Lifting her head, her eyes met Quentin's. He paused midsentence, losing his train of thought, but quickly recovered. He was terrified, she realized. He was terrified of her, and that was why he was being so nice.

The class was over and the students were filing past the professor's desk, picking up their Carlyle papers. From their disappointed expressions, it looked as if few had gotten the grade they were hoping for.

Lucy got to her feet, picked up her bag, and walked woodenly to the front of the room. If he can smile, she told herself, I can smile.

"Is everything all right?" he asked, his voice tight. "You look a little pale."

"Something's going around," she said. Her face felt as if it would crack, she was smiling so hard. Her heart was racing, and her hand trembled as she reached for her paper.

"You're shaking," he said, his lips twisting into a crooked smile. "I hope you're not worried about your grade. I understand how difficult it is for you, with all your other obligations."

"Thank you," she whispered, not quite knowing what he meant. Was he being sarcastic? Was he telling her it was all right with him, that there were no hard feelings?

She walked out of the room and down the hall, flipping through the paper. Finally she got to the last page. A big "A" was scrawled in red ink. She was so surprised that she stopped in her tracks.

"How'd you do?" came a friendly voice from behind. She recognized a fellow student, a man she had seen working on the fish pier.

"Much better than I expected," she said. "I got an A."

"I'd faint if I got an A," he joked. "Listen, you don't look so good. Do you want me to walk you to your car?"

"Thanks," said Lucy, grateful for his companionship. "It's a pretty interesting class . . ." she began, intending to keep up a steady stream of chatter. She didn't want to think about Quentin anymore, and she certainly didn't want to think about how afraid she suddenly felt. She just wanted to go home.

CHAPTER TWENTY-FIVE

The next morning, Lucy attempted to catch up on the house-work she had neglected while she was working at the newspa-per. Zoë followed along behind her as she cleaned, pretending her popcorn popper push-toy was a vacuum cleaner. The flu had taken a toll, however; the little toddler soon ran out of energy, and Lucy put her down for an unusual morning nap.

While Zoë slept, Lucy spread the notes and papers she had accumulated about Carol Crane out on the kitchen table. As she went through her notes, carefully checking and cross-checking her sources, a picture began to emerge.

Lucy imagined Carol as a bright, pretty little girl who had grown up poor in rural Maine. Lucy had driven through impover-ished towns like Quivet Neck, where people lived in dilapidated mobile homes and decaying farmhouses. Miles from anywhere, without even an IGA, their diet consisted of overpriced white bread and canned goods from the general store. The winter was long and cold, and the motherless Carol would have been stuck at home, alone with her father.

It was certainly a less than ideal situation for a teenage girl, thought Lucy. Nowadays there was a growing awareness of incest and sexual abuse, but that wasn't the case when Carol was left alone in the care of her father.

Recalling that Quentin had told her what Carol's father did, Lucy rummaged through her notes. Flipping through the pages, she finally found it. He was a school janitor.

Lucy smacked her head. No wonder Carol had hated Mr. Mopps. She had even called him Pops, remembered Lucy, and had accused him of spending too much time in the girls' room. What had Lucy heard her say? *I know all about you.* That was it. Mr. Mopps had the misfortune of reminding Carol of her father, so he had to go.

For the first time since she'd started investigating Carol's past, Lucy found herself feeling sorry for her. Carol had always seemed to be the manipulator, tricking and maneuvering others, but now Lucy suspected she was driven by powerful emotions and memories she couldn't control.

Working at the country club, Carol must have learned of a different way of life. Lucy could picture her sitting in her lifeguard's chair, carefully observing everything that went on. She heard how upper-class people talked; she saw how the girls dressed and did their hair. She might even have copied them, but there was little point. There wasn't anybody to impress in Quivet Neck and the locals would just make fun of her for putting on airs. The best she could hope for was to marry young and get out of her father's house and into a place of her own. Her husband might scratch out a living lobstering, or repairing cars. She could work for the summer people, but there wasn't much employment for women in the winter.

Then, when she saved that little boy, a brief window of opportunity opened for her. She was recognized as a hero, probably lavished with attention for the first time in her life. It must have been a heady experience, and one that made an indelible impression on her. She accepted the grateful parents' offer of a college education, and never looked back.

Lucy thought of Carol's apartment—the light-colored fabrics, the blatantly feminine Georgia O'Keeffe flowers, the immaculate kitchen and bathroom. Nothing could be farther from the grubby, crowded, makeshift houses inhabited by poor folks in rural Maine. It was Carol's way of reminding herself how far she had come, and Lucy was convinced that Carol would have done anything to avoid going back to Quivet Neck.

Hungry for respectability, she must have loved working as an assistant principal. She had discovered that it didn't matter that she lacked the credentials as long as she could convincingly play the part. Besides, once she had staged one of her heroic stunts, nobody was likely to ask any questions.

Being in a role of authority must have been the icing on the cake. Lucy bet Carol had derived a great deal of satisfaction from making others suffer, as she had suffered as a child. Poor Mr. Mopps had gotten the treatment Carol would have liked to deliver to her own father.

Was her father still alive, Lucy wondered. If he was, Carol had successfully broken all ties with him. He hadn't claimed her body or arranged for a funeral; he hadn't even collected her furniture and belongings.

Hearing Zoë stirring, Lucy brought her downstairs. They had a quick lunch, and then Lucy planned to go into town to do some errands. But first, there was something she wanted to check out.

Lucy dropped Zoë at the day-care center, where she was enthusiastically greeted by Sue. "It's nice to see you're feeling better, Miss Zoë," she exclaimed, taking the toddler's hand and leading her to the Play-Doh table. "Let's make some cookies for the dolls to eat."

With Zoë happily occupied, Lucy headed straight for Carol Crane's apartment complex. She was just climbing out of her car when she noticed DeWalt Smythe hurrying toward his own car. There was something slightly furtive about his movements and Lucy wondered if he was coming from one of the prolonged prayer sessions Miss Tilley had told her about.

"Hi!" yelled Lucy, giving him a big wave.

DeWalt stopped suddenly, and something fell from his pocket. Recognizing Lucy, he waved back.

"Visiting a parishioner?" asked Lucy, walking toward him.

"Ah, yes. It's one of the most rewarding parts of my work," he said, opening the door to his big black sedan. "I wish I had time to chat, but I'm late for a Bible Circle meeting."

"Wait a second," said Lucy, bending down to retrieve a white envelope. "You dropped this."

In his haste to snatch the envelope, DeWalt clumsily dropped it once again. This time the contents, which appeared to be photographs, were caught by the wind and scattered.

DeWalt raced around, frantically trying to gather them before they were carried away. Lucy watched him for a moment until she realized the wind was getting the better of him and she joined in to help, chasing down the photos that skittered just beyond her reach.

As she waited for him to return to the car, Lucy began straightening the handful of photos she had managed to catch. Glimpsing the top one, she gasped. It was a naked man.

Looking more closely, she realized it was a picture of DeWalt. He was smiling coyly, stretched out on Carol's bed beneath her Georgia O'Keeffe flowers.

Lucy tried to pretend she hadn't seen the photo, even though she was pretty sure DeWalt had observed her reaction.

"Here you go," she said, handing them to him face down.

"It's not what you think," said DeWalt, whose face was very red. Lucy wasn't sure if it was from embarrassment or the exertion of catching the windblown photos.

"It's none of my business," said Lucy, backing away.

"She tricked me," insisted DeWalt, pulling himself up to his full height and adopting his ministerial voice. "Like Delilah tricked Samson."

This was too much for Lucy. "I suppose she promised you a modeling contract," she snapped.

"Let me explain," he begged, reaching for her arm. "Please. I don't want you to think I killed her."

"I don't think anything," said Lucy, putting up her hands in denial. "I have to go."

"Lord knows I sinned," he said, abjectly bowing his massive head. "I've been carrying this around for so long—I have to tell someone."

"I don't think I'm the one . . ." objected Lucy, but DeWalt ignored her. She began to understand how enormous his ego really was and his need for instant gratification.

"Lord knows I never intended to sin, but one thing led to

another and we became intimate. Next thing I knew, she was snapping photos. I didn't mind—I was flattered. I thought she wanted to have something to remember me by, but that wasn't it at all. A couple of weeks later she told me she would show them to the congregation's executive committee unless I . . ." He sputtered and stalled; the urge to confess seemed to be weakening. "Well, unless I did what she told me to do."

"What was that?" asked Lucy.

He heaved a big sigh, and forced the words out in a rush.

"She wanted me to plant a bomb in the school."

"You did it?" Lucy was stunned.

"I had to," explained DeWalt, matter-of-factly. "I would have been ruined if these pictures got out. Think of Zephirah."

"But what about the children?" she asked, outraged. "You decided your reputation was worth the lives of innocent children! Didn't you even think about them?"

"Of course I did. I begged and pleaded with her not to do it, but she was determined. Said it would give her the leverage she needed, since I wouldn't fire Sophie like she wanted me to. She told me it was a very small explosive, and it wouldn't do much damage, and she promised nobody would be hurt. She told me exactly what to do, how to hook it into the wiring. Black to black, red to red and all that."

"Did she make the bomb herself?" asked Lucy.

"I don't think so," said DeWalt, nervously fingering the packet of photos. "It was all written out for me, but it wasn't her handwriting. She told me to make sure to destroy the paper and I did."

"When did you do this?" Lucy could hardly bring herself to believe it.

"The night before the first day of school. I had to do it after eleven-thirty, because that was the time it was set for and she didn't want it to go off until the next morning." He quickly licked his lips. "I had keys and the school was deserted. I didn't have any problems and nobody saw me."

"How could you do such a thing? You call yourself a pastor, a minister!" Lucy curled her lips in disgust. "And if all that wasn't bad enough, then you went and started accusing Josh Cunningham!"

"I never accused him of the bombing," said DeWalt, who had carefully measured and delineated the precise limits of his guilt. "I knew I hadn't killed her and it looked like the police had a good case against him. It seemed that the best way to keep the police from discovering my involvement was to keep them focused on him."

Lucy had an idea. "Let me see the pictures," she demanded.

"I don't know who the others are," said DeWalt, handing them over.

Lucy flipped through them, counting about a dozen in all. There were several of DeWalt, and a couple each of men she couldn't identify. The last three were what she was looking for: snapshots of Quentin, embracing a pretty young thing on the steps of the Winchester College library. Lucy groaned out loud.

"How come the police didn't find these when they searched her apartment after the murder?" she asked.

"They were in the freezer, hidden in a bag of frozen vegetables. She was clever."

"So clever she got herself killed," said Lucy, coming to a decision. "I think you better take these to the police, right now."

DeWalt began to protest, but she cut him off. "Get your lawyer and get over there. I'll follow, but there's something I have to do first."

DeWalt nodded agreement and climbed in his car. He started the engine, and peeled out of the parking lot so fast that he left rubber tire tracks.

It was only a few feet to the landlady's apartment, but it felt like miles to Lucy, who walked slowly and heavily. She was weighed down and depressed by her discovery. She knew DeWalt was a hypocrite, but she hadn't expected him to be capable of such evil.

She knocked softly on the landlady's door.

"Oh, it's you," she said, a cigarette dangling from her mouth. Today, Lucy noticed, she was wearing a turquoise sweat suit decorated with little rhinestones around the neck and shoulders.

"Is the apartment still available?" asked Lucy.

"It sure is, honey. Are you still interested?" She raised her penciled eyebrows inquiringly, and Lucy saw that her eyeshadow matched the pantsuit.

"I don't know. Like I told you, it's quite a bit more money than I'm paying. And I'm not sure my furniture will fit." Lucy produced a tape measure. "Do you mind if I take another look?"

"Not at all, but you've got to go by yourself. I'm waiting for the plumber, and I've got to keep an eye on that landscaper."

She gave a nod toward a man who was clipping the hedges, then turned to pluck a key off a board covered with hooks. "Be sure to bring it back," she said, making a quick calculation. "If you want it, let me know. I might be able to adjust the rent."

"Okay," said Lucy, feeling a bit guilty. She shouldn't lead the poor woman on like this, since she was probably having a tough time renting the apartment. It was, after all, the scene of a brutal murder.

Walking along the concrete pathway that connected the units, Lucy observed the groundsman who was industriously trimming the privet bushes that softened the square appearance of the brick buildings. The apartments really were nice, she decided, and the owner took good care of them. It was too bad that Carol had been killed here; it would probably take quite a while for the stigma to wear off.

Pulling open the door to the vestibule, Lucy went in and unlocked the door. Stepping once again into the dead woman's apartment, she couldn't help feeling uncomfortable and hurried through the living room into the bedroom. All she wanted was a quick peek, and she'd be on her way to the police station.

In the bedroom nothing had been disturbed and the watch was still lying on the dresser, where Carol had left it.

Lucy picked it up. As she suspected, it wasn't working. It had stopped, so Carol had put on her other watch, the sport watch she rarely wore. Like Lucy's, it might well have been an hour behind due to daylight savings. If that was true, it meant she had died at seven-thirty, not eight-thirty as the police believed. It also meant that Josh couldn't have been the murderer, because he had been having breakfast at Jake's at seven-thirty, in the company of plenty of witnesses. Lucy carefully replaced the watch and turned to go.

"Imagine meeting you here," said Quentin Rea. He was standing in the bedroom doorway, blocking her exit.

Startled, Lucy gasped. "What are you doing here?" she asked.

"I might ask you the same question," he said, putting her on the defensive.

"I was looking for something that might clear Josh Cunningham," she said, her voice betraying her nervousness. She didn't want to stay in this room where Carol had died, especially with the man she suspected of killing her. The photographs she had seen practically proved it. Carol was blackmailing him, threatening to produce photos that would show he was up to his old tricks of sexually harassing students. Lucy wanted to get out, but was reluctant to try pushing her way past Quentin.

"Did you find it?" he asked, not moving from the doorway.

"I'm not sure," said Lucy, making an effort to keep her voice steady as her unease increased. "It's awfully stuffy in here. Do you mind if we go outside?"

"Don't leave," he said, crossing the room to open the window. "There's something we have to get straight."

Lucy edged her way to the doorway. She desperately wanted to get away. "Okay," she said, trying to act as if nothing were the matter. "But I don't have much time. A friend is expecting me."

Quentin looked at her curiously. "You're afraid of me," he said. "Why?"

"Because of the other night," said Lucy, lying in a high, squeaky voice. "I thought you'd be angry with me." She was so frightened that she could hardly breathe.

"Believe me, I've got more to worry about on that score than you do. Sit down." He indicated the bed.

"I'd rather not," said Lucy, breathlessly, squeezing her hands together.

Quentin cocked his head to the side. His lips twisted into a grimace. "You think I killed her, don't you?"

"Oh, no," lied Lucy. "I would never think that."

"Look at you. You're terrified. You think I killed her, admit it."

Lucy didn't dare say anything. She was wondering if she should risk making a dash for the apartment door. As if he could read her mind, he moved back from the window, standing once again in the bedroom doorway.

"But why would you think that?" he asked, thinking aloud. Gradually, his puzzled expression was replaced with one of realization. "You found out about the sexual harassment, didn't you?" He stared at her, shaking his head slowly from side to side, letting the idea simmer. "You knew more than you let on. You're full of tricks, aren't you?"

"I was honest with you that night," said Lucy. "I didn't know until Monday."

"When did you begin to suspect me?" he demanded. He was angry now, and his voice shook.

"I don't suspect you," said Lucy, hoping to defuse the situation.

"Sure you do. After all, I had quite a motive. Carol could have made things very awkward for me at Winchester."

"Did she?" Lucy wanted to keep him talking. It was her best chance of escaping.

He stepped closer to her. "Actually, she didn't." He shrugged and his lips made a crooked little smile. "I don't think she knew I was here. If she had, I'm pretty sure she would have taken advantage of the opportunity. She would have done something. Threatened me, demanded blackmail. Something. But she didn't know, and I didn't kill her."

Lucy thought of the photos, and decided not to mention them. The less she appeared to know, the better.

"Besides," he continued, "I teach composition every morning at eight-thirty. I couldn't have done it."

"She could have died at seven-thirty." Lucy blurted it out, then wished she hadn't.

"Oh-ho." He raised his eyebrows. "So you still don't believe me." He stepped closer, grabbing her upper arms with his muscular hands.

"I believe you, I believe you," said Lucy hysterically. "Please let me go."

He dropped his hands immediately. "I'm sorry. I didn't mean to frighten you. I just wanted to explain."

Lucy wanted to believe him. "Why did you come here?" she asked, again thinking of the photographs. Perhaps he was looking for them.

"I don't know." He paused and looked around the room. "We go back a long way. We shared a lot of bad times, and a few good times. I wanted to say goodbye, I guess."

Despite herself, Lucy was beginning to believe him. "Well, if you didn't kill her, who did?"

He sat down on the bed and rested his elbows on his knees. "Knowing Carol, I don't think there's any shortage of suspects."

"I think I've eliminated most of them," said Lucy. "At least the ones in Tinker's Cove. I think it must be someone from her past."

"So that's why you thought it was me," said Quentin.

Lucy nodded. "I didn't have time to go through all the newspapers at the state college. Did she have any other victims there?"

"Only her husband," said Quentin. "She dumped him after she was there a few months."

"I didn't know she was married," said Lucy. "What was he like?"

"He was from her home town. He was older. He had a job in the science department—maintaining apparatus, setting up equipment, stuff like that. She once told me she only married him because he could get her out of Quivet Neck." He scratched his head. "At the time I thought it was a joke, but now I'm not so sure."

"That makes sense," said Lucy. "She made use of whoever was available."

"He was a pretty smart guy, as I remember. Great at fixing things and making stuff. His name was Sal, no, that wasn't it." He scratched his head. "Mel. His name was Mel something."

"Mel Costas?"

"Yeah," he said, surprised. "You know him?"

"No. But he was here the day she died. In a car accident, at eight-thirty." Lucy was excited. "He told police he was an old family friend . . ."

Quentin snorted.

"He even told them he had spent the night here," continued Lucy. "In Carol's apartment, because he was having trouble with his truck. But they figured he couldn't have been the murderer because he was in that accident at eight-thirty."

"But if she died at seven-thirty—why do you think it was earlier?" he asked.

"Because of daylight savings. The police said she died at eight-thirty because her watch stopped then. It got broken in the struggle. But . . ." Lucy went over to the dresser and picked up Carol's gold watch. "This is the watch she usually wore, but it's stopped. I think she put on a watch she hadn't worn in a while. It said eight-thirty, but it was really only seven-thirty."

"Lucy, you've got it wrong. If her watch was running on standard time, it would mean she really died at nine-thirty."

"Are you sure?"

He nodded. "Think about it."

"I was so sure I'd figured it out." Lucy was crestfallen.

"Unless Costas came back?"

"I don't see how. He must have been involved with the

accident for quite a while, plus, he wouldn't have had transportation after he crashed his truck."

"Maybe the watch was broken earlier—say the night before," offered Quentin.

"There was an autopsy," said Lucy. "She died in the morning."

"I still think it's worth taking to the police," said Quentin, standing up. "Especially since they didn't know she was married to him."

"That must be why she set up Josh Cunningham," said Lucy. "He came from Quivet Neck, too. He probably would have recognized Costas and remembered they were married. She had to get him out of the way."

"Chances are Costas made the bomb for her—he set up all kinds of scientific apparatus at the university," said Quentin, taking her elbow. They turned to go, only to freeze in place.

A man, the groundsman Lucy had seen clipping the hedges, was standing in the doorway, holding a gun.

"Mel Costas," said Quentin under his breath.

Belatedly, Lucy recognized the face in Jewel's photograph. Costas hadn't looked happy when he was trapped in his overturned truck, and he didn't look happy now. She remembered the open window; he must have heard everything they said.

"Pair of nosey-ass troublemakers, aren't you?" he sneered. "Couldn't leave well enough alone, could you? Couldn't wait to rush off and tell the cops all about me. Now, why'd you want to do that? Think you'd get a good citizen award or something?"

Lucy didn't answer; somehow she didn't think Costas was interested in anything she had to say. He was the last person she could imagine as the fastidious Carol's husband—he looked to be at least fifty, with a graying stubble of beard. His clothes, a pair of jeans and a NASCAR T-shirt, were worn and oil-stained.

"Mel, think about this," cautioned Quentin. His voice was strong and calm. "We don't really know anything—we were just guessing. Put the gun down, and let us go. This can't help. It's only going to make things worse."

"Shut up!" Costas stepped forward, waving them away from the dresser with the gun. Yanking open a top drawer, he pulled out a handful of stockings and pantyhose.

"You!" He pointed the gun at Lucy. "Take these and tie him up. Wrap his wrists together, behind him."

Lucy's eyes met Quentin's, and she whispered an apology as she obeyed with trembling fingers. She tried to make the knots loose, while appearing to tie the nylon tightly.

"Tight—don't think you can trick me," said Costas. "Now his ankles." His eyes were dark points, fixed on her. He was watching every move she made.

Lucy knelt to obey, trying desperately to think of a way to escape. "Is this what you did to Carol?" she asked. "Is this how her watch got broken?"

"Shut your mouth," he growled. He was jumpy, and the gun was shaking in his hand.

"You don't want to shoot us," said Lucy. "There are people all around us. Somebody would call the cops."

"She's right," said Quentin. "Just let us go. Nobody has to know about any of this. Think about it—nobody would blame you." His voice was silky, seductive. "Carol asked for it."

"You're right about that," said Costas. The energy seemed to drain from him, and he slumped on the foot of the bed. He didn't drop the gun, however, but kept moving it back and forth from one to the other, keeping them in his sights.

"She didn't treat you right," said Quentin. His voice was soothing. "You loved her, but she didn't love you. She used you."

"She was so beautiful. Like a doll. With long blond hair and those big blue eyes." Costas's tongue darted out and he licked his thin lips; the gesture reminded Lucy of a snake. "I couldn't believe she was mine, but she was, as long as I did what she wanted."

"She counted on you to get the job done," said Quentin.

"Yeah." Costas's eyes were far away. "She'd watch while I changed the oil in her car, or fixed some little thing, and tell me how smart I was. Made me feel like a million dollars. I would've done anything for her."

"You did, didn't you?" Quentin spoke slowly and softly. "You rigged the bus accident, you even made a bomb. Whatever she wanted, you did. But she didn't keep her end of the bargain, did she?"

"She was getting a divorce." There were tears in Costas's eyes and he clumsily brushed them away.

"You didn't want that, did you?" Quentin was sympathetic.

"I didn't have to live with her," said Costas, now eager to explain. "I knew how important her career was to her. She was right. She was too good to have to wait on rich bastards in a restaurant, or clean their bathrooms. I didn't try to hold her back, just so long as she'd let me come around every so often."

"She wanted you out of her life, didn't she? She told you that night."

"I showed her." Costas stood up, waving the gun wildly. "Thought she could tell me what to do, just like she always had. 'I need a picture hung,' she said, 'and my car is making a funny noise.' I told her there was something we had to do first." His eyes glittered.

"She said, 'Maybe later, after you're done,' but I said it had to be now. I put my arms around her but she struggled, as if I was trying to kill her or something. Tried to knee me. That made me mad." His eyes glittered. "I think that's when the watch broke."

"But you didn't kill her then," said Quentin.

"I tied the bitch up—right there on the bed."

Lucy looked at Carol's quilted silk bedspread and felt sick.

There was a note of triumph in Costas's reedy voice. "She didn't sound so high and mighty then. Wasn't telling me to wash my hands before I touched her, not then." He laughed, and the sound was awful. Lucy wanted to cover her ears; she didn't want to hear anymore.

"I did everything I ever wanted to. She was my wife, after all. It was my right. I touched her hair, I washed the makeup off her face. I touched her all over. I was a real husband to her, for the first time. Whaddya think of that? Married for ten years, but we never did it. I thought it was high time. I thought she'd like it, and then I wouldn't need to keep her tied up. In the morning, when I woke up she was there beside me, just like a wife ought to be. I took the gag off her mouth, so I could kiss her, real gentle like. But she started screaming. I tried to shut her up, but she wouldn't. She kept yelling and screaming. I had to put the pillow over her face to get her to be quiet and that's when she died."

He looked up and Lucy decided he must be mad. His eyes were round and clear, his expression peaceful and innocent. "It was too bad but I was gonna lose her either way."

Suddenly, the bedroom door flew open. Lucy and Quentin stared in amazement as a glittering vision in turquoise marched into the room.

"Ah-ha!" exclaimed the landlady, waggling a finger at Costas's back. "I hired you to cut the hedges, not to stand around talking!"

Costas turned, showing her the gun. Her eyes widened in shock and she started to scream. Deciding she might never have another opportunity, Lucy gathered all her strength and threw herself at Costas. She knocked him off his feet, and as they fell to the floor, the gun went off.

CHAPTER TWENTY-SIX

"What happened then?" asked Miss Tilley, shoving her wrinkled face right into Lucy's.

Lucy slid back in her seat in the high school auditorium, where she was waiting with the rest of the family for the annual talent show to begin. Toby was in the show, performing the rap song he had been practicing with Lance.

"Well, when the gun went off, the neighbors called the police. That wasn't much help to me, however, because it took them at least ten minutes to get there and I was struggling with an armed man. That landlady wasn't any use at all—she just kept screaming. Fortunately, Quentin was able to work himself free and helped me. We had Costas neatly tied up when the cops arrived."

"All's well that ends well," said Miss Tilley. "But you had an awfully close call. I hope you'll be more careful in the future."

"I will," promised Lucy, feeling she had done something

wrong. Miss Tilley often made her feel that way. It didn't matter that she had solved a murder and proven Josh Cunningham's innocence, never mind the fact that her profile of Carol Crane and her account of Costas's confession as published in *The Pennysaver* had been picked up by the wire services and printed in papers as far away as San Francisco. When scolded by Miss Tilley, she always felt like a little girl caught with her hand in the cookie jar.

"Look," said Lucy, pointing to a couple seated a few rows in front of them. "It's Josh, and he's with Sara's teacher, Ms. Kinnear. They make a nice couple, don't they?"

"I was terribly upset when they charged him," said Miss Tilley. "He always impressed me as one of the system's finest teachers."

"The kids love him," agreed Lucy, opening her program and looking for Toby's name. After a bit, she resumed the conversation. "I'm a little surprised you came tonight. I wouldn't have thought a high school talent show would have much appeal for you."

"Nonsense," snapped Miss Tilley. "I have always taken a great interest in the youth of the town."

"So you have," admitted Lucy, nevertheless convinced that Miss Tilley must have had a compelling reason to attend the show. Like many older folks, she rarely went out in the evening anymore.

"What are your plans for the future?" demanded Miss Tilley, studying her closely. "Will you be taking any more courses at Winchester College?"

"I don't think so," said Lucy. "They're too expensive and Ted has asked me to work twenty hours a week at the paper."

"That should be interesting."

"I think it will work out fine," said Lucy. "Full-time was really more than I could manage, but twenty hours should be just about right."

"I was a little concerned about you," said Miss Tilley.

"Really? Because I was working?"

"No," said Miss Tilley, placing a wrinkled hand on Lucy's arm. "Because you were taking that course from Quentin Rea. His field is really the Elizabethans—he doesn't know his Victorians very well at all. I once commented to him about Elizabeth Barrett Browning's 'dear little Pen' and he didn't realize I was talking about her son. She called him Pen, you know."

"I know," said Lucy.

"Well, Professor Rea didn't. He actually said it was likely that her pen was the same size as everyone else's!"

Miss Tilley slapped her knee and cackled merrily; she loved nothing better than exposing someone's ignorance.

"I thought he was a bit shaky on a few points myself," said Lucy, unable to resist adding, "but he did give me an A."

"Are you sure it was for your course work?" asked Miss Tilley, grinning wickedly.

"What else?" asked Lucy, indignantly raising her eyebrows.

"One hears things . . ."

"One should know better than to believe everything one hears," said Lucy self-righteously. She glanced over at Bill, who was sitting beside her, and was relieved to see he was busy going over the program with Sara and Elizabeth. Zoë was snoozing in his lap. "Although I must admit you were absolutely right about DeWalt. It's too bad he didn't stick around to face the music. I bet Judge Ryerson would have locked him up and thrown away the key."

"I think he was planning to leave town pretty soon anyway,"

said Miss Tilley. "Word of those prayer sessions was getting around, and there was talk that most of the missionary fund had disappeared. Some members of the congregation were getting a bit suspicious."

"Well, Zephirah seems to be doing a terrific job. I heard the Revelation Congregation has really changed since she took over. She's started a ministry for single mothers, and is leading a study group about women in the Bible."

"Oh look!" said Miss Tilley, standing and craning her neck. "There she is!"

"Who?" asked Lucy, twisting her head to see the back of the auditorium.

"Norah!" Miss Tilley's ancient face had taken on a pinkish glow. She was even smiling.

"Norah?" asked Lucy, getting up and looking toward the entrance, along with everyone else in the auditorium.

"Norah Hemmings—the queen of daytime TV," hissed Miss Tilley. "Surely you've heard of her."

"Of course I have," said Lucy. "I even watch her show once in a while. But what is she doing here in Tinker's Cove?"

"Recuperating," chimed in Dot Kirwan, who had been sitting nearby. Now she was on her feet like everyone else, hoping for a glimpse of Norah. "She's recovering from liposuction and some other plastic surgery. I read she had a complete makeover and has been in seclusion while she recovered. No interviews—no photos. She's been staying in her family's place out on Smith Heights Road."

Lucy remembered the night she took Lance home and he insisted on being dropped at the foot of Smith Heights Road even though she offered to take him to the door.

"Don't tell me she has a son with her?" asked Lucy.

"She does," said Dot. "His name is Vance or something."

"Lance?"

"That's it, Lance. He's a nice boy, even if he does have one of those rings in his nose."

Looking around the auditorium, where everyone seemed to have suddenly become members of Norah's fan club, Lucy wondered how she could have been so dense. Everyone in town seemed to know all about the famous star's presence, everyone except her and Ted, and they were the very ones who should have known. How did they miss such a big story?

There was a smattering of applause and Lucy saw Norah herself standing in the doorway. The star's newly trim figure was encased in a shiny red vinyl jumpsuit that zipped up the front. Her hair was arranged in one of those deceptively casual styles that only work when cut by a master. Her smoothly sculpted face betrayed no wrinkles, sags, or bags. She was smiling, an enormous smile that revealed dazzling white teeth.

"She looks wonderful," cooed Miss Tilley, star-struck.

"It won't last," predicted Dot, who was a grandmotherly size 18 and not about to diet. "Give her six months and I bet she'll be back in her fat clothes."

All eyes were on Norah as she made her way down the aisle, accompanied by two anonymous companions who faded into drab insignificance beside her radiance. After a brief consultation, they chose seats a few rows from the front. The three sat together, with Norah in the middle.

Then the lights went out and the audience began clapping, in anticipation of the show. The curtain did not go up, however, and after a few moments the lights were back on. The audience responded with a groan.

Mr. Mopps soon appeared on the empty stage, and was

greeted with cheers and stamps from the rowdy high school students. Sara couldn't resist jumping to her feet and joining in the applause. He gave the crowd a little wave, adjusted the microphone, and gave a signal to someone offstage. Once again the lights went out, and this time the show began.

Lucy thought Miss Tilley was paying rather a high price for a glimpse of her favorite TV personality, as she endured seemingly endless amateur acts, badly performed by the town's youth. Becky Flynn tumbled across the stage in a series of gymnastic flips, Elizabeth's friends Melissa Burke and Emily Anderson tottered about in their toe shoes in a dance duet, and Eddie Culpepper played a squeaky "Minute Waltz" on his violin for what seemed to be a very long minute.

Finally the moment Lucy had been waiting for arrived, and the curtain rose on Lance and Toby. Dressed identically in baggy black jeans and shiny sports jackets, with woolen watch caps pulled down over their heads, they struck casual poses and waited for someone offstage to start the music.

When a rap beat began thumping out, they began to bounce on their knees in time with the music. Gradually, with gestures and dance steps they began acting out the story described in the song, in which they were rivals for a girl's attention. When Alison Crowley, the police chief's daughter, appeared on stage as the girl, the crowd applauded enthusiastically.

As Alison twisted and gyrated her hips to the music, Lucy wondered what Chief Crowley thought of her outfit—baggy silk pants, a tube top, and a chain around her waist. Alison was adorable, however, and when she shook her finger at the boys and strolled offstage alone, rejecting both her suitors, she brought down the house.

After the show, Lucy and Bill took the kids backstage to

congratulate Toby on his performance. He was standing with Lance, and Norah was generously lavishing attention on both of them.

"Weren't they fabulous?" she asked, flapping her fake eyelashes at Bill.

"They sure were," agreed Bill, somewhat dazed to be chatting with a TV star.

Lucy reached in her handbag and pulled out her camera.

"Do you mind?" she asked.

"Not at all," said Norah, flashing her signature smile.

Lucy snapped the picture, not quite believing her luck.

"By the way," she said, "I happen to work for the town newspaper. It's only a local weekly, *The Pennysaver*. Would you let me interview you, for just a very little story?"

"Of course," exclaimed Norah, throwing open her arms and engulfing Lucy in a perfumed hug. "Anything for Lance's friend!"